HOUSECARL

Laurence J. Brown.

1

HOUSECARL
First published in 2001.
Revised second edition reprinted 2002

PUBLISHED BY
PAUL MOULD PUBLISHERS U.K
In association with
Empire Publishing Service, U.S.A

U.K   ISBN   0 9528708 4 3
U.S.A. ISBN   1 58690 004 8
Simultaneously Published in Australia, Canada,
U.K. U.S.A.

Library of Congress Cataloging-in-Publication Data

Brown, Laurence J.
    Housecarl / by Laurence J. Brown.
        p. cm.
    ISBN 1-58690-004-8 (alk. paper)
    1.Great Britain--History--Edward, the Confessor, 1042-1066--Fiction. 2. Harold, King of
England, 1022?-1066--Fiction. 3. Hastings, Battle of, England, 1066--Fiction. 4. Anglo-
Saxons--Fiction. I. Title.

PR6102. R69 H68 2002
823`.92--dc21

Also by Author:

COLD HEART, CRUEL HAND

For Kaye, with love.

ACKNOWLEDGEMENTS.

I thank the many people who contributed directly or indirectly to the writing of this book: my father who taught me a love of history; my school friend Paul Howden for his enthusiastic commentary; Geo Fowler for his careful review and critique; and my wife Kaye for her unflagging confidence that enabled me to complete the novel.

I would also like to acknowledge my debt to the following sources: the scholarly and erudite monks who laboured by the light of candles a thousand years ago to record the events of their time in what are now called *the Anglo-Saxon Chronicles* and the seamstresses of Normandy who undertook a massive labour of love in creating the brilliant and beautiful *Bayeux Tapestry,* the source of much of our knowledge today.

I also acknowledge my debt to the following contemporary sources: Richard Humble for his authoritative review of the period, *The Fall of Saxon England* and last but by no means least Terence Wise for his meticulous account of perhaps the most significant year in English history, *1066 Year of Destiny.*

To those whose contributions I have neglected to note here from sheer failure of memory or neglect please accept my apologies. To all I owe a great debt.

PROLOGUE

BONNEVILLE – SUR –TOUQUES

ROUEN, NORMANDY.

1064

It was dark in the cell, dark and cold and damp. The Saxon, huddled in the corner, shivered into his cloak and wondered when they would be coming for him. He sensed that it was daylight but he had no real way of knowing since he had been incarcerated far below ground and it had been over two weeks since he had last seen the outside world. He could only guess at the time. He knew that it had been several hours since his last meal, some cold stew and a skin of foul water that his captors might have pissed in for all he knew.

A rat scuttled about in the far corner and the Saxon hurled his platter at the noise, more in anger than in the hope of driving it off. The platter missed its target and the rat resumed its patrol of the cell. The Saxon cursed, and closed his eyes. He could only wait. He knew what would be coming, and had spent the night if night it was, reconciling himself to what he must do.

He lay with his back against the far wall so that he could face the door. It was solid, impenetrable. At first he had hammered on it until his knuckles bled but no one had responded to his desperate cries and eventually he had subsided into a fitful sleep. In his dreams he was in England, safe from harm, the master of his own destiny, and this had all been a dreadful nightmare, but then he had awoken to discover that this was the reality and his sanctuary in England a mere illusion. He had almost broken at that point but he rationalised that if his Norman captors had wanted him dead he would be. Instead he had been thrown into this stinking hole in the bowels of the earth whilst they decided his fate and the thought had somehow sustained him.

Eventually, after what seemed an eternity, but had only been a matter of days, he had received a visit from his host, Duke William of Normandy, otherwise known as William the Bastard and the full enormity of what was required of him was made clear. He had protested of course; he had ranted and railed in a way that would have had his servants in England piss their pants. But he was not at home, in England. He was in Normandy, the prisoner of the Duke, and the Duke was having none of it.

And so he had rotted his time away far below ground in the bowels of the fortress whilst his straw became fouled and the Duke laid his plans. And what plans they were. And if the Saxon had calculated correctly, today was the day. Perhaps it was, but he could not be sure. He managed to find a dry piece of straw and curled up on it. After a while he slept.

He awoke to the sound of footsteps, several footsteps, echoing on stone slabs. They were growing louder and so he raised himself from the straw into a sitting position so that he could watch the door. A key turned in the lock; heavy bolts scraped back. The door swung open on rusty hinges to reveal three heavily armed men. They approached him with drawn swords and for a moment the Saxon felt a frisson of fear.

"Out *cochon*!" The Captain of the Guard gave the Saxon's foot a kick, causing a sharp pain to lance through his ankle. The Saxon grimaced and rose to his feet.

"Follow me!" The Saxon felt the point of a sword in his back and obediently followed the Captain.

He was led, stumbling, up a long stone staircase lit only by the occasional torch until another door was opened and he was suddenly, unexpectedly, in bright sunlight. The unaccustomed brightness after weeks spent underground caused him to throw up his hands to shield his eyes but they were quickly pulled from his face by the soldiers flanking him and held tightly to his side so that he could not move them. The sword point prompted him forward again and the Saxon reluctantly obeyed.

Blinking furiously against the glare of an August sun he stumbled along on little-used limbs through grassy meadows redolent with the scent of wild flowers that only served to emphasise the squalid conditions in which he had been existing. Gratefully he filled his lungs with the sweet Normandy air, the first he had breathed for weeks. After a while he saw in the distance a large oak tree standing in splendid isolation and guessed that this was to be his final destination. As they approached the tree the Saxon saw that his guess had been right. An audience of Norman nobility had already begun to gather beneath the shade of its generous branches; young and old alike, dressed in their finery, preening and posing to impress their ladies, and those of their friends. They had all come to witness his humiliation. He saw too, that the chosen reliquaries had been placed in the shade of the tree although whether that was for his benefit or for that of his onlookers, or simply to preserve the fragile relics from the glare of the sun he was uncertain.

He knew that he had no means of escaping the ordeal that was to come, and as he stood before the Holy Sacraments his eyes reflected the inner torment of his soul. He had known for several days what he must do, here, today; of the Oath that he must swear to Duke William, but now that the moment had arrived he felt his resolve waver. He determined to look at no one, to stare blindly ahead, to deny his captor the satisfaction of seeing him humbled.

His arms, like his face, were thin and white from weeks spent in permanent darkness deep in the bowels of the fortress with only the rats for company, and now they were seized by the soldiers-at-arms and spread wide, placed firmly upon the Scriptures. They grinned at each other as they left him standing there, arms spread wide at the horizontal, and after a moment the Saxon realised that there was something about his pose that was familiar, that reminded him of a picture, or sculpture, or something. He had seen it often, but for a moment longer it escaped him. And then he had it; it had hung on the wall over his bed: Christ, on the Cross, at Golgotha. The Bastard was mocking him. He was *mocking* him. The realisation caused a flush of anger to course through his veins and as his cheeks coloured the Saxon silently swore revenge.

A priest emerged from the crowd and made his way up to the relics so that he faced the Saxon. After a few moments spent scrutinising the Saxon, and obviously disliking what he saw, he began to speak in the nasal tones that the Saxon had come to recognise as Norman. The words themselves meant nothing to him as he did not speak the language, but as the priest reached the Oath itself, the wording of which had been hammered out during exhausting weeks of negotiation, the crowd spontaneously burst into applause. Duke William rose from his seat to acknowledge them and the applause increased. It was all smiles and laughter, a great game played out on this glorious August day. But now the priest was speaking in English, and motioning to the Saxon that he should repeat the words as a bride repeats her wedding vows. The Saxon held his breath whilst he silently damned the man and desperately fought for some way out of his predicament. There was none.

"Swear the Oath, Godwineson." William the Bastard spoke for the first time, the words uttered quietly, his English poor, but the menace in his voice carried clear across the hushed crowd. The Saxon turned to look at his tormentor, a glance only, but it was

10

enough. There was no choice, no choice at all. He was, after all, nothing more than a prisoner, a pawn in William the Bastard's grand strategy; a strategy that would hand him the Throne of England, the richest prize in Christendom.

And so the Saxon repeated the words of the Oath, each word, each act of obeisance stripping away his pride, layer by layer, until, finally, he was laid bare. He was the Duke's man, even unto death. Tears of shame, invisible to those watching the spectacle burned into his cheeks and with each tear the Saxon swore revenge. He would never forget what had happened here, today.

Never.

CHAPTER ONE

5TH JANUARY 1066

LONDON.

The snow drove hard into the men's faces, blinding them so that they could not see. It stung their reddened cheeks and clung to their beards, turning them white. Their hands were frozen and their feet were numb and the men buried their heads ever deeper into the folds of their cloaks and prayed that the blizzard would soon end. The streets of London were treacherous underfoot where the snow had settled and turned to ice and the men painfully inched their way forward, racing against time as the wind screamed about their ears and like some evil, elemental force mocked their attempts to make headway against it.

There were five men in the party, three of them brothers. The other two were unrelated but as close as though they were twins. But it was the man in the centre of the group that was the reason for their being abroad on such a wretched night, and despite the appalling weather his eyes, red, and circled with dark shadows, blazed with fire for after eighteen long, tortuous months he had finally received the call that he had been praying for.

Many times since his return from Normandy Harold Godwineson, Earl of Wessex, had despaired of life, had thought of ending it all there and then; a slash of the knife across the wrist and it would be over. He was no coward, and his own death would mean little to him but something, *something*, had held him back and instead of taking the blade to his wrist he had buried himself deep in his work, spending months at a time in his beloved Wessex or at his home at Bosham managing the affairs of his great estates, or the business of the County. There was always something to do, someone with a petition for this or that; disputes to resolve, tenants rights to be determined, tithes to be agreed, criminals to be tried, and summary justice, Harold's own justice, to be handed out to those deserving. And whilst he was doing this England's King, Edward the Confessor, was abdicating his responsibilities as he gave himself over to his life's ambition, the completion of the magnificent edifice on the banks of the Thames that was to be the new Westminster Cathedral; a fitting monument to the Glory of God, and, some would say, to himself.

And when Harold Godwineson was not running the affairs of the West Country he would take his leisure; the days spent hunting with his hounds and his falcons, the nights with his lover Edith Swanneshals, the mother of his three young children.

But despite this, the long full days, the equally filled nights, the nightmares had never left him and he would wake in the small hours, a cry choking in his throat, to find himself soaked with sweat. Not in the Normandy field of his dreams, surrounded by his enemies, but in his own bed, in the arms of his lover, whilst she tried to comfort him as he cried out his fevered imaginings. For a time she would succeed, holding him in her arms until dawn broke over the gently rolling hills and the day brought problems of its own. Then the nightmares would recede, retreat into the darker corners of his subconscious until he had almost forgotten their malign existence. But always they were there, lurking, simply biding their time before returning to haunt him with renewed vigour in the small hours of the night; a permanent reminder of his folly.

And through all of this he had waited; waited for the call that he prayed would one day arrive. And then, at last, it had. On Christmas day the Confessor's messenger had arrived in Wessex on a sweat lathered mount bearing a summons from a dying King. And like the obedient servant he was, had *always* been, Harold Godwineson had hastened to obey. Despite the winter weather, the wind and the snow, the death of his horse, its heart broken by his demands, he had made London in just five days. With him were his brothers, the Earls Gyrth and Leofwine, and making up the party, Ranulf Redbeard, Captain of his housecarls, and Guthrum Hard-Axe, Ranulf's second. Both men, like all of Harold's housecarls, had sworn a solemn blood-oath to die on the field of battle for him. Their lives were his, to do with as he wished.

"Just ahead Lord!" Ranulf Redbeard turned a pinched, weary face to his own. His voice was raised, the words shouted, and still they were whipped away by the wind. But Harold Godwineson had heard them and he lifted his bearded chin from the folds of his cloak to follow Ranulf's outstretched arm. A blast of snow obscured his vision and he cuffed a frozen hand across his face to clear it from his eyes. It was difficult to see anything at all but his senses told him that Ranulf was right for in the distance was the unmistakable glow of torches burning in their beckets, orange pinpoints against the blackness of the night. It was Westminster Palace, and inside its massive walls laid the King of England.

"Pray God he still lives," Harold muttered, more to himself than to anyone in particular as he quickened his step toward the gatehouse and a brief respite from the bitter weather.

The acrid smell of guttering torches greeted Harold Godwineson as he entered the dimly lit bedchamber of King Edward the Confessor. The others were waiting in the antechamber out of deference to a dying King. It was Harold he had demanded to see, and their presence could only be regarded as an unwanted intrusion into the King's last moments on earth.

The silence inside the bedchamber was deafening, broken only by the King's shallow breathing and the whispered prayers of the priest at his bedside. He paused momentarily inside the threshold before stepping forward into the chamber, his eyes quickly taking in the scene.

A log fire raged in the hearth, spitting and cracking, casting giant shadows on the heavily tapestried wall opposite. In the far corner of the chamber stood the King's bed, and beneath a heavy pile of bedclothes laid the prostrate King. It was very warm in the bedchamber, almost oppressive, but despite the heat and the bedclothes the King was shivering uncontrollably. His face was pale and drawn, his skin glistening like ivory. Knelt in prayer beside the priest was Edith, the King's wife, Harold's own sister. It had not been much of a marriage, a political necessity forced upon her and the King by her father, and there were no children of the union. The Godwine family had never expected her to love him. But as the years had passed she had grown fond of him and now it showed. She turned at hearing the footsteps and rose to greet him. He was taller than her and she had to reach up to kiss his cheek. It was still wet with melted snow but she hardly seemed to notice.

"I came as soon as I heard," he said, his eyes exploring his sister's face, the lines and wrinkles, the cares of the long years etched there.

"He said you would come." Edith glanced toward the bed, at the figure shivering beneath the coverlets. "His conscience weighs heavily upon him. He talks much of you, when he is lucid, of how he has wronged you; of his regret at what happened." She paused to reflect upon what she had just said. "He is troubled Harold, much troubled. And he has little time...." Her voice tailed off, as though she had said too much.

15

"You look exhausted brother," she said suddenly, changing the conversation. He studied his sister. Her own eyes, lined and dark from lack of sleep betrayed the weariness that she herself was feeling.

"A hard ride," he replied absently, but it was more than that of course, much more. He noticed that Edith had more grey in her hair than when he had last seen her and he realised with a start that it had been almost eighteen months. Eighteen months since those dreadful events in Normandy and his return to England a broken man.

"How long does he have?" It was plain from his own brief observation that the King was, indeed, dying.

"A few hours perhaps, maybe less." Edith turned towards her husband. The priest was still at his bedside, his tonsured head bent low over his psalter, engrossed in his prayers.

"Come over to the bed," she said. "Edward will speak with you, if he can." She took him by the hand and led him to the bedside of Edward the Confessor, King of England and Wales, the greatest Ruler in Christendom. For twenty- three years Edward had held the Country in an iron fist clothed in a velvet glove whilst he gradually, painfully, moulded it into the power it was today. All Harold saw was an old, sick man.

Edward had always been tall; well over six feet, but now, gaunt and wasted, his body was child-like in its angular frailty. His eyes, sunk deep within their sockets, were closed as though asleep, whilst his face, beaded with sweat, had a mask-like quality, as in death. In truth Harold could see that death could not be long postponed for the fever had the King in a firm grip that seemed to be well beyond the capacity of any physician to loosen. His skeletal frame shook uncontrollably beneath the blankets that seemed to clothe him like a shroud. The priest rose from the bed, his prayers completed.

"The King has been shriven, my Lady; he rests in the safe hands of the Lord."

"Thank you Father. The Almighty knows our hearts. Your prayers will not go unanswered." She pressed a coin into his palm and the priest blessed her before leaving, the coin clutched tightly in one hand, his much-used psalter in the other.

Harold approached the bed and stared at the man shaking beneath the coverlets. Somehow he knew that this would be the defining moment of his life. All that had gone before had simply been to prepare him for this moment. He was not a fatalist, for only fools believed in fate and he believed in shaping his own destiny, but now he felt a tightness in his stomach that he had not felt since Normandy. He took an involuntary breath. *Greatness or oblivion.* It was now or it would be never. *So be it then.*

He reached out a hand and placed it on the King's forehead. It was hot beneath his palm. More than hot; it was a furnace. The Confessor was burning up before his eyes. By the side of the bed stood a pitcher of water and he dipped the end of his cloak into it and gently ran it across the King's brow. Edward stirred and he dipped the end of the cloak again, this time wiping the King's whole face with it, letting the water trickle into the lines and wrinkles about the eyes, then down, into the almost white beard. Edward turned and looked up, towards him. For a few moments it seemed that the eyes would not focus. Instead they stared out from the King's face vacant and unseeing, a blind man groping for sight. And then, as if a veil had been lifted from his eyes the light of recognition dawned and a smile, weary and fleeting, but a smile nonetheless crossed his thin lips.

"Harold," he said, "give me your hand." He offered his hand and the Confessor took it in his own. The King's grip was surprisingly strong but he did not attempt to pull away.

"You came," the Confessor said, rheumy eyes locked upon him. "I knew you would. I know you, Harold....better than you know yourself." The voice was weak but there was iron in his words.

"You commanded me Sire," he said awkwardly, unsure of where the Confessor was leading.

"No, not because I commanded; not that...you came for my Crown."

"No-!" He started to protest, but the Confessor squeezed his hand, silencing his protest, commanding his attention.

"Listen," he said. "Listen. I have something to say and time is short." The Confessor closed his eyes, opened them, and started to speak. It was the longest speech he would ever again make.

"I have made this quarrelsome Country one land," he said. "One land, when before it was many. One land, and now one people. A people at peace...whoever succeeds me shall have that task, to keep the people united, content, and God knows that will not be easy. But do it they must, if England is to remain strong."

He saw that sweat was beading on the King's forehead, trickling down into the eyes. The King shook his head in irritation and Edith leaned over to wipe his face, pouring a little of the water into his mouth. The King muttered something that he didn't catch, and continued:

"I have thought on this matter long and hard, this choice of who shall succeed me." He paused again, as though deep in thought.

"I have wronged you," he said eventually. "Wronged you; and I am sorry for it."

"It is past," Harold heard himself reply.

"But not forgotten." The Confessor forced a weak smile as if to say, *I know.*

"You did what you thought was best."

"And I was wrong," the Confessor said pointedly. "I see that now. Now that it is almost too late."

Harold noted the hint of remorse; a desire to change the past, but that was not possible. Only the future could be changed: today, tomorrow, the rest of his life.

The Confessor had fallen silent again, his breathing laboured and heavy, and Harold wondered for a moment whether the King had finished with him, the audience over. He looked at Edith, uncertain of what to do when the Confessor spoke again. And it was as if he were speaking to himself:

"William will not be King." The words were so unexpected, so quietly uttered that Harold thought that he must have misheard. He leaned closer.

"Not William?" he said. "Not William? Then who?" He shot a glance at Edith.

"You," the Confessor whispered. "You will be King after me. It is what you have wanted and now you shall have it."

"But why? Why now, after all this time?"

"Because you are Saxon," the Confessor said. "And William is Norman. And England needs a Saxon King... In my heart I have always known it, but I fought against it. Your father would have torn the Country apart but I believe you are different." He paused again, clearly tired, and the silence hung between them like a knife.

"Do you love England?" The Confessor asked suddenly, tightening his grip, surprising him with the question.

"Love England?" he said, buying time.

"Yes. Do you love her?" The question was repeated, the voice strident, as though it were the most important thing in the world.

"I do, Sire," he said, regaining his composure. "I love this Country as I love my own kin." It was the truth. He loved the countryside, the rugged Cornish shoreline, the hunting with his hounds and falcons...he loved the power he held and the licence to exercise it, but these things he did not mention, were better unsaid.

"Help me up," the Confessor said, and Harold helped him into a sitting position. The King's hands were hooked, like talons, into his doublet and now he brought his face to within inches of Harold's own. It was like seeing death in the mirror and Harold, unable to hold the reflection, looked away, to cast a glance at his sister.

"Look at me!" The words were spoken harshly, almost too harshly. There was a feverish overtone to their inflection that hinted at the Confessor's anxiety, his awareness of his mortality.

"Look at me!" The words were repeated and Harold turned to gaze into the ravaged face of the King of England. The eyes were wild now, intense; an intensity that burned through him and pierced his soul. He wanted to look away, but could not do so. The eyes held him fast.

"You will be King," the Confessor said, eyes blazing with fever. "You will be King, and you will rule this Country as I have ruled. Do you understand? .... *Do you understand?*"

"Yes, Sire," he said. "I understand perfectly."

"Then my work is done. Done at last." The Confessor's eyes closed and the trace of a smile crossed the thin lips. But soon it was gone, and the King was all urgency once more. The grip tightened again, the fever stricken face filled Harold's vision, became his whole world.

"Harold!" he said, the last words he would utter, "I commend to you my wife and all this land......look after them, for God's sake, for I am going to my maker..."

And for fully ten seconds, whilst Harold sat transfixed, the Confessor locked his eyes upon those of his successor; eyes that blazed like beacons from a death mask, imposing his will even as the grave reached out for him. And then he was gone; a gentle sigh the only mark of his passing and Harold lowered the Confessor onto his pillows. The face, he saw, was calm now, at peace, with no sign of the anxiety that had characterized his last few moments of life. He closed the eyes.

How Edward had found the strength to raise himself from his sick bed, to deny death its triumph for so long, he would never know. Perhaps, as some people said, the Confessor was divine, blessed with the Holy Spirit. And now he sat immersed in his thoughts until Edith came forward to cover her husband's face. He had almost forgotten her existence.

"You knew," he said.

"Yes," she replied. "But it had to come from him. For his own peace of mind, God rest his soul." She crossed herself.

"I will be a good King, Edith," he said. "I will not fail him." He felt that somehow the words were required, even though the Confessor could no longer hear them.

"Do not fail me either," she said, and he saw that she was shivering. A tear suddenly spilled onto her cheek.

"Hold me," she said and he took her in his arms and held her against him. Her body convulsed with sobs and the tears, held in check for so long, rolled down her cheeks. Eventually, after what seemed an eternity she pulled away from him, gathering herself, wiping her eyes.

She moved to the bedside and took the Confessor's hand in hers. She stroked it gently, recalling some private moment, then kissed it once before taking hold of the ring that bore the King's seal of office. She slid it along the finger until it caught against the skin. She twisted it, and just for a moment she felt the hand move, as though in protest, and then it was free.

"Harold," she said, motioning to him, and seeing her intention he held out his right hand. She slid the ring onto his finger and, as she had with her husband, she kissed it, just once.

He heard a noise behind him and turned to see that Gyrth and Leofwine had entered the bedchamber, their faces anxious, concerned.

"Hal," Gyrth said, "Fitz Wimarc is outside, demanding to see the King. He is most insistent."

21

Harold looked to the bed, to the corpse of the Confessor, covered by his shroud.

"He is too late," he said. "The King is dead. Tell him that." And then he paused, and checked himself.

"No, not that. Tell him the King is busy. Tell him that I have a funeral to arrange; a funeral….and a Coronation."

CHAPTER TWO

WESTMINSTER CATHEDRAL

LONDON

6TH JANUARY 1066

The funeral procession wound its way from the Palace towards the newly completed Westminster Cathedral. The mourners following the coffin had their heads bowed in prayer, lost in thoughts of their own as they negotiated the narrow, winding streets that led to the Confessor's final resting place. The day had dawned clear and bright but it was bitterly cold as a January wind whipped through the Capital and the icy breath of the mourners briefly stained the blue sky before dissipating into oblivion.

Watching the rhythmic swaying of the coffin ahead of him, borne on the stooped shoulders of Gyrth, Leofwine, Ranulf, Guthrum and two men chosen from the late King's household, Harold Godwineson contemplated the events of the last twenty-four hours. He had struggled tirelessly to make the arrangements, holding meeting after meeting in private with the Witan, the elected Council members, old men and women, more frightened of their own shadows than any threat he could offer. They had readily agreed to acknowledge his right to the Throne when the Queen had come forward to confirm her late husband's wishes. The arrangements for the funeral and the Coronation had been more difficult. The majority of the Witan had felt that a period of mourning should be observed before the funeral, and, after that, a further delay before the Coronation itself.

But Harold had been persuasive. Delay, he argued, gave room for the dissenters to voice their objections. Delay meant that England would have no King to rule her, and the absence of rule meant chaos. Delay, he said, bred uncertainty. Delay and Duke William will be hammering on the doors of the Palace with his army. That had clinched it. That and the fact that they could keep their positions and their Titles. Men were the same the world over, he mused, and he was no exception. After all, he was a Godwineson, and the Godwinesons' had been born to rule. And today he would prove it.

He should, he thought, be mourning; reflecting upon the late King's glorious reign, and the sorrow of his passing. Instead he was filled with the most wonderful feeling of being alive as he walked alongside his sister, the late King's grieving widow. He cast a glance at her. Dressed all in black, her face covered by a veil, head erect, she proudly followed her husband to his final resting place. But today belonged to him: *Harold the Second by the grace of God King of England.* It sounded well, and by nightfall he would be King. And then his real work would begin.

He had made a promise to the Confessor to rule as he had ruled but he had already decided what his first task would be: to rid England of the Norman scum that infested the Capital like a disease. And Fitz Wimarc would be the first to go. God, he would enjoy that. He had never liked the arrogant Norman, not since he had first encountered him in Rouen eighteen months ago. He could still recall the sneering look on Fitz Wimarc's face as he had taunted him that bright August afternoon whilst hiding behind the skirts of his Lord and Master, William the Bastard. Yes, that would be a pleasure worth waiting for, to send him packing to Normandy. Fitz Wimarc, and the rest of them. A smile crossed his lips at the thought and he tried to imagine the reaction of William the Bastard when he heard the news. What a picture that would be. God, but life could be good! And for him, it would all start today.

A tolling bell brought him back to the present and he glanced again at his sister to see whether she had noticed but her head remained proudly erect, her face pale beneath the veil. She had seen nothing, and her tear-stained face told him that her thoughts were not on him, but upon the man in front of them, the man who, until last night, had been her life. He felt a pang of guilt at his own pleasure and reaching out he caught her hand in his and gave it a squeeze.

"Whatever you desire, you shall have," he said. "You shall want for nothing."

"What I want you cannot give." She turned her eyes, reddened with tears, towards him. "But I thank you for your kindness.... I shall survive," she said, after a pause, " for I too am a Godwineson, remember." She smiled at him then. It was a thin smile, the smile of a woman newly widowed, but it was a start. He smiled back. She was right of course; she would survive. They were both Godwinesons, from the same mould. A mould that had been fashioned by their father, Earl Godwine so many years ago and which had, at last, seen his soaring ambition achieved; not for himself, but vicariously, through his daughter, who had been Queen, and now, through himself, as the next King of England. *King Harold the Second.* If only his father could see him now. The thought flashed across his unconscious only to be replaced by another. *Yes, and the bastard would try to steal my Throne too! Just as he had tried to steal the Confessor's.* He laughed inwardly, his heart singing. He had succeeded where his father, for all his ruthless ambition, had failed. Would his father have been proud of him? Perhaps. But there would be jealousy also. His father was like that. And Tostig, the youngest brother, more like their father than any of them. Where was he now? Off God knew where, seeking his fortune no doubt. Well, he could seek it elsewhere. That was another matter to consider once he was King. Tostig could be dangerous, to himself, and to others. He would have to watch him. Perhaps the Earldom of Wessex, his own Earldom, could be offered to Tostig to keep the peace. Perhaps....but that could come later, once the Normans had been sent packing...

He looked up and noticed that whilst he had been happily day dreaming they had reached the steps of the Cathedral. Inside the cavernous interior the choir now struck up, young, angelic voices raised to the heavens. Up the steps they went, the bearers so careful with their charge, until they were at the great double doors. Archbishop Stigand, persuaded against his better judgement to perform both great ceremonies in one day paused momentarily to allow the mourners prepare themselves. A few moments only, and then they were inside, the gloom of the vast interior relieved by the light of a thousand candles and the most glorious altar-piece imaginable, the crowning glory of the Confessor's genius.

The Confessor was coming home, to rest for eternity in the sepulchre that he had built. And he, Harold Godwineson, would be the first King of England to hold his Coronation here. *King Harold the Second.* His eyes were solemn, his face impassive, giving nothing away as the procession followed the coffin up the aisle toward the High Altar, but inside his heart was filled with joy. For today he would be King, and the world would be at his feet.

CHAPTER THREE

10TH JANUARY 1066

A FOREST OUTSIDE ROUEN, NORMANDY

The boar was beginning to tire. For over three miles the wolfhounds had relentlessly pursued him through the snow-covered forest and the spear, deeply embedded in his heavily muscled hindquarters was taking its toll. The boar desperately needed to find cover and as he tore through the undergrowth his small rounded eyes cast about for a safe haven from the ravening pack that dogged his trail. The boar knew the forest well. He had hunted and killed for many years in the solitary seclusion of the ancient forest, but always for food for himself or his sow and her offspring. Now the tables were turned and he was the hunted, and the hunter was man, the most dangerous enemy of all. Unlike the boar, man hunted simply for sport, for the thrill of the chase, and, finally, the kill. And aiding and abetting him were his wolfhounds, vicious, ill-tempered animals trained by man to hunt the wolves that inhabited the great tracts of forest around the Rouen area. But it was not only wolves that they hunted, and now the wolf-hounds were on his trail, the blood from his wound staining the snow crimson, leaving an indelible path for the hounds to follow. And the path led, inevitably, to him.

The boar had already accounted for one of them, its throat ripped open by the needle sharp tusks that protruded from his heavy lower jaw, but the victory had been expensive. A lucky throw by one of the

27

spear-men had caught the boar in his flank just as he was turning to face an attack from another of the hounds. He had had to flee from the fight, badly injured and pursued by the remainder of the frenzied pack. In the distance the baying of the wolfhounds echoed around the forest, increasing in volume as they gained ground on him, eager for the kill.

The boar knew that he must find cover. Instinctively he splashed through a narrow stream swollen with melted snow, tore up the embankment on the far side and saw, nestling against the side of a rise in the ground, a thicket of fallen trees, overgrown with brambles and ivy. He had used it on hunting trips in the past. Unhesitatingly he headed for it. The thicket was familiar territory, and perfect cover from which to surprise his prey. And he had done so on countless occasions. The boar did not possess a sense of irony, or even fear, but his instinct for survival was overwhelming and like any cornered animal he would fight, to the death, if needs be. And so despite his weariness, his senses dulled by the spear-shaft buried deep in his flank, the boar held fast to the knowledge that this was the perfect place to hold the hounds at bay. Perhaps, if he was lucky, he might surprise one or two of the hunters before he was finished. With the baying of the wolfhounds growing ever louder, ever closer, the boar went gratefully to ground, to rest, to gather his strength for the final encounter.

Duke William loved the forest. Even more, he loved hunting. Stag, hind and boar - especially boar - were his favourite prey. Of late he had had little time to indulge the sport, but he had taken the Christmas break as an opportunity to spend time with his wife Matilda and their children. His three sons, Robert, the eldest, Richard, his second son and the youngest, William, nicknamed Rufus because of his blonde hair and red face, were with him on the hunt as were several of the members of his Court. He could never truly be alone, and indeed he did not seek such isolation. Duke

William was happiest when he was involved in the affairs of his province; a province fashioned through his own efforts, his astonishing courage, his skill as a battle commander and above all his ruthless, driving ambition. Normandy was the envy of France. Envy, and a constant threat to its neighbours.

For William did not intend to limit his horizons to Normandy. Far from it: he was still ambitious and his acquisitive eye had settled on the neighbouring provinces of Brittany and Maine, and if he had to resort to the sword to annex them to Normandy he would not hesitate to do so. William had lived in the shadow of violence all his life. Ever since his personal steward had been murdered, stabbed to death in front of his eyes, in his own bedchamber, at the age of ten he had been familiar with its sting. Violence was a part of his life and he had not shrunk from using it himself when necessary.

And beyond Normandy, beyond the cold, grey, stretch of sea that was called the Channel was the greatest prize of all, *England.* And it had been promised to him. By the Confessor, whose time was surely near, and by Earl Harold Godwineson who had sworn a solemn Oath to support his claim to the Crown when the time came. Duke William cast his mind back to the day that he had learned of Godwinesons' misfortune. Of the storm that had blown his ship off course and of his capture by Count Guy of Ponthieu.

The Gods had surely been smiling upon him that day. To place his greatest rival for the Throne in his hands to do with as he wished was an almost unbelievable stroke of luck, but it had happened. And he had taken his full measure from it. And so all he must do was to wait. For a King to die, and for the Crown to be placed on his head. And for once no blood would be shed. But if men had to die in order that he achieve his destiny he would not shrink from that either. The Crown *would* be his.

"Father! Father! Can we watch the kill?" Duke William's eldest son Robert reined up hard beside him, his face flushed with excitement.

Behind him his younger brother Richard struggled to control his lively mare, a present from the Duke that he had not quite mastered. Bringing up the rear was William Rufus, his red face, like Robert's, flushed scarlet. The Duke's sons would wage war on each other in the future, many years from now, but as they tried to control their mounts their only thoughts were on the fight to come. The boar had been tracked to its lair and the wolfhounds were closing for the final act.

"Yes, watch," he said, "but do not get involved. And stay close to Osmond. The boar still has fight in him. He could yet spill some blood. I don't want it to be yours!"

The boys laughed, and Robert and Richard spurred ahead, racing to join the mounted spear-men riding close behind the hounds.

"Can I stay with you father?" William Rufus looked up from the saddle of his pony with round, fearful eyes. Only nine, Duke William thought that perhaps he was too young for this. He reached down and tousled his son's blonde hair.

"Yes lad, you ride with me. Your time will come." Rufus smiled at him and suddenly the fear was gone. So young, thought the Duke, so young, and yet he had succeeded to the Dukedom of Normandy whilst still only eight. *Eight*. It was a miracle he had survived, but he had. It occurred to him that he had, all things considered, led a lucky life. If only his luck would hold a little longer...........

He watched Robert and Richard racing off into the distance, whipping their mares for the last ounce of pace. Robert was the elder by three years and was the better rider, but Richard was learning fast. In time he would catch, and then surpass Robert, both as a rider and as a student of warfare. And then there would be trouble. For Robert, being the elder, was Duke William's successor, and in Normandy the law of primogeniture dictated that the first-born inherit everything. But it was not the Duke's problem, and as he watched them leap a fallen log, their sure-footed mares making a perfect landing, almost in unison, he felt only pride that he had fathered such fine boys. They could fight their own battles when the time came.

Ahead of Duke William the baying of the hounds indicated that they had finally tracked the boar to the thicket that harboured him. The trick now was to flush him out so that one of the spear-men would have the chance to finish him with a well-aimed thrust to the heart. Amidst the cacophony of noise, the nervous snickering of the horses, the snarling and baying of the hounds and the squealing of the boar the spear-men formed a loose circle around the thicket. Duke William noted that despite his cautionary warning both Robert and Richard had manage to manoeuvre their mares into the circle of spear-men where they waited with their spears held tightly in their leather-gloved hands. With a sense of pride he saw that neither of them looked nervous. On the contrary there was good-humoured banter coming from the riders either side of them and Richard was animatedly pointing out a pool of blood at the entrance to the thicket. He was on the point of calling to the boys, ordering them to move back, out of the circle, when he suddenly checked himself and decided to let them have their day. They had to learn some time and now was as good as any. *Boys into men.* He had seen it so many times in his forty odd years. It happened overnight in his province of Normandy, a hard, cruel land where only the toughest survived. It had happened to him and he was not the worst for it. Let the boys stay then. At least the enemy was not man.

A horn sounded on the far side of the circle and the blast sent the wolfhounds into a frenzy. Bared fangs and a terrible deep-throated growl greeted the horn, the signal to seek out the quarry. One by one, almost in turns, the hounds launched themselves ferociously into the narrow confines of the thicket where the boar determinedly awaited them and after a bloody struggle repelled them with bared tusks that slashed like razors.

For fully five minutes the first scene was repeated; the hounds making forays, one by one, or in pairs, into the thicket, only to be repelled, bloodied and beaten by the boar that was making a defiant, an heroic, last stand. Duke William was about to order the firing of the thicket in attempt to smoke him out, something which he would have preferred not to do, when unexpectedly the boar emerged from cover, its stocky legs propelling him quickly over the snow-covered ground. He was through the wolfhounds before they could react and William realised with a pounding heart that the boar was heading straight for his eldest son.

"Robert!" he exclaimed as he jabbed his spurs into his stallion, drawing blood, but even as he did so he knew that he would be too late, far too late, because the boar was almost upon him. The boar hit Robert's frightened mare square in its belly, opening up a savage wound with its razor-sharp tusks. The mare reared and staggered from the impact and Robert was thrown to the ground, landing heavily on his back. To his dismay Duke William saw that instead of leaving his hunters behind, of quitting the field of battle, some primal instinct caused the boar to halt, to turn, and now it charged the prone figure of his son. Robert lay frozen with fear, unable to move as the huge beast bore down on him, its head and ferocious tusks levelled for the impact. Only two people were close enough to offer assistance: his brother Richard, and Osmond de Bodes, a knight in the Duke's service.

"Do something!" he cried, whipping his stallion even harder, a sob in his voice for the first time in years. He looked anxiously at Richard, gazing down at his brother as though in a trance, unable to help. It was hopeless. He was about to look away, unable to watch any longer when a figure flashed across his vision, lance point twinkling in the sun. In a moment it was over. The point found its mark, plunged deep into the boar's chest, hurling it backwards in a spray of blood. And now it lay thrashing just feet from where Robert sat shivering with fear, his eyes round and wide as he watched the thrashing subside into the last quivering moments of the doomed animal.

"Thank God!" Duke William said as he hurriedly dismounted and strode over to his son, hugging him hard against his chest. "Thank God you're safe."

"Thank Osmond father." Robert cast an accusing glance at Richard, still astride his mare, not having moved since the drama began. Richard looked away, as though it were nothing to him and Duke William wondered, just for a moment, whether Richard had wanted his older brother dead. It was nonsense of course, and he instantly dismissed the thought.

Osmond de Bodes walked over to the cadaver of the boar and brusquely pulled the lance point from its chest. The point had pierced the heart and there was bright red blood on the steel from the tip to the shaft. He wiped it on his breeches. The charge of the boar had done his work for him, fatally impaling itself on his point.

"A clean death, Lord," he said.

"You did well," said the Duke. "I owe you my thanks."

"It was nothing." Osmond de Bodes shrugged. "I simply had to hit the target. The boar's charge did the rest."

Duke William clapped him around the shoulders.

"The life of my son is *not* nothing. And you *did* do well. You are too modest. Lance work like that deserves a reward. Dine with us tonight."

"With pleasure, Lord." Osmond de Bodes knew an order when it was given.

"Well, then, that's settled." The crisis over, the Duke was himself once more. He looked at the boar stiffening in the snow, its blood slowly turning the ground red.

"He fought hard. He also deserves a reward. We must find a fitting end for him." The day had ended well and tonight they would feast.

He was about to mount his destrier when a rider, unknown to him, galloped into view. He absently noted the flecks of sweat on the stallion's neck and withers, the exhaustion etched into the man's face. He felt the hairs on his neck stiffen. There was something not right about this. The rider dismounted and handed him the note. He saw the fear in the man's eyes, the refusal to meet his own and knew that his intuition had not been wrong.

"What is it?" he snapped.

"A message from Fitz Wimarc, Lord....from England."

The courier withdrew to tend his lathered mount and Duke William opened the note, breaking the seal. He quickly scanned the contents.

And when he had finished reading his renowned temper, barely controlled at the best of times, finally erupted. The boar, the feast, his sons, Brittany and the Maine were quite forgotten as Duke William poured forth a torrent of vitriol such as those present had never heard, and would never hear again.

For Harold Godwineson was Crowned King of England, his oath to the Duke forgotten, the Duke consigned to history...

CHAPTER FOUR

THE SOUTH COAST OF ENGLAND

MARCH 1066

King Harold Godwineson had not forgotten his oath to William the Bastard. He had not been allowed to forget. And now he stood motionless on the highest point of the cliffs at Dover staring out across the bleak grey sea whilst the wind whipped his hair across his face and tugged at his grey-flecked moustaches. One day, that sea which was now almost empty would be filled with ships: the ships of William's fleet. And when they came he must be ready to hurl them back.

It had been a tumultuous three months since his Coronation, since he had sworn the threefold Oath sworn by every King of England at his Coronation since Edgar had first framed the vows in 973 AD: *To guard the Church of God; to forbid violence and wrong; to keep Justice, Judgement and Mercy.* He had already broken one oath but that was excusable since it had been necessary to maintain the others. On the day of Fitz Wimarc's expulsion he had had to force the Norman Earl into the ship that saw him depart England's shores, cursing and swearing eternal damnation on him for ignoring his Oath to Duke William. The man had stood arguing on the jetty, protesting his rights, the loss of his land, the sanctity of the oath, when Harold had drawn his sword and pushed him gently backwards. Fitz Wimarc's men had had to fish him out of the water.

He should not have done it but it was sweet revenge for the ignominy he had faced at the hands of his Norman captors.

And now they had all gone, departed England's shores forever. He had cleansed the Capital, the Country, of them. There would be no traitors, no Norman spies at his Court sending reports back to William or spreading dissent amongst the people. But that had only been the beginning. Soon rumours of Duke William's terrible outrage, his lust for revenge, his plans for a spring invasion, were being whispered throughout the Capital. And then the messages had begun to arrive.

In January William had offered his youngest daughter, Agatha, in marriage to him. It was a thinly disguised attempt to claim the Throne by the back door but of course Harold had rejected her.

"What do I want with the Norman whore of a Norman bastard?" he had replied. "I already have a woman." Then William had simply demanded the Crown, reminding him of his solemn Oath.

"An Oath given at the point of a sword is no Oath at all," he had replied peremptorily. And then the most serious news of all had arrived: William had petitioned the Pope to support his cause, his "holy crusade" as he had called it. And he had succeeded beyond his wildest expectations.

Not only had Rome given its support to the "crusade," calling upon all true believers to support the invasion, they had also issued a Papal Bull, excommunicating him from the Church of Rome as a perjured liar, as a breaker of oaths, indeed, as the Anti-Christ himself. So now he was damned by God and by the Church of Rome. The injustice of it had appalled and angered him when he had first received the news, but now it gnawed at him like a festering sore that would not go away. It occupied much of his time, time that should be spent on preparing for the battles ahead.

"Are you a religious man, Ranulf?" He turned to his senior housecarl, now the King's Champion. Ranulf had an honest, open face that most women found handsome, but it was weatherbeaten and worn, touched with hardness by years of campaigning, the permanent threat of violent death. He tore his eyes from the Channel to answer the question.

"Religious, Lord?" he said, surprised to have his beliefs questioned by the King, as if they somehow mattered. "I suppose so," he said. "Some great being must have created us, otherwise we would not be here."

Harold Godwineson grunted, considering Ranulf's answer.

"Yes," he said, "but do you believe in God, in heaven, and hell?" He pressed his point, needing reassurance.

"I believe the Gods watch over us, Lord," Ranulf said, unsure of the reason for these questions, "but as for heaven and hell, I suppose I shall just have to wait." Harold grunted again. It was not the answer, the reassurance, that he had been seeking, and now he turned to Guthrum Hard-Axe.

"And you Guthrum, what do you believe in?"

The reply he received was uncompromising, like the man himself, but ultimately of even less help:

"I believe in keeping my blade sharp, Sire," he said as he squinted along the edge of his axe, "and I believe that if William the Bastard trades blows with me I shall crack his skull like an egg!"

Harold laughed, despite his inner concerns.

"You may soon have your chance!" he said. Then, on a more serious note:

"William is set on the Crown. Even now he is making his preparations. We must be ready for him."

"He cannot hope to succeed, Lord." Ranulf's eyes were turned again towards the grey water of the Channel. "We are too many for him and Normandy is just a province, no bigger than Wales. He must know he has no chance."

"True enough," Harold acknowledged, "but his reason, his….judgement, is clouded. Clouded by hatred of me, and lust for revenge. He had England in his grasp. I gave it to him and then took it away. He is not a man to cross…and now he has God on his side."

He followed Ranulf's gaze out to sea, lost for a moment in thought. He had done all he that he could for the present. In the north he had secured an alliance with the Earls of Northumbria and Mercia: the brothers Morcar and Edwin. His own brothers had been despatched to their Earldoms to raise men for the army and here, in the South, preparations were already well in hand.

He looked along the coastline, first to the east, and satisfied, to the west. All along the coast he had ordered that huge, wooden pyres be built, perched on top of the white chalk hills, ready to be lit in an instant, the moment the invader was sighted. He had mobilised the fyrd, his volunteer army, each man required to give six weeks service to the King and now those men, the militia, were stationed along the coastline, tending the pyres, watching and waiting for William the Bastard. Just like himself.

He sighed a small sigh and stared far out to sea. The coastline of Normandy was obscured by mist and he could see nothing. Nothing, save for the seagulls crying their raucous cry as they circled endlessly above the water and a small fishing boat risking the run of the ebb tide, the demons of the sea, whilst they fished its murky waters for a catch. If only it could have been otherwise.

His hand was drawn to his scabbard and he touched the hilt of his sword as if to draw strength from it. This was no ordinary sword but *Requitur,* the Sword of Kings. It had been presented to him at his Coronation and it was magnificent. He slid it easily from its oiled scabbard and examined it as he had done on numerous occasions. It meant more to him than the Crown, the Orb, or the Sceptre, the symbols, the vestments of power. It had been fashioned by Alfred the Great after his great victory over the Danes at Edington and it had been worn by all the Kings of England ever since. And now it was his. He turned it in his hand, admiring the fine filigree work on the handle, the beautiful gold inlay chased into the razor-edged blade, and the huge rubies, diamonds and sapphires set into the pommel, giving the sword its perfect balance. It was a work of genius.

"A beautiful weapon, Lord." Ranulf, ever the warrior, knew fine workmanship when he saw it and there was admiration in his voice.

"Yes, Ranulf," he said. "But it is more than a weapon. It betokens the wearer as the true, the legitimate, King of England, just as much as the Crown itself." He slid *Requitur* smoothly back into its scabbard and felt momentarily cheered. Eternity was not yet at hand and he *was* England's true King, whatever William the Bastard or those other bastards in Rome might have to say about it.

He looked out to sea one final time but nothing had changed; the mist had thickened and now hung over the sea like a shroud. Even the little fishing boat had disappeared. There was no point to this. William the Bastard would come, of that there could be no doubt. In Normandy great swathes of forest were already being cleared for their timber. Timber for William's fleet. But his great fleet was still under construction; not yet ready to sail. And in the meantime he had a Kingdom to rule, an army to prepare, and by God, or the Devil, if God had turned his back on him, he intended to do so.

"Back to London," he said. "There is work to do."

CHAPTER FIVE

THE HOUSECARL'S CAMP, SUSSEX.

EARLY APRIL. 1066.

The spear-point flashed in the sun, aimed unerringly at his heart. At the last moment, the last fraction of a second, he parried to his left and the point, caught by the shaft of his own spear, whipped past him, piercing only the air. Without a pause, in the same fluid movement, Ranulf Redbeard went into the riposte, hoping to catch his opponent unaware but the boy was quick to react. With a turn of his arm he deflected the thrust with ease, catching the blunted end of the spear-point on the face of his shield so that it too slid away, harmlessly, into thin air. The boy was good; he was very good. The best Ranulf had seen all morning. He called a halt.

"Excellent," he said. "Where did you learn your spear-work boy?"

"My father taught me," the boy replied. His face was a little flushed with the effort but otherwise he was quite calm. He had a good temperament, a quality that would be essential if he was to stand in the shield-wall.

"Your father taught you well," Ranulf said. "What do they call you?"

"Cnut," the boy answered, "after King Canute. My father always said that we could trace our ancestry back to him."

The boy had long blonde hair and blue eyes. His father could have been right.

"What does your father do now?" Ranulf asked. "Perhaps I know him?"

"My father is dead," Cnut said. "Killed in the Welsh Wars five years ago, fighting for the Confessor."

"Wales," Ranulf said, remembering his own experience of it. "An ungodly land. A poor place to die. I am sorry, boy."

"No need for sorrow," Cnut replied, "he died doing what he did best. He knew the odds."

"And you?" Ranulf said, "You wish to fight for the King? The shield-wall is a brutal place to earn a living."

"It is what my father wanted," Cnut said. "It is what he trained me for. And why I am here."

Ranulf turned to Guthrum who had been watching the proceedings.

"What do you think?" he asked. The King was desperate to recruit as many men to his Standards as possible. There would be enough willing volunteers when the time came but Harold needed trained men, skilful warriors to stand in the shield-wall: Men who would not flinch at the horror of battle; men who would be loyal to their blood-oaths. Such men were hard to find.

Guthrum looked at Cnut, sizing him up.

"Take him," he said. "He came as close to skewering you as anyone I have seen…except myself, of course." He laughed.

"Alright Cnut," Ranulf said. "I will see you later."

Ranulf walked over to the crowd of young men anxiously waiting their turn to test themselves against the King's Champion.

"Next one!" he cried. "Lets see whether you can get through my guard! But remember – if you don't get me, I will get you. That's the way of it." Another hopeful stepped forward from the ranks, young, eager, another boy. There were too many boys he thought, not enough men. He was about to begin when Earl Gyrth rode into the camp, dust and sweat covering both himself and his stallion.

"How is it going?" Gyrth asked as he dismounted.

"Slow," Ranulf said, "but one or two useful looking ones have been found. Why?"

"We will need more than one or two," Gyrth said sourly. "We have just heard that Hardraada has decided to chance his arm."

"Hardraada?"

"Harald Hardraada, the King of Norway. Claims he can trace his blood-line back to Canute, and that gives him the right to the Crown."

"The world is full of them," Guthrum joked, overhearing the conversation. "There is another of them over there." He pointed to Cnut. Gyrth ignored him.

"The point is," Gyrth said forcefully, "we may have to fight on two fronts and to do that we need men. Lots of them."

"So?" Ranulf asked.

"Recruit more men, and then train them. Train them hard, from dawn until dusk." He mounted his stallion with practised ease and eyed the crowd of hopefuls waiting to be tried.

"That lot look promising," he said as he reined the stallion around. Ranulf shrugged. "Perhaps," he said. "Time will tell."

"Time and *training*," Gyrth emphasised the last word. He dug his spurs into the stallion's flank, kicking up a cloud of dust as the stallion leaped forward.

"Remember Ranulf!" he cried as he rode out of the Camp, "Dawn until dusk!"

Ranulf sighed and went back to the recruits. If Gyrth was correct, and they had to face Hardraada too, the odds had lengthened dramatically.

CHAPTER SIX

LONDON, ENGLAND.

24TH APRIL 1066

The beer had flowed freely again and Ranulf, sitting alone in the corner of the ale-house that he had started to frequent stared idly at the throng of people packed inside its squalid accommodation. He was drunk, and his head rang with the sound of laughter coming from the table adjoining his. Quite how he had fallen into the routine of frequenting this particular establishment on a nightly basis after training he was not entirely sure.

There was little to commend it, save for the price of the beer, watered down, no doubt by the landlord. He was large and round and hearty and kept his customers until the small hours. But it was not this that had attracted Ranulf's custom. It was the young serving maid that the landlord employed to wait on his tables and to keep his customers in their cups. She was a lively vivacious girl with raven hair, a lean, hard, body beneath her shift that set his imagination on fire, and dark, dark eyes like limpid pools that a man could lose himself in for ever.

Ranulf had seen the way the other men looked at her, lusted for her, devouring her with their eyes as she placed their tankards in front of them. But whilst she had flirted with them, laughed at them, shared their jokes, she had never shown the slightest interest in a deeper attachment to any of them. And that small fact had fuelled Ranulf's own hopes, for deep down, buried beneath the layers of tissue and bone that made him the most feared warrior in the Country was a desire for this girl that burned brighter than he could ever have imagined.

He had not yet spoken to her but their eyes had met across the crowded tavern floor and she had smiled at him before her attention had been drawn away elsewhere. He had made enquiries and discovered from careful questioning that her name was Alice and that she was an orphan, forced into taking this position just to live.

Ranulf was not proud of the fact that he had drifted into somewhat lax ways, but the training was hard and even a housecarl was entitled to have some fun. There had been precious little of that since Gyrth's visit three weeks earlier. Harold himself had visited the housecarl camp on four occasions in the past few weeks, closely questioning Ranulf on how the new recruits were progressing, whether they would stand in the shield-wall when the enemy were closing upon them, the numbers that he had he recruited, and question after question along those lines.

Harold had changed in a subtle way that Ranulf could not precisely identify. Whenever he tried to raise the matter with him, Harold had simply shrugged and changed the subject. It was as though Harold was waiting for something to give, for the enemy to show himself. Ranulf understood the King's concerns as to what was happening on the other side of the Channel, and he felt sure that Harold's excommunication by the hypocrites in Rome had not helped matters, but what was there to fear? Harold had, with the men loyal to his brothers and those of his new allies, the Earls Morcar and Edwin, nearly twenty thousand men at his disposal. This number was far more than William the Bastard or Harald Hardraada could ever hope to match. A problem only arose if they made their invasion plans together, or within a few weeks of each other so that Harold would have to divide his army to deal with them. But that was most unlikely, and could be discounted. So what Harold's problem was he really could not tell.

He downed the remains of his tankard and looked around. The girl had not yet appeared and he felt a tinge of disappointment.

Perhaps she was not working this evening. He cast about again, hoping to spot her amongst the crowd, but not seeing her he bowed to the inevitable and picked up his long, double-edged sword. He threw some coins on the table and moved towards the door. Recognising him as the King's Champion the crowd nearest the door respectfully parted to let him pass. He was not a man to cross. He grunted his farewell to the Landlord and made his exit into the cool night air. His head swam and he gulped lungfuls of fresh air in the hope that it would clear his mind. He decided to make his way back to their London barracks. Perhaps Guthrum or some of the others, Aelfgar, or Eadgar, would have some entertainment laid on. It would be all work in the morning; more raw recruits, more eager young men without the slightest notion of what it was like to stand in the shield wall and not run for your life when all of your senses were screaming at you to do just that. He sighed, and Gyrth's parting words, *from dawn until dusk,* echoed in his subconscious. He was strangely restless to make the most of the night.

As he turned the corner of a narrow alley he had his wish, but not in the way that he would have supposed. Two men, one large and burly, the other wiry, with a face marked by the smallpox were holding a young girl to the ground. She was struggling violently, kicking wildly with her feet whilst the larger man held a knife to her throat, his other hand over her mouth to prevent her from screaming. The smaller man was reaching greedily under her gown with a leer on his face. Their intention was obvious and Ranulf felt sickened by what he saw. Shouting a challenge he drew his sword and hurried towards them. The larger man had to withdraw the knife from the girls' throat to pull his own sword from its scabbard and the girl quickly ran off in the direction of the tavern.

The danger for her was over, but now Ranulf had two opponents to face. For common cut-throats they were clever. Whilst the larger man faced him from the front, the smaller man, wielding a long stiletto, circled around to take him from behind. He guessed that they would time their moves simultaneously, hoping to catch him with his guard down, his back unprotected.

There was only one move to make and he made it quickly. Lunging towards the large man he put a distance of five paces between himself and the man threatening his rear. It was little enough, but it gave him the precious seconds that he needed to deal with the immediate threat. The large man was quick, but not quick enough, despite the drink that Ranulf had consumed. Ranulf swung at his head and the large man brought up his sword to parry the blow, but it was only a feint, practised a thousand times on the training ground and lowering his point at the last second he went under the big man's guard and caught him clean through the heart. The man seemed surprised at first, it had all happened so quickly. He looked at Ranulf then down, to the gaping wound in his chest, the blossoming crimson stain. He had started to cry, blubbering like a child before his eyes glazed over and he toppled forward. He was dead before he hit the ground. It had taken mere seconds.

Ranulf now turned to face the threat from the rear but the smaller man, seeing how decisively Ranulf had dealt with his friend decided that armed with only a stiletto he stood no chance against this interfering stranger. Pausing only to hurl the knife at Ranulf he disappeared into the shadows. It was a lucky throw. The knife caught him on his left shoulder, lodging in his flesh up to the hilt. It was sufficient to stop him in his tracks and prevented any thought of pursuit. He gritted his teeth and pulled the stiletto from his shoulder, the exit of the weapon causing a surge of blood down his arm. He tore a piece of cloth from his cloak and started to dress the wound, painfully, clumsily, when a soft voice caught him unawares:

"Let me tend to that." He turned to see who had spoken and looked into the dark eyes that he had been dreaming of all night. It was the

46

girl from the tavern. She had been crying, he saw, but it only added to her beauty, a goddess with a human heart.

"You," he said. Then softer, remembering that they had not yet spoken: "What happened?" He handed the rough bandage to her.

"I was making my way to the inn when those men" - she glanced fearfully at the torso of the dead man - "set upon me. With a knife at my throat I dare not cry for help. It was lucky you came along when you did. If not for you…." She did not finish; she did not have to. Ranulf understood what she meant. She looked at his face, at the red beard covering his cheeks.

"Does your shoulder hurt? How is that?" She finished dressing the wound. The bandage had finally staunched the flow of blood.

"It hurts like hell but I won't die from it." He examined the stiletto.

"If I see that bastard again I will skewer him with this." He wiped the blood from the blade and tucked the knife into his belt.

"I know you don't I?" the girl asked suddenly, surprising him. "From the tavern?" She stared into his face with her dark eyes, the question still on her lips.

"I have been drinking there lately," he said guardedly.

"I thought so. I have seen you sitting alone in the corner. You always seem to be so serious, so deep in thought." She paused to reflect. "What is troubling you?" she asked.

He looked at the girl, at the limpid eyes fixed enquiringly upon him. She really was beautiful. And, he had to admit, very young. She was dangerous, but he felt like a little danger. Perhaps it was the drink but he doubted it.

"Why don't I tell you whilst I walk you home," he suggested. "The streets can be dangerous at night."

"I didn't know!" She laughed, her eyes alight, and realising his mistake, he laughed too. He was nervous, he realised, nervous of a slip of a girl. Unbelievable.

"I live not far from here," she said, "with an elderly couple. They took me in when I was young. They have been very good to me. I do what I can to help them."

"By waiting upon drunkards! That is no life for someone like you." He hoped it sounded like gallantry but he wasn't sure that it did. Gallantry was not his usual style.

"And what am I then?" she said, her eyes still alight, still fixed upon his, and he knew that she was teasing him. He hesitated before saying: "A beautiful woman, who deserves better." It sounded so crass he almost blushed beneath his beard.

"Its not so bad." There was a serious note to her voice now, as though she knew she had caused him embarrassment. "Most of the men are usually too drunk to cause any trouble." She made it sound like nothing. Astonishingly, Ranulf realised that he was no longer drunk, although whether it was the fight, the wound, or just the beautiful girl on his arm he could not say.

"I have seen you in the tavern," he confessed. "I sometimes watch you serving the tables. I didn't see you tonight, and when you didn't appear I decided to leave..." He tailed off, unsure of himself once more.

"So you watch me do you?" The girl laughed softly and now she brought up her hand to touch his cheek, the first intimacy between them. He could feel her fingertips on his beard; soft, like her laugh.

"Why do you watch me?" she said, her face tilted towards his own, her eyes gazing into his, as though to see into his soul.

"You know why," he said eventually. His hand folded over hers, holding it to his face, not wanting to lose the moment.

"Yes," she said, "I know. I know, and it's alright." She pulled her hand away but he didn't mind; the compact had been made.

She led him to her lodgings and as she did so he told her of his life: of what it meant to be the King's Champion, of his blood-oath, of the troubles besetting the King.

"But surely," she said, "We have nothing to fear? If men like yourself, your comrades and the rest of the Country stand behind him the King must prevail?

"Yes," he replied, "that's right. Or I believe it is. But the King is not convinced. Dark thoughts trouble him, and the more he thinks on them the worse it gets. It is the waiting, I think. Fear is always worse than the reality." He sighed, not for the first time. "Enough of the King," he said, "for tonight, at least."

They made their way back to Alice's home, a small tumbledown dwelling in one of the poorest parts of the Capital. She lived in a small, damp room under the roof eaves. The remaining occupants, her "mother and father" as she called them, had retired to their bed long since. She lit a single tallow candle and Ranulf could see in the poor light that the room contained only a straw bed, covered by a patched blanket, and a stool, one of the legs of which were missing.

The roof, which let in the rain, sloped down to the floor and it was only by positioning himself carefully that he could stand without having to crouch double.

He went to the window and briefly looked out. Hearing a noise he turned around and saw to his astonishment that the girl was naked. And that she was beautiful. Her slim body, darkly shadowed in the gloomy light was lithe and hard, and he could not help staring at her. She opened her arms and he went to her. He held her against him, feeling strangely vulnerable even though she was naked and he was still clothed. After a while she gently pulled free of his caress but it was only to undress him, which she performed slowly, carefully, gently kissing the parts of him that she unveiled. She lingered over his wound, as though to kiss it better, and she was almost like a child as she did so. But she was not a child and he felt himself harden with arousal, a desire for this woman that he had not felt in years. He gave himself to her completely.

49

They made love with a passion, as though by doing so they could exorcise their fears: the pain of the night, her attack, his wound, all the ghosts of their past. And after they had made love they lay in the light of the solitary candle, her head across his chest, her hair damp with sweat, her breathing light and easy in sleep. He thought of what tomorrow might bring, of how he would reconcile his life with what had just happened, for his life, so simple, so ordered, had irrevocably changed and he would never again be able to return to it. Not entirely.

He rose from the mattress carefully, softly, so as not to wake her; she was sleeping soundly. He walked over to the casement window and threw it open to get some air. He looked into the clear night sky, his thoughts far away. And then he saw something that caused his heart to miss a beat. He rubbed his eyes, not trusting, not believing, what he had seen, and he looked again. But there was no mistake: The long-tailed star not seen for nearly a hundred years was shining brightly over the London skyline. It portended the overthrow of a nation, the death of a King. He thought of William the Bastard, of Harald Hardraada, and of Harold Godwineson, his King, his *friend,* and a shiver went down his spine.

"God preserve England," he said, taking a final look before quickly closing the shutter. He offered up a silent prayer and hoped the Almighty was listening.

CHAPTER SEVEN

THE GREAT HALL,

THE PALACE OF WESTMINSTER,

THE END OF APRIL 1066

The Great Hall echoed to the footsteps of men going late to their beds as yet another Council of War ended. Everyone agreed that it was only a matter of time before William the Bastard or Harald Hardraada put in hand their plans for their proposed invasion and Harold's War Council had debated long into the night the means by which the threats could be met. They all agreed upon one thing; that the threat from Duke William, from across the narrow stretch of the Channel, was by far the greater, and the one that posed the immediate problem.

Harold was tired. It was nearly two a.m. and his bed beckoned, but he was reluctant to sleep. He was as satisfied as he could be that everything possible had been done, and was still being done, to secure the Country's position. The southern fleet had been posted all along the south coast, and the fyrd, his regular troops, had been held in reserve, a little inland, ready to move to wherever the threat might come. Ranulf and his comrades were busy recruiting new warriors for his elite housecarl regiment and his brothers' had rallied their own hearth troop to his Standard. Everything that could be done had been done, but he had a terrible foreboding nonetheless.

Ranulf had been watching the King during the course of the long night, and was concerned for him. With every day that passed it seemed that Harold's demeanour grew more restless, his mood swinging from depression to exultation with very little explanation or cause. The long-tailed star that had shone so brightly that unforgettable night had shaken him to the core and he knew that he was not the only one with grave misgivings as to what it might portend. All over Europe eyes were turned towards England, awaiting events. He caught the King's eye and decided to seize the moment.

"A word, Lord?" he said. It was an old habit, the use of the word "Lord," a habit he had been unable to break despite the fact that Harold was now his King. Harold never objected; they were old friends though the social divide was a chasm.

"Yes, Ranulf," Harold said, "What troubles you?"

Ranulf hesitated before plunging ahead with what he had intended to say.

"It is what troubles you, Lord, that concerns me." The King gave him a quizzical look but he pressed on regardless.

"Since your excommunication you have not been yourself. We have long been friends and have shared our problems; I would know what is troubling you." For a moment he thought he might have pressed his point too hard for he saw the King's eyes flash, a spark of anger, but then it was gone.

"Perhaps I can help?" he said.

Harold turned reddened eyes, circled with dark shadows, towards him, and this time held them there.

"Something is troubling me," he admitted after a pause, "but it is not a matter one can speak openly about." He appeared to debate the point with himself before speaking again.

 "I have your word that what I say will not be repeated, to anyone?"

"Yes, Lord."

"I have your blood-oath on this?"

"Of course, Lord."

"Then I will tell you," Harold said at last. Even so there was a long pause before he began.

"I have this dream," he said finally, "the same dream each night."

"Yes Lord?"

"It started soon after I was declared excommunicate from our Saviour's grace, from the light of His salvation." He paused again, as though trying to frame the words so that they made sense.

"Do you believe in destiny, Ranulf?" he said suddenly. "That whatever path we choose our fate is always the same?" His eyes, his voice, demanded an answer, and Ranulf considered the question carefully before responding.

"No Lord," he replied truthfully, vaguely recollecting a similar conversation on the cliffs overlooking the Channel. "Man makes his own destiny, or so I believe."

"Yes, Ranulf," the King said. "So have I also believed. But now I have this dream, this… nightmare, some would call it, and I question myself."

"Nightmare, Lord?"

"In my dream, my *nightmare*, I am lost in a red mist. The mist blinds me so that I cannot see. I turn, around, and around, but still I see nothing for the red mist covers my eyes. I lay down, as if to sleep, but I do not wish to sleep, and yet I wish I had slept, for as I lay four …spectral figures, brilliant figures in silver and gold and scarlet approach through the mist. And then I feel pain, such pain that cannot be described, and then I awake, Ranulf. And when I awake I am covered in sweat. From head to foot, covered in sweat. And yet I am cold, so cold…"

Ranulf looked at the King not knowing what to say. He had not expected this.

"What do you make of it Ranulf?" the King asked and the haunted eyes seemed to look right through him. Ranulf did not answer, indeed had no answer.

"I have considered the meaning of this dream," the King said softly, "and it allows only one interpretation. It is my belief that the red mist is the fire of Everlasting Hell; that the four spectral figures are avenging angels sent from Heaven to punish me.... This is my belief, Ranulf; this, I fear, is my Fate."

Never had Ranulf seen the King look so distraught. The dark circled eyes, the fear reflected in them were confirmation of it. And what the King had said troubled him more than he could admit.

"Punish you for what, Lord?" he said at last. "You have done nothing to reproach yourself for. You are the Crowned King of England, appointed by God, and anointed by his servant here on earth. You have said as much yourself."

"But what if I am wrong?" The King's voice shook with emotion and Ranulf could almost touch the fear in it.

"You are not wrong, Lord," he said with a confidence he did not feel, "but you are tired. And these are the dreams of a tired man. These dreams are nothing to concern yourself about. Consider this Lord," he said in a moment of inspiration. "I too am excommunicate, for the Papal Bull included all of your supporters. Myself, your brothers, all of us. And yet the fires of Hell do not trouble our sleep. Avenging angels do not visit our bedchambers to torment us. You are simply tired, Lord. Tired, and troubled by the fight to come."

He watched the King's face as Harold considered his reply, weighing his words, but he could see that he had failed in his attempt at reassurance. Eventually the King spoke, but in a voice that was as bleak and chill as winter:

"Then why me Ranulf?" he said. "Why me?"

The question was rhetorical for the King knew the answer. He had stolen a Crown.

And now he must pay the price.

CHAPTER EIGHT

THE ENGLISH CHANNEL

EARLY MAY 1066

Beneath a leaden grey sky the long boats with their high, dragon headed prows made their way slowly towards the land. Their sails billowed as the southerly breeze that had brought them across the Channel now carried them towards the shore where, with a resounding crash the waves broke upon the shingle and died.

Standing in the prow of the leading vessel Tostig Godwineson, younger brother of King Harold Godwineson, former Earl of Northumbria looked upon England for the first time in a year. The Isle of Wight had always been a strong supporter of the House of Godwine, and Tostig, eyeing the green fields and valleys of the approaching island hoped to rally that support to his cause. He sailed with a fleet of thirty-five ships and nearly one thousand two hundred men. Not enough for his purpose, but it was a start.

For the past year he had been in exile in Flanders, fretting about what was happening in England and hoping against hope for a recall. He had not been idle, however, and had spent his time gathering support, recruiting troops, and making allies wherever he could. And those allies included Harald Hardraada of Norway and Duke William of Normandy. Whilst the old King, Edward, had been alive there had always been the chance of reinstatement to the Earldom of Northumbria, but now, with the Confessor gone and his brother Harold on the Throne his position was hopeless. He hated his brother with a blind, unreasoning hatred that consumed his soul. The thought that Harold was now wearing the Crown of England whilst he was a penniless exile only served to add fuel to that hatred. So now his brother would pay and he, Tostig Godwineson would once again be a power in the land. That, or he would die in the attempt. He had sworn an Oath to himself and it would be so. He would not accept an Earldom now even if Harold offered it to him. Not that Harold would be likely to do that anyway. No, he would have to take what he wanted, what he deserved, by force. And by God he intended to do it.

As the long ships entered the surf Tostig pulled on his eagle winged helmet, a gift from his cousin, Sven Erithson of Denmark, and tightened the strap under his chin. Leaping over the side he plunged into the icy, foaming water. The cold hit him like a knife but he did not care. Ripping his sword from his scabbard he held it tightly in his fist and the feeling was wonderful. He was back on English soil, and the Country would tremble at his touch before he had finished with her. With a wave of his sword he ordered his men forward and waded through the surf towards the shore.

Duke William stood for a long time on the quayside at Le Havre, watching the sails of Tostig Godwineson's fleet slowly disappear from view. The breeze that carried the long ships away from Normandy whipped his hair and stung his face and he gathered his cloak tight about him against the cold. He could not hazard a guess as to what prospects of success Tostig's enterprise faced as the gaily coloured sails of the fleet became smaller and smaller. He shrugged. It was all one to him whatever happened, although he had been stunned when Tostig had appeared at his court offering his services for his crusade. In return he had wanted the Earldom of Northumbria. He must have been mad. William had politely declined because the last thing he wanted was a Saxon Earl to deal with after he had gained the Crown. In any event, he had already promised to carve up the land between those who supported him in return for their ships and their men. There would be no room for Saxons in his England once he had gained the Crown. But he could not tell Tostig that.

The prospect, however, of setting brother against brother was simply too good an opportunity to miss. And so he had given Tostig just enough ships and men to cause Harold trouble; real trouble if Tostig could gather any support, something which he thought doubtful on his assessment of Tostig's character. Still, there was always the possibility that the two barbarians would kill each other and save him the trouble. He was not a man easily given to smiles but he smiled to himself nevertheless.

His invasion plans were proceeding at a pace. Rich in oak forests, Normandy had been systematically plundered by shipwrights and carpenters anxious to obtain the finest timbers for his fleet and now the first vessels were being launched and assembled in the estuary of the Dives, a large tidal lake ideal for the gathering of the invasion fleet. Furthermore men were flocking to his banner. Word of the Pope's support for his Holy Crusade had spread far and wide and volunteers were pouring in, not only from Normandy but from the adjoining provinces of Maine, Brittany, Ponthieu, Flanders, Isle de France, Anjou, Picardy and Aquitaine. Men had even travelled from Germany to join his crusade, and from across the Alps, from Italy, and Sicily. Some of the volunteers, such as Eustace of Boulogne and Guy of Ponthieu were great Lords with many followers but most were simple knights, attracted by the lure of adventure and the prospects of riches, and land, in England.

Feeding and accommodating such a host was proving to be a considerable problem and the young knight, Osmond de Bodes, who had saved his son's life had been drafted onto his staff to help with the many problems that the mercenaries were beginning to cause.

Osmond now approached the Duke who was standing stock-still watching the horizon, his eyes narrowed against the wind.

"The beginning, Lord?" he asked. Osmond was fired with the thought of the Holy Crusade and was itching to be off, doing the Lord's work in England. Even though it was for William the Bastard.

"A small beginning, I think," Duke William said without taking his eyes off the horizon. "How much longer before my invasion fleet shall follow them?"

Osmond was not sure whether this was a question directed at him or whether the Duke was talking to himself. He knew the Dukes' temper, however, and so ventured a reply:

"If all goes well, by the autumn, Lord."

The tiny points of colour had now disappeared from sight, the fleet gone from view. William the Bastard turned to face the land again.

"I am sure you are right, boy," he said. "I am sure you are right."

CHAPTER NINE

THE GREAT HALL,
THE PALACE OF WESTMINSTER, LONDON.

MAY 1066.

So it was Tostig, his brother. Not William the Bastard, not Hardraada, but his own brother that had brought the first challenge against him. Harold Godwineson studied the faces of the four men gathered about his Council Table as they debated what to do. Gyrth, Leo, Ranulf, Guthrum. They were mostly in shadow but even so he could see that they were grim, concerned, for this was a turn of events that with all their other problems they could have wished to avoid. But Tostig had made his play – to what end he could not be sure, but it was clear that William the Bastard was behind it – and so they had to deal with Tostig. And deal with him quickly.

Torches burning in their wall beckets threw long shadows across the flagstone floor of the Great Hall and for a moment Harold imagined that he could see in those shadows the spectral figures of his dream. But this was no time for dreams. The threat that Tostig posed was very real. No time for dreams then, but for action.

Harold had pressed his argument with his brothers: William was not yet ready; his fleet not yet built. Hardraada was the other side of the North Sea. Tostig had only thirteen hundred men and had not yet established any support. Their course was clear, he said: march on Tostig now, take him quickly and regroup. There would be no need to use the fleet; that could stay on station. But take a third of the fyrd, *a third,* and use it as the anvil upon which the hammer of his own housecarl regiment would smash Tostig.

Leofwine put a skin of wine to his lips and wiped his mouth on the sleeve of his doublet.

"Who will command the fyrd?" he asked.

"Yourself, and Gyrth." He glanced at Gyrth, saw him nod his agreement.

"And yourself?"

"I will bring my hearth troop south, with Ranulf. We shall catch him in a pincer movement. If he moves against you, I will take him in the rear. If he moves north, against me, then you shall move against his rear. Finish."

Leofwine passed Gyrth the wineskin and asked the question that had been uppermost in his mind from the moment they had learned of Tostig's landing.

"And Tostig? He is our brother. What of him, Hal?"

Harold looked at Leofwine for a long time before giving the answer that he knew he would one day have to give.

"Tostig is no longer our brother," he said. "No longer a Godwine. Tostig is now the enemy, an ally of William the Bastard. And enemies of England can expect little mercy."

He looked around the table, at the four men seated opposite him. And as his eyes met theirs he knew that in their hearts they were agreed.

CHAPTER TEN.

THE KENTISH COAST, ENGLAND

MAY 1066.

Watery sunlight penetrated the cracks in the timbers of the old barn, warming the young couple that lay spent, their naked, sweating bodies entwined together in the hay. They had been meeting clandestinely in the barn for three weeks and the girl thought that she had never been so happy. She looked down at her young lover, his head across her breast, his eyes closed against the sunlight. He was so beautiful. She stroked his golden hair and slowly ran her fingers through it, enjoying the feel of it against her skin. He was breathing gently, easily, and murmured in mock protest when she curled a lock of his hair around her finger and gently pulled it. He was seventeen and she was just sixteen, and for both it was their first love.

They had met only recently, and for her it had been love at first sight. She and her father had travelled to Romney from Lincolnshire seeking work and all had gone well until they had reached the outskirts of the village. Without warning, a wheel had come off the cart in which they had been travelling and try as they might they did not have the strength to lift the cart sufficiently to refit the wheel. And then Edmond came along. Stripping off his shirt and bracing himself against the cart, he had managed to lift it long enough for her father to refit the wheel to the axle. Her father had thanked Edmund for his help and they had continued on their way. But she had not forgotten him; had looked back wistfully as the cart jolted over the rutted road, and had seen that Edmund was looking at her.

She had smiled at him, and waved, and he had waved back. When they bumped into each other the following day they had quickly taken up where they had left off and now they were meeting secretly in the barn each afternoon, exploring each other, loving each other, all else forgotten.

What her father would say if he knew she could not imagine, and she giggled at the thought. Edmund smiled, kissed her breast and closed his eyes again.

"I love you," he said, and the way he said it, hearing those words, made her heart melt. She thought that they might get married, and she wondered what it would be like to be married to Edmund. They would have children, she thought, two boys and two girls. She wondered which of them they would look like; herself, or Edmund. She hoped that they looked like him because he was so beautiful. She giggled again and closed her eyes, her head turned towards the sun, enjoying the warmth of it on her face. She was so happy.

Her happiness, her daydreams were shattered by the door of the barn bursting open. Her immediate fear was that her father had discovered them but it was worse, much worse. Not her father but four large, heavily armed men. Their leader had a scar running from his eye to his jawline where it ended in a puckering of the skin, twisting his mouth into a permanent sneer.

"What do we have here?" he said, and he laughed, and the other men laughed with him. The girl, frozen with fear, could not move.

"Time for a little sport I think." He laughed again and went to close the door.

Edmund had awoken at the sound of the door bursting open but remained across the girl's breast feigning sleep. He had a small knife in his breeches pocket, and if he could reach it, it might give them some small chance until help arrived. The thought flashed through his mind that there might be no help; that they might be the only two still alive, but he instantly dismissed it. All his energies had to be on reaching the knife. Judging the moment as best he could he suddenly leapt sideways, to his feet, towards the knife. Unfortunately one of the men – Edmund never saw his face – had anticipated the move and as Edmund made his leap he was tripped by a large booted foot. He fell to the ground, landing heavily. A kick to the head broke his nose and mercifully he did not see, was barely conscious of, the sword that was thrust down to snuff out his young life.

The girl, who moments before had been dreaming of marrying the young man, started to scream. Her screams rang around the barn disturbing the cattle and startling the hens. It did not prevent the men taking their turn with her.

An eternity later and barely conscious from her beatings she became aware that a man was standing in the doorway. Behind him, through the open door, flames were leaping from buildings, her village being fired. She could not see the man's face, silhouetted by the flames, but he looked at Edmund's corpse, taking in the fact of his death before his eyes flicked towards her. They were cold, emotionless.

"Finish her and burn it," she heard him say. And as a knife was drawn across her throat, before she lost consciousness, she could have sworn that he was wearing a strange kind of helmet that she had never seen before.

It appeared to have eagles wings.

CHAPTER ELEVEN

SOUTHERN ENGLAND.

MAY 1066

The fields and roads of southern England shook to the sound of marching feet as King Harold Godwineson hurried towards Sandwich with three thousand housecarls, the elite of his army. To the south, marching east, Gyrth and Leofwine hastened to close the jaws of the trap with the fyrd; and between them stood their brother Tostig, holed up in Sandwich, an outcast of his own making. Rejected by the citizens of the Isle of Wight he had departed the island to ravage the south coast, killing, burning and looting until he had reached Sandwich and found that he had nowhere else to go. And now he was trapped, unable to go north, unable to turn west. And soon the noose would tighten about his neck and that would be the end of him. One rival accounted for.

At the head of his army, beneath the twin banners of the Dragon of Wessex and the Golden Fighting Man, Harold rode his stallion in stoic silence whilst he reflected upon a time, long ago, when he was just a child. He and Tostig had been rivals even then. Rivals for their fathers' attention; rivals in their ambition to be the first to ride; to hunt; to love; and later, to achieve power: as now. Nothing had changed in Tostig since he was a child. And perhaps, Harold thought, nothing had changed in himself. The only difference between them was that he had won, and Tostig had lost. But Tostig could not accept that. So now he must pay.

Harold glanced up at the red windsock that was his Dragon of Wessex banner. It billowed proudly in the sun, the wind filling its silken limbs and giving it life. Beside it, his second banner, the

Golden Fighting Man glinted in the warm Kent sunshine. *The Fighting Man*; a golden warrior embroidered onto a blue background. This was his personal Standard and wherever he gave battle it went with him. And it had never tasted defeat. Wales, the north country, the south. It was all the same to him. Victory had followed victory until the Confessor could ignore him no longer and had appointed him his right hand man. He had earned the right to be King, was damned if he would relinquish his Crown without a fight. The land would run with blood first. It occurred to him that since he had learned of Tostig's landing on the Isle of Wight he had not had the awful nightmares of which he had spoken to Ranulf. Perhaps, he thought, Ranulf had been right. He had just been tired. It was good to be his old self again, in control, in charge.

He turned in the saddle and looked behind him. Ranulf was there, as ever, with Guthrum at his elbow, two old friends, two great warriors, and behind them row upon row of the finest fighting men in Europe, perhaps the world. Sunlight glinted off polished helmets and spear-points, off mail hauberks and axe heads and like a silver stream it seemed to go on forever. And seeing it he felt for the first time in weeks that the worst was over. William the Bastard could come, Hardraada could try his hand. But *he* would prevail, for no army in the world could stand against his housecarls. *Let them come,* he thought, *let them all come,* for he was Harold Godwineson, the King of England. And he was a warrior.

For Ranulf, marching behind the King, the last few weeks had been tumultuous. There had hardly been a night when he had not seen Alice, not spent long, languid hours lying with her, laughing with her, planning their future. In truth he was exhausted, physically exhausted from the long hours on the training field as he put the newest recruits through their paces, and exhausted from the lonely journey into London, to see Alice, or to attend a Council of War with the King. He was glad that Harold appeared to have recovered most of his old spirit, his old elan, but the King's revitalised mood had simply meant that he had more to achieve day after day than ever before. He had arranged new lodgings for Alice, a room in the tavern where he had first seen her, a room that was warm, and dry, and with a roof that did not let in the elements. He was paying for it himself, out of his Captain's pay, and begrudged not a penny of it. He was in love and he had never been so happy, or, in many ways, so confused.

The problem lay in his oath to the King. His blood-oath, that required him to die on the field of battle for his King. Men's lives were governed by oaths, he reflected, and his blood-oath meant that his life was the King's to do with as he wished. And how did his love for Alice sit against the oath that he had given, freely, of his own accord, to his King? It didn't. It could not possibly do so for the two were mutually incompatible. Ranulf could not precisely articulate his dilemma to Alice for he knew that she would not understand. He only knew that he loved her, would do anything for her, make any promise to her that she asked of him, and yet, in the same moment could be asked to give his life for his King.

The problem gnawed at him just as Harold's dream had gnawed at him. And as yet he had no answer. He was, he had to admit to himself, in a foul mood. And his mood was the cause of yet another problem, this one entirely self-inflicted. Just two days ago on the training ground, Cnut of the golden hair, Cnut, who was descended from King Canute himself had almost breached his guard and Ranulf, for once losing his iron control reacted so violently that he had broken Cnut's arm. It was unforgivable. Worse than that he actually liked the lad and now felt an enormous guilt bearing down on his broad shoulders to add to his other problems.

His mind inevitably returned however, to Alice; to the slim lithe limbs of that darkly shadowed body that he loved so much. Her raven hair, her jet black eyes; the beautiful lilting voice that sent raptures through him each time she spoke.

"Come back to me soon," she had said as Ranulf prepared to leave for the march south. And of course he had promised that he would; he would promise her anything in her presence, his oath to the King forgotten.

And Ranulf did return to Alice that day for the sun that had shone so brightly on Harold's splendid army had also betrayed their presence to Tostigs' lookouts. And so it was that just moments before the jaws of the trap closed on him Tostig Godwineson put to sea and slipped from his brother's grasp...

CHAPTER TWELVE

BOSHAM, SUSSEX.

THE END OF MAY 1066

The oars of the small craft dipped and rose, dipped and rose, the water sparkling in the sunlight as the banks of oarsmen ferried King Harold Godwineson up the estuary to his home at Bosham. Sitting alone in the stern of the boat Harold could see to his left, far in the distance, the dragon ships of his fleet moored off the coast of the Isle of Wight. Some were swinging to their anchors in the shallow water, others drawn up onto the beach for minor repairs.

Overhead, seagulls circled above the fleet in their endless search for food, titbits left by the sailors of the fleet as they hurried to obey the commands of their seniors. Harold had spent all morning with his Captains, impressing upon them the need for constant alert, for a perpetual state of readiness. He turned to look ahead and studied the crew of the boat. The faces and arms of the men were covered in sweat, their faces contorting each time they pulled on their oars; propelling the flimsy craft through the shallows towards the shore.

Harold became lost in his thoughts as he considered the train of events that had lead to his present predicament. He blamed himself for Tostig's escape from Sandwich, although it had not been entirely his fault. It was impossible, he told himself, to hide an army of three thousand men, and had the sun not given such early warning of their presence Tostig would, in all probability still have had sufficient time to make good his escape. Nevertheless it was a severe blow for Tostig was still on the loose, creating havoc along the East coast as he slowly made his way north. Those people, the inhabitants of Lindsey, where Tostig was last reported as being seen were his subjects, entitled to his protection and he had failed them. On the contrary here he was, tied to the south coast with both army and navy, watching and waiting for William the Bastard to materialise, if he did. Like Prometheus of Greek legend, chained to a rock for eternity, so he felt chained to the south coast of England in case William should suddenly appear through the mist with his invasion fleet. *William,* he thought. *Always William.* Ever since he had gained the Throne the wretched man had been with him; in his dreams, in his plans and hopes for the future, in his every thought. How much longer could it be? It was now almost June and every message that he received from his spies in Normandy spoke of ships being built, of a massive fleet being assembled in the Dives, of mercenaries arriving from all over Europe, and, of his own doom, foretold by the death star.

"Damn the man," he said aloud, startling the oarsmen from their labours; causing them to lose their stroke. The lead oarsman looked at Harold quizzically and he shook his head. The man bent back to his oar.

It seemed to Harold at times that he had not had a moment's peace since the Crown had been placed on his head. But did he regret it? He asked himself the question for what seemed the hundredth time and back came the answer: *Not a bit.* He would rather be King of England, even under these trying circumstances than nothing at all. And because he *was* the King he would see it through, to the bitter end, whatever that was.

He shook himself from his reverie, saw that they would shortly be landing and allowed himself the luxury of picturing the welcome he would receive from Edith and the children. He had spent so little time with them since his Coronation and eagerly looked forward to a few days relaxation before returning to London. He shaded his eyes against the sun and realised that the small party on the jetty were not Edith and his children but a group of men, and weary men at that.

They were standing stock-still, staring out into the estuary at his approaching boat. Behind the men a groom attended to their horses. They were lathered in sweat, their flanks and withers covered in white froth. They had obviously been ridden hard, but from where, and for what purpose? He could only assume that it was more bad news. He sighed and rose to his feet, prepared to disembark.

As the boat reached the jetty the lead oarsman leaped out with a practised ease to secure it to a mooring post. He had done this trip many times but never with his King in the stern sheets.

Harold braced himself as the boat came to rest against the barnacle-covered timbers and one of the men stepped forward, reaching for his hand, helping him, almost *pulling* him onto the jetty; the leader of the group, no doubt. He was a large untidy man, but he had a warm smile. Harold noticed that most of the man's teeth were missing, and those that remained were blackened and rotting. His breath was foul and he endeavoured to keep his distance as the man now addressed him in a broad, northern accent. The tale he told was tortuous and convoluted, but the essence of it was sufficient to banish the woes of the morning.

They had ridden from Barton on Humber with news of his brother. Tostig had landed near their village early one morning, unaware that he had been spotted by one of the villagers. Earl Edwin had called out the Lindsey fyrd and they had lain in wait for him to arrive. It was a misty morning, visibility down to just a few yards. When Tostig entered the village they had completely surprised him, slaughtering most of his men. Once again Tostig had escaped, but with most of his men dead and only twelve ships left he would hardly be a threat in the future.

"Where has he gone?" Harold asked.

"North, to Scotland we believe."

"Let him rot there then."

He looked at the bedraggled group and suddenly felt for them. They had ridden hundreds of miles to tell him this.

"You have done well," he said. "Stay and enjoy some refreshment." He looked at their mounts, sorry beasts, covered in sores, not much better than the men that rode them. "And rest your horses," he heard himself say. "There is hay and fodder in my stables."

How the hell he would explain this to Edith he could not imagine. Almost five months without sight of him and he was returning home in the company of these men. She would crucify him. But for all that the day had turned out much better than he could ever have dreamed. Perhaps, he thought, his luck was turning at last. One enemy accounted for. *But there was still William. And Hardraada...*

They would have to wait; at least for today.

He turned to the men from the north and beckoned them follow him up the hill. He was going home.

CHAPTER THIRTEEN

EARLY JUNE 1066.

From the window of his bedchamber Harold Godwineson looked south along the estuary. Twelve miles away, obscured by haze, the ships of his fleet lay at anchor off the coast of the Isle of Wight, strategically placed to sweep down upon William the Bastard whenever he appeared. How much longer he would have to wait he had no idea but he was determined he would be ready. It was now early June and England was at its most glorious. Yet a shadow was cast over the land. A mixture of fear and boredom permeated his thoughts, and those of the people surrounding him as they maintained their vigil upon the grey waters of the Channel. Someone must soon make a move, he felt sure of it.

He moved away from the window and cast his eyes to the bed, to the supine figure laid within its folds, the tentacles of sleep still wrapped around her.

Edith had surprised him upon his return home. Instead of being angry at the rough company in which he had greeted her she had kissed and embraced him as soon as he had crossed the threshold, and then she had given her attention to the men of the Lindsey fyrd. With startling efficiency she had organised food and ale for their guests and had kept up a desultory conversation until, at last, they had departed for their homes in the north. The men had fallen over themselves to thank her for her hospitality, bowing and kissing her hand as one by one they had taken their leave. They had been awed by her beauty, and flattered by her close attention, and Harold realised that they had probably never met anyone like her before. When he considered it he was certain that they hadn't for he, the King of England had not met anyone quite like her either.

When finally they had left, Harold had briefly embraced his children and handed out gifts to them all: A beautiful jewelled dagger of Celtic design for Godwine, his eldest; a dress of fine woven wool for Eliza, and for little Morgana, a baby of just two years, a pair of leather bootees made from the softest doeskin imaginable.

The formalities completed the children were surrendered to the care of their nursemaid, who fussed over them before whisking them off into the garden to resume their game. Harold and Edith had then made their way to the bedchamber where, for the first time in months they were truly alone. Edith had scolded him for bringing the men to their home, but she was only play-acting, mimicking their strange, north country accent as they had fawned all over her. And then they had made love with a passion that had surprised them both. Whether it was his Crown that proved to be the aphrodisiac, or simply the pent up frustration, neither of them knew. But they had barely left the bedchamber in three days. And now Edith lay exhausted whilst he could not sleep at all.

He moved to the bed and studied her face, tranquil in repose, the small beads of sweat on her forehead, her pale, almost translucent skin. His eyes moved down to her graceful neck, and down, further, to her long, slender legs, entangled in the bedding. "Swan-like," he thought. Edith Swanneshals was well named. He bent to kiss her cheek and as he did so she turned to look at him.

"I thought you were asleep," he said.

"I was, but you woke me. Can you not sleep my love?"

"I have spent enough time in bed these last few days," he said, smiling.

"But not sleeping though!" she rebuked him, her eyes laughing. "You appear to have acquired a royal appetite along with your Royal title!"

"Any man would have an appetite for you," he said.

73

"Then let me take the edge off it." She laughed again, and held out her arms to him.

They made love slowly, languidly, in the early morning sunlight, and for a while afterwards they slept. Later, her head and hand resting on his chest, her fingers curled into his hairs she asked: "William – what kind of man is he?"

Harold lay silent, considering the question for a long time before replying.

"To know William, to appreciate what drives him, one must first know that he was born a bastard," he said at last. "His father, Duke Robert of Normandy took a fancy to a tanner's daughter and William was born out of wedlock. His father eventually tired of the girl and she was given away to one of his followers; he never saw her again. He died on the way home from pilgrimage to Jerusalem. He had no other sons, no obvious successors, and so William found himself Duke of Normandy at the age of eight."

"At that time Normandy was a minor state, ravaged by private wars and threatened on all sides by her neighbours. For twelve years after he became Duke, Normandy was in a constant state of anarchy. His guardians were murdered and William had to seek refuge on several occasions simply to survive. Yet within twenty years he has brought Normandy to the position where it is now independent of France, is the envy, and fear of its neighbours, and is totally, utterly dependent upon him."

He paused to consider what he had just said. *Eight.* It was no age at all. He turned his face toward her.

"How has he achieved this Edith?" he said. "By force of personality; by blind ambition; by political awareness. By being utterly ruthless to his enemies - and by his genius on the battlefield."

"It sounds as though you admire him."

"Admire, yes, and hate," he said after some thought. "He has achieved a minor miracle in Normandy with help from no one save his own personality and a soaring ambition. But he rules men's lives by fear, by bloodshed. I have seen it at first hand." Edith noted the bitterness in his voice and felt compelled to speak.

"And now he seeks your Crown," she said. "I fear for you my love." Harold pulled her towards him and wrapped his arms around her. He stroked her hair softly as though to sooth away her fears.

"Now, my angel," he said, "there is nothing to fear. For all the Duke's ambition, Normandy is just a small province, scarcely bigger than Wales. He does not have the men or the resources to seriously challenge us. And there's twenty miles of water separating us – quite an obstacle in itself."

"Perhaps," she said hopefully, "he will not come after all?"

"Oh, he will come, my love," he said, not wanting to disappoint her but acknowledging the inevitable. "He will come. Sooner or later we shall have William to deal with. Not only has he made a vow to claim the Throne; he also has the Pope's blessing for his crusade, as he cares to call it. He cannot back down now even if he wanted to. He would lose too much face. His enemies would take it as a sign of weakness, and he cannot allow that. Besides, he thinks he can win."

"He will kill you," Edith said softly, her eyes distant, faraway in the future, as though she had somehow seen his death for herself. Harold looked at her as though she had slapped him in the face.

"What makes you say that?" he snapped irritably. She had hit his raw spot and he knew it.

"I don't know," she replied quickly, conscious of the fact that she had hurt him. "I don't know. I'm just being silly." She hugged him, child-like, eager to make amends, wishing she hadn't spoken.

" I am sorry my love," she said. "Sorry for upsetting you."

Harold laughed, but it was a hollow laugh without sincerity, for her words had disturbed him more than he cared to admit.

"He will try, I have no doubt," he said. "But my enemies have tried before, and failed. He will also fail. I swear it."

She smiled at him then, and he smiled back, proof of his confidence, his inviolability.

But he did not tell her of his dreams, of what he truly felt inside.

CHAPTER FOURTEEN

THE HOUSECARLS CAMP, SUSSEX

MID JUNE 1066

It took several seconds for Ranulf's eyes to adjust to the dark interior after the brightness of the sun outside. Gradually he was able to make out the figure of Cnut lying disconsolately in the corner of the tented hospital, a dirty bandage wrapped untidily around his head, his left arm strapped loosely to his chest. Cnut's eyes, normally sparkling blue, were sunk deep into his skull, his face ghastly pale, like parchment. As he approached he became aware of the stench of what he knew to be corrupted flesh, and he was shocked to realise that it emanated from his young protégé.

Ever since he had shattered Cnut's arm in training he had taken a fathers interest in the recovery of the young recruit, constantly pestering the surgeons, such as they were, for information as to his progress. He had been dismayed to learn that far from making a recovery Cnut was slowly sinking into a pit of infection and disease. He felt guilty enough as it was, that his pride had caused him to retaliate against Cnut in the way that he did. To learn that his wounds may prove to be fatal had moved him to make this visit for himself.

"When was this last looked at lad?" He indicated the untidily bandaged arm. The smell was overwhelming, nauseous in its intensity. Cnut stared at him with glazed eyes, as though returning from some far away land. He seemed to be on the point of exhaustion and his words, when he replied, confirmed this to be so.

"I'm not sure." The voice was weak, his words slurred, as though he were drunk but Ranulf guessed that it was fever.

"Let me look at it," he said. Gently he undid the filthy bandage to examine the wound. It had clearly not healed: far from it. The wound was livid and angry, running with pus. And on the periphery of the lesion the skin had taken on a familiar grey hue that he knew from experience to be the beginning of gangrene. He cursed under his breath. He had seen enough wounds turn gangrenous to know that if it was not treated soon Cnut could lose his arm; perhaps even his life.

"We must act quickly," he said. "What do the camp medics say?"

Cnut gave the most imperceptible shrug, as if to say that they had very little idea, and moreover that they couldn't care less. He stared at the putrifying arm, the gaping infected wound, lost in his private world of misery. His brow beaded with sweat and he wiped it with his good arm to clear the moisture away. Ranulf noted the movement and suddenly felt angry: angry with himself for causing this injury. Anger that the surgeons were doing so little.

"Sorry Ranulf," Cnut suddenly spoke, as though waking from a dream. "I shall have to learn to fight one-handed." He smiled a thin smile. It was as if the boy had read his thoughts.

"Not if I can help it lad," he murmured. "And it is I who should apologise to you." The anger had still not left him, and he determined to do something about it. He fell silent, wondering what to do when an idea, born out of desperation, suddenly came to him. It was a small chance, but he must do something. His conscience gnawed at him just as the corruption was gnawing at Cnut's arm, draining the life from him.

" I must go now," he said, "but I will return. And I must have your word on something." Cnut shrugged again, as though it were all one to him.

"Whatever you do, don't let the camp butchers remove your arm. There is someone who may be able to help. If anyone lays a finger on you without my consent they will pay with their life." His eyes took on a fierce intensity as he attempted to drive the message into Cnut's feverish mind. "Tell them that," he said, "they will pay with their lives." He turned to leave; there was little time.

"I will be back by dawn."

"Where are you going?" Cnut's curiosity was finally rousing him from his lethargy.

"To see a necromancer," Ranulf replied. "A little magic is called for I think."

He pulled the flaps of the tent aside and emerged into the bright sunlight. His stallion was ready and waiting and he leaped into the saddle, put his heels to its flanks. Cnut's life hung by a thread, all his hopes pinned upon him. He hoped to God he was right.

Down winding streets and narrow alleyways as dark as the night above them, Alice lead Ranulf until they came to the door that they were seeking. He had ridden all afternoon, and well into the night to reach London, and Alice. And now they were anxiously beating upon a door, bidding the occupant let them enter.

It was whilst talking to Cnut that Ranulf recalled a conversation with Alice some weeks earlier. She had mentioned that the tavern was the regular haunt of prostitutes, allowed to ply their trade provided that the landlord received a share of their earnings. He had been relieved to hear that she had not stooped so low herself, despite pressure from her employer to do so, but he had asked her what these ladies did when they contracted the pox or one of the other consequences of their chosen careers. She had told him of a woman, now very old, who professed to be a descendant of the Druids, a long lost cult that practiced medicine and performed strange rituals at the circle of stones far to the west. Alice had explained to him that this woman – Ceilwyc – was skilled in the ancient arts of the druids and often prescribed remedies to cure the infections with which her colleagues and their clients habitually suffered. So here they were, hoping against hope for a cure for Cnut.

Presently the door opened on creaking, rusty hinges, and an old, a very old, woman bade them enter. She had only the one eye, an eye that now stared at them from beneath beetling brows. They stepped over the threshold, their senses assaulted by the sights and smells that suddenly greeted them. Row upon row of earthernware jars were stacked along the shelves that lined the walls of her room. Not only stacked upon shelves, they covered the table in front of her, the floor beneath her, they were stacked on top of books, dry, ancient books that had not, it seemed to Ranulf, been read in years. All of them, the great paraphernalia of books and jars that made up her life were covered in a fine layer of dust.

The aromas emanating from the jars were myriad. One moment Ranulf detected a sickly, cloying smell, the next the pungent odour of what seemed to be rotten egg but which Ceilwyc informed him was the spore of the *Phallus impudicus* or, to give it its common name, Stinkhorn.

"And what can I do for you at this time of night?" The tone of her voice was disconcerting and Ranulf instinctively looked to Alice for support. She squeezed his hand, encouraging him to reply.

"We understand you may be able to help us," he said lamely. Now that he was here he was much less sure of himself. Ceilwyc gave him a sideways look.

"Are you a soldier?" The question was spat at him abruptly.

"Yes," he replied. "Captain of the Royal Housecarls."

"A Captain indeed!" She laughed. "I have never had to treat a Captain before!" She cackled with laughter again, her mouth showing blackened stumps that had once been teeth.

"No, no," Ranulf said quickly. "You misunderstand. Not for me – or either of us."

"What can I do for you then *Captain?"* She emphasised the last word, her voice heavy with sarcasm. This was not going well. He again turned to Alice, an unspoken plea for help. To his relief she obliged him, taking up the tale.

"A friend of my...husband has a wound," she said. "It is a serious wound that may yet kill him. It has become infected with gangrene." She looked at Ceilwyc and then at Ranulf. He saw that she had conjured up that little girl look that he knew so well, found so hard to resist.

"And tell me," said Ceilwyc, "is this friend of yours also a soldier?" She fixed Ranulf with her one good eye, her question clearly directed at him.

"A soldier, yes," he replied simply, thinking it better not to volunteer any more information than necessary.

"Soldiers!" Ceilwyc spat the word suddenly, violently. "The Romans were soldiers," she said, taking an obtuse line of conversation that seemed to have no relevance to the issues, the problem, at hand. She glared at him again, her one eye like a beacon.

"Efficient soldiers the Romans were! Before my time, of course. They changed things forever. Before they came my people, the druids, ruled this Country."

"The druids?"

"Not like you understand the word," she snapped at him. "They ruled it in their own way; quietly, gently, nurturing the land, taking from it only what they needed and giving back what they didn't."

This was not what Ranulf had heard. The stories that he had been told had all indicated that they were bloodthirsty, murdering bastards who liked to sacrifice virgins on great stone slabs. But he was not about to contradict her. She continued, still in full flow:

"And then the Romans came," she said, warming to her theme. "The Romans, with their Legions and their golden eagles and their Roman Gods and their weapons of destruction. What did they know of my people, my gentle people? Within a decade the power of the druids was broken forever. Soldiers! Pah! What good have soldiers ever done us?"

Ranulf pretended not to hear this; was unsure in any event whether an answer was expected.

"But you," he said, "You have their secrets?"

Ceilwyc smiled, showing the blackened stumps.

"I have their secrets," she said quietly, and he saw the unmistakable glint of triumph in her eye.

"Then how, if…?"

"Because my forefathers were determined that their Gods, the old Gods, the *true Gods* would not simply pass into history; that their secrets would not die with them. From generation to generation, from father to son, for a thousand years, the lessons have been handed down until my father taught them to me many years ago.

"So you will help us?" he asked. "I will pay you well."

"Soldiers pay!" she spat again. "I do not want your soldiers pay!" Her voice was vehement in its denial.

"Then what?" he asked. "What is your price?" She appeared to consider this.

"Your soldier friend, " she said. "He is young?"

"Too young to die," Ranulf replied caustically. "He is nineteen."

"Then I will help him. But if I save him, I want him. You will send him to me when he is cured?"

"What do you want of him?" he asked, curious at the request.

"He will owe me his life," she said. "And it is no concern of yours. Now, do you agree? If not, there is the door."

He didn't like it but he had no choice. He glanced at Alice and nodded his head.

"Good. Then it is settled. Now to begin."

She moved to the far wall of the room and began to search amongst the jars. With each one she handled a small layer of dust was disturbed so that after a short while she appeared to be working in a fog.

After a few minutes she returned with three jars, two identical, the third with tiny holes in the stopper. Lifting the stopper she showed Ranulf and Alice the contents. Hundreds of maggots wriggled and squirmed over a small piece of rotting apple. Alice looked away in disgust and Ceilwyc turned her one disapproving eye towards her.

"Before we can treat the infection we must rid the arm of gangrene. These little beauties should do the trick."

She raised the jar to her one eye and studied them almost with affection. She noted the doubtful look on Ranulf's face and turned to him.

"Some innate sense dictates that they eat only rotting flesh, leaving the healthy tissue untouched. Place these on the young mans arm, directly upon the gangrenous flesh, and they will soon start to feed." She cackled to herself. "Much cleaner than the instruments of torture your butchers use, I do assure you."

Ranulf continued to look doubtful, but nodded in acknowledgement of the instruction.

"Now," she said, "Once the rotten flesh has been removed we can start to treat the arm, the source of the infection." Opening the second jar she poured a little of the contents into an earthernware bowl.

"Tansy," she said. "Or, to give it it's Latin name *Chrysanthemum vulgare*. Do you speak Latin, Ranulf?" she asked him. "No, I suppose not," she said noting the bemused look on his face.

"What is it?" Alice asked.

"A herb, my dear, to staunch wounds. It is reputed to have been eaten by the Jews at Passover, but who knows?"

She mixed the Tansy with a little water and then added the contents of the third and final jar.

"Woundwort," she said. "*Stachys sylvatica,* in the Latin. It is used for dressing wounds – hence its name. Helps to draw the infection." She added a touch more water and vigorously mixed the two herbs together until they formed a paste.

"Now," she said. "This should be applied to the wound each morning under a clean – I said clean – bandage. By the third day of treatment – after all signs of gangrene have been removed – you should see an improvement. If not, well...." She did not have to finish for Ranulf well knew what the consequences would be.

"Finally," she said, reaching for a fourth jar, "this is to be taken orally." Ranulf frowned.

"Through the mouth." Ceilwyc pointed to her own, as though teaching a child. He nodded, embarrassed.

"It will help him relax...but a word of warning," she said. "The young man may crave more. Do not give it to him unless he is in real pain."

"What is it?" he asked.

"The crushed seed of the poppy. It helps the victim to fight the pain, or at least not care about it."

"We are grateful," he said as Ceilwyc handed him the maggots, the herbs and the seed of the poppy.

"I do not want your thanks," she replied pointedly. "But I do want the boy. Send him to me when he is cured." The door closed behind them.

He accompanied Alice to her new lodgings in London. He would have stayed the night but time was pressing, a cure hopefully found. He rode back to the housecarl camp alone, hoping it would not be too late.

CHAPTER FIFTEEN

THE DIVES, NORMANDY.

EARLY JULY 1066

From the saddle of his war-horse William the Bastard looked down upon the massive fleet assembling at the mouth of the Dives. He considered it the most beautiful, and certainly the most impressive, sight he had ever seen. The instrument of his conquest of England – in the name of Holy Mother Church he quickly reminded himself – his fleet was now nearing completion.

Hundred upon hundred of long ships lay at anchor in the great lake, gently swaying to their cables. And surrounding each one, like an army of ants, the shipwrights and carpenters worked busily away with saw and adze, drill and bit, fitting out the ships with oar holes, masts and rudders. Sail makers too, were in abundance; steadily, patiently, fitting the sails to the masts, or embroidering intricate and fantastic designs upon the tough canvas that would, God willing, carry them safely to the shores of England.

William absently fished an apple from his saddle-bag and fed it to his war horse. The horse happily accepted the proffered fruit and noisily devoured it, turning its head and nosing the saddle-bag, hoping for more. William ignored it. Studying the fleet he mentally calculated the number of ships that had actually been promised to him: his half brother Robert of Mortain, one hundred and twenty ships; his second half brother, Bishop Odo, one hundred. William, Bishop of Evreux had promised eighty. William Fitz Osbern, seated beside him on his great war horse had promised sixty. How many was that? Three hundred and sixty. Three hundred and sixty long ships.

And then there was Roger of Montgomery and Roger of Beaumont, both members of his Curia, his inner Council, who had each promised sixty ships. Four hundred and eighty. Who else? He quickly calculated. Hugh of Montfort, fifty ships; Fulk le Boiteux and Gerald Dapifer, forty each. How many was that? Six hundred and ten. Walter Giffard had promised thirty ships. Where were they? Not here yet. He must speak to him. If he wanted some of that rich English soil he would deliver. He had better.

Who else? A Bishop. Yes, that was it. Vougrin, Bishop of Le Mans. Thirty ships. Six hundred and seventy so far. But there were more. By God the list was endless. Perhaps there would not be enough land in the whole of England to reward them all. Who else had promised him ships? There was one other, he felt sure of it. And then he had it: Abbot Nicholas of St Ouens; twenty ships. Six hundred and ninety. Add the ships that he himself had commissioned. Eight hundred ships, near enough. Eight hundred. He played with the figure in his mind and tried to visualise what eight hundred ships would look like. Lord, he thought, they would stretch from one side of the Channel to the other.

He quickly calculated the number of ships now lying at anchor in the Dives. Six hundred and fifty, give or take a few.

"Mid August, I think," he said, turning to Fitz Osbern, "if the weather holds."

"Very good, my Lord," Fitz Osbern replied. "The Godwinesson will rue the day he crossed you."

Duke William loved flattery of this kind. He turned to Fitz Osbern, a slight smile playing around the corners of his mouth. He rarely smiled, but what he had learned had cheered him immensely.

"I am sure you are right," he said confidently. "Although my sources tell me that our rival for the Throne of England is himself preparing an invasion fleet. We may not be fighting Harold Godwineson after all."

"Hardraada?"

"Yes. I have had word that Hardraada has himself prepared a fleet off the Solund Islands, north of Bergen. They can only be gathering for one purpose. An invasion of England."

Duke William looked down on his own great fleet, but his eyes and thoughts were far away to the north.

"Harald Hard-Council has long thought of himself as another Canute," he said, "and I fancy he desires a tilt at Godwineson himself before long. We may not be fighting Saxons, Fitz Osbern, but Norsemen." He gave Fitz Osbern another of his rare, enigmatic smiles.

"Its all one to me," Fitz Osbern replied. "They die just the same."

"True, true," Duke William acknowledged, "but I should not wish to have to fight two opponents when I could fight just one."

"Two? How so?"

"If Hardraada invades, and succeeds, in the north, and then reaches a truce with Godwineson, they might decide to divide England between them."

"Godwineson would never agree to that! He is too proud!"

"I agree; but he may have no choice. If Hardraada defeats him on the field of battle Godwineson may sue for peace. His strength, England's strength, lies in the south. He may consider it preferable to give a little to retain the southern realm."

Fitz Osbern looked doubtful. "It is possible, I suppose, but I would lay odds on a fight to the finish between those two."

"And that, my friend, is what I am counting on." Duke William smiled another of his rare smiles but soon it was gone. "Now," he said, "to other matters. The horses."

"Horses?"

"Yes, we have not yet devised a method of ensuring their safety during transportation. The crossing may be rough, and we shall require some form of stabling, some sort of pen, to prevent them panicking. I want you to give...." His words were lost as he recognised one of his couriers riding hard towards him. The stallion that he was riding was breathing hard as it came to a halt a few yards in front of the Duke's own mount, kicking up dust as it did so. The courier, a young man, leapt off his horse and ran, almost tripping in his haste to deliver his message to the Duke. William gave him an icy glare then bade him to speak. The courier bowed, too quickly for etiquette to be properly observed, and then blurted it out:

"Lord!" he cried, "Lord! Duke Conan of Brittany has issued an ultimatum! Cede to him the lands you stole in your last campaign or he will invade Normandy the moment you set sail for England!" The courier saw the anger flare in his masters' eyes and stepped back a pace. Then another.

"I am sorry, my Lord," he said, as though it were somehow his fault.

Fitz Osbern had seen the flash of anger in the Duke's eyes and knew what would be coming: an outburst to wake the dead. He knew his Lord and Master well enough by now. He needed to act.

"Then Duke Conan has just signed his own death-warrant!" he cried, and he laughed, forcing it from his throat. It was a mighty laugh for it needed to be. It rolled across the valley and went on, and on, until, finally the anger died from William the Bastards' eyes and Fitz Osbern was joined in his laughter by the Duke.

CHAPTER SIXTEEN

THE PALACE OF RENNES, BRITTANY.

Duke Conan was in rare good humour. Sitting alone in the Great Hall of his Palace at Rennes, he congratulated himself once again on his strategic masterstroke. He knew how William the Bastard lusted after the throne of England and he could well imagine how William would be feeling right now. By God, he thought, he would not wish to be in the shoes of William's Council these past few days. William always looked for a scapegoat for his own troubles and like as not some of them would be feeling the thick end of William's tongue, if not his boot this very moment. Life was sweet, he reflected, and revenge was so much the better for being tasted cold.

And he deserved his revenge for all the troubles that the Bastard had brought upon him. His mind returned to the dark days of 1064 when William had smashed everything he had put up against him, and having done so had looted his province for all it was worth.

He had harboured hopes for revenge ever since; had gone to bed each night thinking about it and had woken the following morning, each morning for two years wondering if this would be the day. And now it was.

Duke Conan went over the plan - again – in his mind. He looked for any pitfalls, any loopholes there might be but could find none. William the Bastard had two choices and two choices only: forget about England, about his "crusade" as he had cynically chosen to call it, or cede to him the land and possessions he had stolen in 1064. He felt sure that the Bastard would never call off his invasion – he had gone too far for that – so he would have to give back what he had stolen as being the easier of two alternatives. After all that was a small price to pay for the Throne of England. Yes, he thought; that is what I would do; that is what William will do.

Duke Conan allowed himself the luxury of picturing William riding into Rennes under a white flag, a flag of truce, and then, on bended knee ceding to him the lands and chattels he had stolen. What a day that will be! And then he considered it more than likely that the Bastard would send an envoy, one of his Curia, to do his grovelling. That old fool Roger of Beaumont perhaps; or that arrogant *cochon* Fitz Osbern. Whoever it was by God he would make them grovel. That would be a day to cherish.

He realised that he was feeling hungry. The anticipation of receiving William the Bastard – or his envoy – in abject surrender had given an edge to his appetite. And his flagon was empty. He rang for his chamberlain. After a few minutes the chamberlain, an elderly, quiet man appeared.

"You rang, Lord?"

"Of course I rang you fool! Where were you?"

"I am sorry, Lord. Call of nature. When you get to my age..."

"Yes! Yes! No matter. Send for one – no – two of the chicken that we purchased yesterday. And some more wine. The decent stuff from the Loire."

"Yes, my Lord." The chamberlain disappeared as slowly as he had arrived.

"I shall have to replace him," Duke Conan considered. Never liked him much anyway. Too slow, too secretive; something about him not quite right.

The Duke's thoughts took him naturally to the question of the chamberlain's successor. None of the present domestic staff would do, he thought. The gardener was young and good looking but his place was outside. The groom? No. None of the others were even close. Adele would be upset but he could appease her. Buy her a new dress or something. The thought of Adele, the latest recruit to the domestic staff turned his mind to events earlier that morning. The young chambermaid had been sleeping with him for several weeks now but had come into his bedchamber unannounced – damned cheek; his wife might have been there – to announce that she had missed her monthly flux. She had accused him of being the father. He had angrily denied it. What had it to do with him? Besides, Lord knew where else she was bestowing her favours. But he had promised to find her a better position if he could. Well, he was not going to appoint her as his chamberlain. Not a woman. Unheard of. Certainly not.

Now, where was that damned chamberlain with his meal? He angrily rang again, and presently the chamberlain appeared, carrying a tray laden with cold chicken and a large flagon of wine.

"Apologies for the delay, my Lord," he said. "I have had to open a new cask."

"Never mind, just put it down there," Duke Conan said, pointing to the empty space directly in front of him. The chamberlain bowed, and made his customary exit.

Duke Conan poured himself a generous cupful of the wine from the flagon and, with a relish, tore a wing off one of the fowl. The meat was delicious, and his mood, which had taken a downward turn at the thought of his staffing problems quickly improved. He gulped down a large mouthful of the wine and washed the chicken down with it. The wine appeared to taste a little bitter, a little tart. The new cask, he thought. He took another mouthful and helped himself to some more of the chicken. And then the pain hit him. A burning sensation rose up from the centre of his chest and, for a moment he thought he was having a heart attack for he could not breathe; but his throat was burning like it was on fire and his vision was blurred. The pain was indescribable. He lurched unsteadily to his feet, sending his chair sprawling across the cold flagstones. He grabbed for the bell pull and hung onto it for dear life, his senses reeling. Soon he could no longer breath, could not see, could hardly control his limbs. *The pain...* Dear God where was that chamberlain?

He found that he could no longer control his legs and as they buckled beneath him he slowly slid down the bell pull to the floor. He tried to focus on the door, to see if help was coming, but he could not do so, and as his heart stopped beating as a result of the massive dose of strychnine administered to his central nervous system Duke Conan stared up at the vaulted ceiling of the Great Hall with unseeing eyes.

CHAPTER SEVENTEEN

THE HOUSECARLS CAMP, SUSSEX.

MID - JULY 1066

In the event it took eight days and nights to arrest, and then reverse, the spread of the infection in Cnut's arm. Ranulf had hated administering the carnivorous parasites to him. Cnut had screamed and shouted, contorting his face into a grimace as the maggots were dropped into the wound, sweat pouring from his tortured, infected, body. Ranulf had had to enlist the aid of two colleagues to hold him down as one by one the maggots were placed on the rotting flesh to begin their grisly meal.

Ranulf had to admit that they were effective. After just five days they had eaten their way through the corrupted, rotting flesh, their bloated little bodies near to bursting with the amount of flesh that they had consumed. When all sign of the gangrene had been removed he carefully and gingerly removed the sated parasites from Cnut's arm and disposed of them, grinding them beneath his foot.

Next, as instructed, he applied the poultice prepared by Ceilwyc and carefully dressed Cnut's arm with a bandage. The fever still raged within him, turning his dreams into haunted visions of hell, his days into delirium induced nightmares. For three more days Ranulf religiously followed Ceilwyc's instruction, all the while watching Cnut grow weaker and weaker, slowly slipping away. Only the powder from the poppy seed appeared to give Cnut any respite from the infection that threatened to take his life and Ranulf used it liberally. It had been an extremely close run thing, and, during the evening of the sixth day when the fever had still not broken, and Cnut's arm was burning up from the infection it had seemed hopeless. On the morning of the seventh day he had once more changed the dressing and had been appalled and alarmed to note the congealed, evil smelling discharge that had soaked the bandage, infusing it with its dark, corrupting malignancy. He had almost given up, had been on the verge of calling for a priest when, unbelievably, the fever broke at dawn on the ninth day of his vigil.

Ranulf himself was near exhaustion, having hardly slept since arriving back at the camp just after dawn nine days ago. Nine days that seemed like an eternity. Cnut lay on his cot, in the corner of the fetid tent, a sweat soaked blanket wrapped loosely around his ravaged torso. His face was pale and drawn, the flesh stretched tightly over his cheekbones, and his wasted body told its own tale of the battle that had raged within him. He was asleep now, the fight having exhausted his last reserves of strength. Looking down at him Ranulf felt that not only had Cnut won his fight against the infection that had threatened to carry him off but that with Cnut's victory he too, had exorcised the feelings of guilt that had so directed his actions over the past few days.

It was strange, he reflected, that he should have felt as he did when he realised that all was not going well with Cnut's recovery. Before he had met Alice such thoughts had never entered his head, such feelings had never touched him. Death was part of a soldier's life, and came in all manner of guises. That he had acted as he did was simply a measure of the extent to which he had changed. The realisation dawned on him that it was not simply that he had changed – it was a measure of the profound effect that Alice had wrought upon him. He found himself wishing that Alice were with him now, in this tent, sharing his joy at seeing Cnut sleeping like a baby, the fever gone from his body, the infection, finally, under control.

He turned to go; he had neglected his duties for long enough, but Cnut's voice, weak, strained, called him back.

"Don't go."

Ranulf turned at the voice. "I thought you were asleep."

"I was; until I heard you enter. I was dreaming. It was so vivid, so real; as though it were really happening."

"What was it about?" Ranulf asked.

"Gone now," Cnut said. "Completely gone."

"That would be the draught I gave you. Ceilwyc said to be sparing with it."

"Ceilwyc?"

"The woman that saved you. You owe her your life."

Cnut digested the information. He recalled the maggots being dropped into his suppurating wound one by one until he thought he would go crazy but after that everything was a fever induced blur. Reality was indistinguishable from the nightmares of his dreams, the fever raging unchecked through his body, and then the drug-induced calm that finally came to him and provided peace, and rest, when he most needed it.

"Thank her for me," Cnut said. He was tired, he realised. Very tired. He lowered himself back onto his cot.

"You can thank her yourself," Ranulf replied. "She demanded to see you in return for her help. I agreed."

"To see me? Why?" Ranulf shrugged.

"I don't know," he said. "I don't know. Take some leave when you are fit. Go see her. But for now be quiet and rest – and for God's sake look after that arm. I want you fit and well when William the Bastard shows his face."

CHAPTER EIGHTEEN

THE SOUTH COAST, BOSHAM.

THE END OF JULY 1066

Harold Godwineson picked from the beach a singularly round, smooth, pebble and turned it around and around in his hand enjoying the cool heaviness in his palm. To the east a thin sun was just rising above the horizon, casting an orange glow upon the longships of his fleet drawn up on the beaches of the Isle of Wight. They looked like toys from where he stood, carelessly placed there by a bored child. Another day of waiting had begun; another false dawn; the invasion fleet of William the Bastard had yet to make an appearance. He threw back his arm and hurled the pebble far out to sea, watching it arc in the air until, its velocity spent, it dropped into the surf.

To left and right small groups of men huddled together, gathered around fires of driftwood and kindling, as they maintained their eternal vigil upon the horizon, but Harold studiedly ignored them. He was not in the mood for talk. Turning his back on the sea he walked slowly up the beach, his feet slipping and sliding on the wet shingle.

No matter how much he tried to persuade himself otherwise, the plain fact was that his problems were beginning to mount. William, Hardraada, his brother Tostig even, all of them still unresolved, undefeated, and it would soon be autumn. He had discovered that he could best think matters through by taking solitary walks down to the sea where, unencumbered by domestic or other problems he could apply his intellect to them, turn the problems around in his head, and hopefully reach a solution. But solutions were becoming hard to find.

He had already held his fleet in place, and his army in the field, longer than any English King before him. Yet this was little consolation for he knew that William the Bastard could arrive at any time; and if he were not prepared William would be able to land unopposed. Worse, there was still no news of Harald Hardraada from his allies in the north. The young Earls, Edwin and Morcar, supplied him with regular bulletins as to their state of readiness but they, like Harold, could only keep their troops in the field for a short while longer. Autumn was fast approaching.

August and September were crucial months for the gathering in of the crops that must sustain the populace during the long, cold, winter months. Having harvested the crops they must then be properly stored so as to prevent them from rotting. Livestock must be slaughtered and properly preserved for food. If any of these tasks were not completed before winter finally set in, starvation and death would inevitably follow. And what price his Kingdom, his Crown, then?

He had already received reports of desertions, in admittedly small numbers, but he was certain that the numbers would gradually increase as the days and the weeks wore on. He could hardly blame the men – they had wives and families to feed and support just as much as he had. He needed the answer to one, burning, question for in that answer lay the key to his dilemma: When will William come?

He had now reached a small dirt track at the head of the beach and he turned to gaze far out to sea. The sun was a little higher now and its reflection sparkled on the gentle swell, but there was no warmth in it. He sat on a small hillock and gave the problem his full attention. He knew that the autumnal equinox occurred around the 16th September. After that date it would, or should, be impossible to launch an invasion. The days would be too short. There would be insufficient daylight to make the crossing, disembark the troops and horses and all of the other detritus that must inevitably accompany him. Surely William will not leave it until then? Surely not. After the 16th it will be too late; too late to cross the Channel, too late to disembark, too late to plan a campaign. No, after the 16th he must wait. Wait out the winter in Normandy until the vernal equinox came around in March. And a lot could happen in six months. William's army could desert, his fleet could be sabotaged, anything could happen. So *he* must find a way of keeping his fleet in place until then. It was six weeks to the 16th September. Another six. Difficult, very difficult; but not impossible. His Kingdom could rest on it. He would find a way. He must.

Rising from the hillock he shaded his eyes with his hand and looked out to sea. The sun was much higher now, he realised. How long he had been engrossed in his thoughts whilst he tackled the problem he could not say. Time appeared to just slip away. Like the whole of the summer.

The sea was empty, the horizon unchanged. He turned his back on the sea, on his great tormentor, and began to tread the familiar path back to his home.

CHAPTER NINETEEN

THE HOUSECARLS CAMP, SUSSEX.

EARLY AUGUST 1066

Cnut sat in a shaded area of the training ground, his back resting against an oak tree that had stood undisturbed for centuries. Its heavily laden branches protected him from the heat of the midday sun that had slowly, over the summer, turned the ground to dust. His attention was totally focussed upon what he held in his lap, a small, leather bound book barely held together by its ancient and damaged spine that was in danger of falling apart at any moment.

The book had been given to him by Ceilwyc when he had visited her. It was written in an eclectic style, although this concerned Cnut not at all for he could not read. It was not the writing that fascinated him but the drawings that appeared throughout the book. They were mainly in black oakum, occasionally in faded pastel colours, and they depicted couples committing the sexual act in all manner of strange and wonderful positions.

Cnut had dutifully presented himself to Ceilwyc as instructed by Ranulf as soon as he had recovered his health. His arm still plagued him and although the bandage that had protected it had been removed several days earlier, Cnut could still feel it binding his arm to his chest, just as a man who has had a leg removed under the surgeons knife will feel it itch many years after.

What Ceilwyc had said had amazed and confused him. He had promised to think on her offer and to concentrate his mind she had presented him with two parting gifts. The first was the subject of his now rapt attention; the second a small parcel of the crushed poppy seed, secreted inside his leather doublet.

He slowly turned a page, studying the next illustration, yet another delight, and imagined that he was the subject shown performing the impossible act with the lovely young girl. He closed his eyes and debated whether to take another pinch of the addictive powder when a loud Irish brogue interrupted his thoughts:

"And what does the young prince have nestling in his crotch I ask meself lads?" Eiric Mac Eirran stared down at Cnut, his bearded, weatherbeaten face split wide in a grin. Eiric was a huge man, one of the senior housecarls in the regiment. He had fought with Ranulf and Guthrum in the Welsh wars against Gruffyd ap Llewellyn, but his lack of discipline, typical of so many of the Irish volunteers, had prevented him from progressing beyond that of much younger men. For all his failings Eiric had a fearsome reputation with the double-handed axe and men were few and far between who would risk incurring his redoubtable Irish temper.

Eiric had his own following; mainly Irish, they were men who kept themselves to themselves and formed their own small nucleus within the shield-wall. They were loyal to the King, having taken his blood-oath, and fiercely loyal to each other. The shield-wall bred loyalty like no other place on earth, but they lead their own lives within the regiment and generally left the others well alone. Today, however the devil was inside Eiric and Cnut, the new recruit, was the object of his attention. Without warning he snatched the book from Cnut's lap and glanced at the cover.

"Why 'tis a poor wizened piece of leather that our young prince has in his lap!" he cried, "No use to man – or woman!" He let out a huge bellow of a laugh, greatly amused at his wit. Cnut leaped angrily to his feet and attempted to retrieve the book from Eiric's huge fist but Eiric was quick, whisking it beyond Cnut's reach before he could grab it.

"Well! Well!" he laughed, "the prince has a temper! I wonder what could be so fascinating that he should so lose his head!" He opened the book and began to turn the pages, twisting and turning away from Cnut so that he could only stand and watch. Eiric found one particularly graphic engraving and now turned to his comrades, his eyes alight with laughter.

"Would you believe it lads!" he cried, "the young prince has been amusing himself while we have been working up a sweat on the training ground! What say you? Do you want a look?" His comrades laughed and clamoured to inspect the book, responding enthusiastically to his offer.

"Very well lads," he cried, "I am a fair man; there is plenty for you all!" The pages were ripped from the book and flung into the air where they were caught by the summer breeze and chased down by his comrades. Hungrily, and with considerable amusement they devoured the drawings, greatly enjoying their impromptu game. Cnut was beside himself. Ceilwyc had loaned him the book; had told him to look after it and to return it when he called with his decision. And she had promised him more of the crushed poppy if he did. But that promise was now in tatters; just like her book. A great anger welled up inside him, an anger that he could not contain.

"Bastard!" he hissed through gritted teeth and leaped at Eiric, anger coursing through his veins, his control completely gone. He crashed into the bigger man, sending them both sprawling in the dust, arrows of fire lancing up his left arm as he fell onto his side. Arms and legs flailed wildly in a struggle for supremacy; a struggle that was accompanied by shouts of encouragement from Eiric's bemused comrades.

For a moment Cnut thought he had the upper hand as he somehow managed to manoeuvre himself on top of Eiric but the larger mans' vast bulk was critical and just as Cnut thought that he had him Eiric managed to throw him off, turning him as he did so. Before he knew it he was pinned to the ground and Eiric was laughing loudly into his face.

"Now, now, little prince!" he cried. "We were only amusing ourselves. No need for you to take your temper out on old Eiric!" Cnut struggled beneath him, fighting to break free of the stranglehold that he now found himself in.

"Why, 'tis a wildcat we have!" Eiric laughed and turned to his comrades. "If he fights like this when William the Bastard pays us a visit our Norman friends will row straight back to France!" He let out another great bellow, vastly amused at his own joke.

"Little prince," he said, looking soberly at Cnut now, "if you promise not to attack me again I will let you up and we can forget this nonsense. What say you?"

Cnut heard Eiric's voice as though through a fog. He realised, dimly, that he had never before reacted like this; the angry outburst, the loss of control that were so alien to him. His father had always taught discipline; in his conduct as a man, and in combat. The loss of that discipline, of that control, could prove fatal in battle and he had always striven to maintain it.

"You have my word," he said.

Eiric lifted himself from Cnut's chest and with a smile to his comrades began to wander away. He had had his fun and no harm had been done.

Cnut struggled to his feet and watched him go. Eiric's laughter rang round the training ground as he shared a private joke with his men and Cnut wondered what it was. It was too late now but it irritated him nonetheless. His left arm ached, reminding him of his injury, and he fished into his doublet for a pinch of the opiate. He put the powder to his lips and closed his eyes, letting the effect flow through him, soothing, warming, numbing the pain. A thought occurred to him, an unresolved matter, and his mood suddenly changed.

"Eiric!" he called after the Irishman who stopped and turned to face him.

"What?" Eiric said. "What now?" He had thought it all over. It should have been.

"'Little prince," Cnut said. "You called me "little prince?"

"So?"

"Why "little prince?"

"A joke; its nothing boy."

"What joke?"

"Leave it boy," Eiric said, but Cnut could not leave it.

"*What joke?*" He persisted with his question, a strange desire to have the answer forcing him to continue, almost despite himself.

Eiric growled his response, his irritation evident. "Leave it I said. The matter is closed." He turned his back on Cnut, signalling the end of the debate. His throat was dry and parched from the dust and some cold beer awaited him. He wanted to enjoy it in peace. He was to be disappointed.

"The matter is not closed." To his astonishment Cnut found that his sword was free of its scabbard, and was now held tightly in his grasp. How the hell it got there he would never know but immediately the atmosphere changed, the air charged with menace.

"Damn you boy!" Eiric cried. "Pull a sword on me will you? D'ye not know when to let a matter lie?"

"I will have your answer," Cnut said, "and then I shall be content." His eyes locked on Eiric's, unwavering, unblinking, the steel cold in his hand. Eiric returned the stare, weighing matters, a silent battle of wills.

"Very well boy," he said eventually, "we call you "little prince" because we know you. We know your type. Born to lead, weren't you boy? Or so you think. All your life men have run to do your bidding – even Ranulf, who ought to know better." He laughed but there was no humour in it. "I know you boy," he said. "I know that when the enemy appear you will be over the horizon and running for your pretty life. You're dangerous boy. Dangerous because we can't rely on you. I believe you would rather see us dead than risk your own neck for us." There was a scornful look in his eyes that said as much as the words he had just uttered. "You wanted an answer; now you have it." He turned abruptly on his heels, the matter closed. His beer was getting warm and his temper had taken a turn for the worst.

The flash of a sword, bright in the sun, the rending of his doublet, a sudden pain in his arm and bright spots of blood patterning the ground stopped him in his tracks. He checked the wound to his arm, withdrew his fingers, and gave Cnut a baleful glare. "You're dead boy," he said. "Dead." No one blooded him and lived to tell the tale. No one.

"Fetch me Bloodaxe," he called to one of his comrades who hurried away to fetch his battle-axe. "You're a fool boy," he said after a pause. "A damned fool."

Cnut just stared at him, saying nothing. There was no going back now, but why he had provoked this when he could have let Eiric walk away he simply did not know. Perhaps, as Eiric said, he was just a fool. He could soon be a dead one.

Eiric's man returned with the axe and handed it to him. Bloodaxe was Eiric's favourite weapon, a double-handed axe, lethal in his experienced hands. Eiric took it casually, confident in the outcome. Twenty-three men he had killed in his long career; twenty-three that he could remember. There may have been more, bleeding their lives away long after the battle had ended. And today Bloodaxe would again enjoy the sweet caress of skin along its edge, the taste of blood as it bit deep into flesh, even though the flesh would be that of another housecarl.

A shield-circle had formed around the two men, fifty men, shoulder to shoulder, their burnished shields forming a barrier, an arena of death. The two men looked at each other, wondering which of them would live to see nightfall while the noonday sun beat down, baking the ground, careless of the drama unfolding beneath its merciless glare.

Ranulf knew something was amiss the moment he rode into the camp. He could almost taste the atmosphere, the tension in the air. It did not take long for the tale to be told and his mood was grim once he realised that a man must die.

"You must stop this madness," Guthrum said, taking his arm. "Cnut is no match for Eiric. And with his arm…"

"I can't stop it," Ranulf replied. "And I won't. Cnut has blooded him. It is a matter of honour. You know that."

"Eiric will kill him then," Guthrum shrugged. "A pity after all you have done to save him."

"Maybe," Ranulf replied, "Maybe not." He thought of how Cnut had driven his spear point through his own guard just a few weeks ago. The boy was quick and Eiric was not as young as he was. It could yet be an even fight. They walked over to the shield-circle to watch events unfold.

Inside the arena the men eyed each other cautiously; the older, experienced campaigner, quietly confident in his abilities; the younger man all nervous energy, trying to retain his control, remembering his fathers words as he waited for the start.

Cnut felt that Eiric had made a mistake. The battle-axe, although a terrible weapon, capable of inflicting the most awful of injuries, it was not the weapon for single-handed combat. In the shield-wall where space to move, to manoeuvre, was at a premium the axe was undoubtedly the most feared of weapons. With nowhere to hide, nowhere to move, the axe could be used to devastating effect, smashing through shields as though they were paper and then on through bone and tissue into the skull of the enemy.

Here, however, inside the shield-circle Cnut reckoned he had twenty feet to play with; twenty feet to avoid the deadly swinging blade. Even so the slightest kiss of the lethal edge would mean the end for him. On balance though he felt that his sword would give him the edge in single-handed combat. If he could make Eiric tire, prolong the fight long enough for the heavy axe to take its toll on Eiric he could prevail. And that was his plan. With the sword he could cut, thrust, and recover. By contrast there would be no easy recovery for Eiric if his blow went wide – the heavy double-headed blade would continue to carve through air, and in that moment he must seek his opportunity. But first he must stay alive.

As he had expected Eiric made the first move. Hefting the double-headed axe above his head he moved towards Cnut, swinging it in a great arc above his head. The air sang as the blade carved huge circles through it and Eiric closed in for the kill. Cnut backed away, careful how he placed his feet. One slip and that would be the end. Suddenly he felt something behind him and realised that he had backed into the shield-circle. He had nowhere else to go. Eiric's face lit up in triumph. He had the whelp cornered. Cnut swore under his breath, cursing his mistake; his carelessness. He prepared for the hammer blow to land, his senses singing as he tried to anticipate it; to avoid it.

When it came it was like a thunderbolt from heaven, the only clue to its arrival being the extra grimace, the tightness of the cheeks, as Eiric went for the kill. At the last second Cnut ducked beneath the whistling blade; felt the air rush past his head as the axe crashed into the shield-wall behind him. He heard a grunt as the full weight of the blow was taken on the face of one of the shields and the housecarl buckled beneath the blow, going down to the ground with a broken wrist. The shield-wall closed up in time-honoured fashion and the fight continued. Cnut danced away into the centre of the circle where there was, once again, room to manoeuvre and Eiric relentlessly pursued him.

"Come and fight little prince!" he cried mockingly. "Come and fight old Eiric; I have seen enough of your yellow spine!" He swung the axe once more, and again the air sang with the noise. Slowly, slowly, he forced Cnut back, but this time he did not make the same mistake and when the blow came he danced out of the way, avoiding it with ease, and the blade found only the soft earth.

And so the pattern was set. Eiric, like a tiger stalking his prey, relentlessly pursuing Cnut around the arena and Cnut doing everything possible to keep the whispering death from caressing his skin. Whole minutes passed and both men began to tire. Eiric from the effort of swinging the heavy blade about his head, for he could not afford to relax his guard in case Cnut struck; Cnut from constantly having to move; to duck beneath, or leap away from the lethal blade. Twice Eiric almost caught him, the axe head grazing his doublet as with an agility born of desperation Cnut managed to sway backwards, away from the singing death as it arced towards him.

Cnut was drained; sweat soaked his whole body, his legs and back ached beyond belief with the need to constantly keep his balance, to leap away from the axe head that arced forever towards him. His left arm throbbed and pulsated wildly and inside his tunic it felt warm and sticky and wet. The wound had opened up again. But he could not think of that for the blade was whirling towards him once more and he leaped away, only to catch his heel in a divot. He fell backwards, into the dirt, the impact knocking the breath out of him. Eiric brought his axe down with a great bellow for surely this time it was the end for the young upstart. He had finally prevailed as he knew that he would. The sun caught the edge as it hurtled unerringly towards Cnut, towards his head, and even as the blade descended Eiric felt a pang of sadness for against all expectation the boy had been a worthy opponent and now he would die.

Cnut saw the blade descend; saw the flash of the sun on its edge and reacted without thinking. At the last moment, almost too late, he rolled sideways to his left, onto his damaged arm. Pain lanced through it like a knife but he ignored it. The blade bit the dust an inch from his head. The act of rolling onto his left brought his right arm, his sword arm, into play, and as Eiric lunged down for his killing blow, Cnut thrust upwards, a great sob erupting from his throat. The point went deep into Eiric's chest, piercing his heart, and on, through tissue and bone until it emerged bright with blood from his back. Eiric gasped; shocked; it had happened so suddenly that he was not prepared for it, for his own death when it should have been another's. His face turned ashen as the blood drained from it and his hands clutched uselessly at the hilt of Cnuts sword, bloodied by the spreading patch of crimson. He looked down, at the mortal wound, at the spreading crimson, and then up, at Cnut.

"I'm sorry, boy," he said. "I'm sorry." He looked up further, to the heavens, to the light that blazed in on him, then suddenly darkened.

Those watching would later swear that there were tears in his eyes as Eiric spoke those final words; the first tears since his wife had died when he was seventeen and he had become a housecarl to forget her.

For a long time no one moved, not a sound was heard. The silence was a requiem for the dead. One or two openly wept for despite his fearsome reputation Eiric had been a good friend to them, a man of wit, of great Celtic humour, their faithful right-hand in the shield wall. Now he was gone.

"Bury him with honour," Ranulf said when finally he recovered his senses. He looked at Cnut, unmoving on the ground, and then at Guthrum.

"Leave him," he said. "He will want his own company for a while. And I want a drink."

He marched off without another word. He needed a drink alright. More than one. A brave and experienced man had died this day. And he had died needlessly when men such as Eiric were desperately needed for the battles to come. *Damn Cnut,* he thought. *Damn,*

damn, damn. It would be a long time before he would forgive him for this day's work.

And when he did it would be almost too late.

CHAPTER TWENTY

THE DIVES, NORMANDY.

MID-AUGUST, 1066

Duke William paced the deck of the vessel and admired her sleek lines, the sweep of her bow which was raked back in the style so popular with his Scandinavian forefathers, and her high, dragon headed prow that stared, unblinking, across the stretch of water that separated him from England. She was a fine ship, he thought, and would surely serve him well. This was to be his vessel, the ship that would transport him, and many of the Norman nobility to their destiny on the shores of England. He had already chosen a name for her, the *Mora,* named after his wife Matilda, whom he adored.

Unlike many of the craft in his massive invasion fleet the *Mora* carried not only a main sail but also a bank of oars enabling the craft to make headway against all but the strongest of winds. Unfortunately for the Duke that was precisely the problem that he was encountering as he paced up and down her deck, for almost simultaneously with the completion of his fleet a north wind had sprung up from nowhere and showed little sign of abating. The numerous vessels now assembled in the Dives bobbed up and down like corks, their sails tightly reefed as they pulled against their anchors. White caps proliferated as, whipped by the cold northerly wind, the angry water in the inland lake beat incessantly against the shoreline and against the hulls of the tiny craft seeking refuge in its normally calm bosom.

Duke William turned to Fitz Osbern, who, like a faithful dog was shadowing his every step up and down the deck. He had to shout above the wind to be heard:

"The English King must be in league with the devil, for how else could he summon this tempest to thwart me? The very forces of darkness are ranged against us my friend!" The Duke's heavy features looked strangely pinched and drawn, but whether from the strain that he was under or from the elements that were plucking his boat cloak so that it streamed out behind him, Fitz Osbern could not tell. The Duke plucked from around his neck the holy relic given to him by the Pope and fingered it carefully.

"We must pray to Our Lady for strength to continue our endeavours, and for perseverance in adversity," he said. "Truly, we are facing the fallen angel himself!" Whether he was serious or simply acting Fitz Osbern would never know, but as he looked on in astonishment Duke William lowered himself to his knees on the deck of the heaving ship, and, bowing his head in prayer, the relic clasped between both hands offered up his silent invocation.

Presently the Duke turned to Fitz Osbern and with a look of disapprobation bade him kneel also. He did as he was bid, dropping reluctantly to his knees, and knelt beside the Duke while he prayed to the Madonna and all the saints for victory over his enemies. Fitz Osbern's thoughts as he knelt beside his Lord and Master were concerned with matters temporal rather than spiritual. *Who is this man,* he asked himself, *that rules our lives so? That prostrates himself like this? That would bend the very elements to his will?* He realised that he knew William, the man, not at all.

Surreptitiously he stole a glance at the man knelt beside him on the heaving deck and felt a surge of envy course through his veins. *Where does it come from, this strength? this single-mindedness?* He was damned if he knew. He shook his head to himself and resumed the attitude of his master. He closed his eyes.

Before he knew it William was shaking his shoulders, urging him to rise.

"The wind! The *North* wind! Think Fitz Osbern! What prevents us from sailing will surely aid Hardraada!" Then, calmer:

"I must send riders north, for if I am correct the Godwineson - and his legions from hell - will soon have their hands full, and with more than they bargained for."

Raising his face to the heavens he added:

"I was wrong, Fitz Osbern. This could be a propitious sign. A propitious sign indeed."

He stood, eyes closed, face raised to the wind, his cloak streaming behind him. What he was thinking Fitz Osbern could only guess. The man's optimism was boundless, he thought. His fleet was ready to sail, his army short of food, but poised on the brink of invasion and now this damned squall prevented them from sailing. Yet the Duke found cause for celebration. He heard himself agreeing with the Duke in any event.

"Yes, Lord," he said. "You are right. A sign from heaven itself."

Two days later, taking full advantage of the Arctic winds Harald Hardaada, the King of Norway crossed the North Sea from Bergen to the Orkneys and anchored his invasion fleet at Scapa Flow.

CHAPTER TWENTY- ONE

BOSHAM, SUSSEX.

1ST SEPTEMBER 1066.

King Harold Godwineson rose from his chair and walked to the window. The damned shutter was driving him mad, banging open and shut in the wind. He reached out and pulled it toward him, wedging it tight with a splinter of wood. *Thank God,* he thought, as the noise from the wind receded into the background. *Now he could think.*

Satisfied that the shutter was secured he walked back to the table, to the men who had been summoned to his family home, to discuss the growing crisis.

It was nearly Autumn but to the tense and tired men gathered around the conference table it felt like Winter. The north wind had continued unabated for two long weeks and the candles lighting the gloomy chamber flickered and guttered in their holders with each blast of the chill wind that caught their fragile flames.

Things were falling apart, slowly, inexorably, and nothing that Harold had done had been able to prevent it. His fleet had been drawn up on the beaches of the Isle of Wight for months. And now his Captains were beginning to haemorrhage sailors in ever increasing numbers as more and more men deserted, to return to their families. He had done all that he could to ensure the fleet was adequately provisioned, even to the extent of imposing a levy on villages in the neighbourhood, but it had not been enough. The men were concerned for their wives and children, and under cover of darkness, night after night had slipped away, never to return.

His fyrd were also beginning to desert, torn between their duty to the King and to their own family. They had given their six weeks and more, and still William the Bastard had not appeared. Perhaps he never would. And so Harold was left with his housecarls, and the men of the Wessex Militia, but they were not sailors, and, in any event, they were needed to patrol the coastline for he still had no idea where William the Bastard would make his landing.

Only one thing remained certain, and that was the wind. Whilst it continued to blow from the north William must remain in port, on the other side of the Channel for he dare not risk his fleet, his invasion force, to the vicissitudes of nature.

Around the table sat the four men that Harold most trusted; his brothers Leofwine and Gyrth, his housecarls Ranulf and Guthrum. All five of them knew the reality of the situation, the fact that if they could not maintain the fleet on station, the army on the coast, William could land unopposed. Where they differed was in what to do about it.

Harold slumped back into his chair at the head of the table. He was tired and irritable, his patience wearing thin. He grabbed the wine-skin by his elbow and poured some of the contents into his mouth. Wiping his moustaches he looked at the faces gathered around him. Gyrth was pressing the case for Harold to return to London whilst he and Leofwine guard the coast. They would act as his sentinels, Gyrth said, his eyes and ears, leaving him free to resume his duties in the Capital. He had, he knew, neglected them for long enough.

Harold considered this; he could see the merit, the plain sense in what Gyrth was proposing but had already decided to reject it.

"My duty is to be where the danger is greatest. And that is here, on the coast."

"But Hal, you have – we have, no fleet! And no men to sail it," Gyrth protested. "What good can it do to remain here any longer?"

he looked at his brother long and hard, hoping that the force of his argument would prevail. Harold sat impassively weighing the matter, reluctant to be torn from the coast, from where the threat must, eventually, materialise. He made no answer and Gyrth looked toward Leofwine for support.

"I agree with Gyrth," Leofwine said. "No need to risk your life brother," he added softly.

Harold studied his brothers' in silence while he continued to weigh the matter. His pre-occupation with William the Bastard was verging on paranoia but still he could not tear himself away from the coastline. When William appeared he wanted – needed – to be there, to hurl him back into the sea before he had barely set foot on English soil. He looked at Ranulf, then at Guthrum. They had both maintained a discreet silence during the debate.

"What think you Ranulf?" he said.

"Your brothers are right Lord," Ranulf said, "but all the same it must be hard to turn your back when the knife is ready to be plunged." He shrugged, apologetically. "I am sorry, Lord. This is a decision for you."

No help there, then. He looked at their faces, one, by one; they were all his men, even unto death. And yet, he knew, that at this precise moment not one of them would trade places with him. He could not leave; *he could not.* He was the King.

"One week more," he said. "One week; then I return to London."

On the 8th September, one week after the meeting, the fleets' provisions ran out. It was the Nativity of St Mary, a day for celebration. There was no celebrating in the King's household. With a heavy heart he ordered the return to London. He kissed his children and embraced Edith Swanneshals. He left on horseback with his housecarls and his Wessex Militia. He took a circuitous

115

route back to the Capital, dropping off groups of men at strategic points along the coast, which, apart from their thin presence was totally unguarded.

That same day, the 8th September, Harald Hardraada sailed his fleet on a northerly wind into the estuary of the Tyne. He was met by Tostig Godwineson who greeted his ally with an embrace and promised him the Throne of England.

CHAPTER TWENTY-TWO

LONDON.

16TH SEPTEMBER 1066

She lay arched like a rainbow across the width of the bed rather than along its length, her raven hair trailing upon the floor. His tongue, warm on her extended neck raises goose pimples on her arms. Then down to her breast, his tongue circumscribing the aureole, her nipple taken into his mouth. A moan. Her? His tongue traces a line, a ribbon of pleasure, down to her navel.

Could she tell him? Could she? The question cut through her thoughts like a knife.

Down further now, to the dark curls at the base.

"God I love you," he said. She must tell him. But would he believe her? And then she is lost, her thoughts drowning in the sea of her pleasure as the waves break over her. Gradually, like a swimmer she rises to the surface and gasps for air. She has to tell him, but later, for now it is his turn. He is inside her now, the tempest blowing outside the darkened room matched by the passion indoors. She has never known him like this. She senses his urgency and clutches his buttocks, drawing him into her. He is above her now, raised on his arms as he moves rhythmically in and out. She feels his muscular body tighten and relax with each surge, sees the white slash on his shoulder, a knife wound caused five moons and a thousand years ago. The night of the death star.

He cries, and it is over; she holds him in her arms. She decides to tell him. The words come out in a torrent, tumbling into each other in her haste to convey the message. Four or five months; probably five. Yes of course she is sure.

"Mine?..."

"Yes, of course."

Then tears on her cheek. His, mingling with hers. Tears of joy, and some of sadness. He holds her to him, drawing her in, arms wrapped tightly around her as though unseen hands might snatch her away. And so they lay until dawn: Alice and Ranulf and God's tiny gift.

CHAPTER TWENTY-THREE

THE GREAT HALL, WESTMINSTER

17TH SEPTEMBER 1066

It was a time of darkness, a time of uncertainty and indecision. King Harold Godwineson had arrived in London just two days ago, having taken his time posting his housecarls along the coast, reluctant even now to drag himself away from the southern boundary of his Kingdom. When he had arrived in the Capital he was greeted with the worst possible news; his fleet had been caught in the first of the equinoctial gales to batter the coast and there had been a substantial loss of both ships and lives. His mood was dark; as dark as those grim days of 1064 and he felt that no matter what he did things always turned out for the worst. *Perhaps God has deserted England. Deserted me.* The thought came unbidden to his mind, only to be replaced by other thoughts, just as grim, as introspective.

He tortured himself with visions of the drowning men, gasping for breath in the icy waters, fighting for the last piece of flotsam; anything that might sustain them momentarily before the seas unforgiving clutches dragged them screaming and cursing beneath its watery veil. He imagined them being dragged down, their lungs fit to burst as they clung to their last breath until, inevitably, they had to exhale and then with his name on their lips and a curse in their hearts they filled their lungs with seawater. And then the contortions as they fought for the air that did not exist. And it was his fault.

He looked at the faces gathered about the Great Hall. Did they blame him? Could they see the guilt hidden in his eyes? They were all there; Gyrth and Leo; Ranulf strangely quiet, lost in a faraway world of his own; several members of the Witan, concerned; afraid, as ever.

He told himself that there was nothing more to fear. The worst was over. It was too late now for William the Bastard; he had missed his chance. Perhaps the Gods were not entirely against him. Perhaps God had sent the north wind to thwart William's invasion, to preserve himself on England's Throne. Perhaps. And still the north wind continued to blow. After all these weeks it had not yet blown itself out; neither had it changed direction. But he no longer trusted his judgement – how could he after consigning so many men to their graves? – and he had hedged his bets by leaving almost a third of his men to watch the Channel. Just in case.

He was unsure of what to do next. He knew he was sick of waiting. That much was clear to him. It seemed that he had spent the whole of his reign waiting for Duke William to make his move. And still he waited. Must he wait forever? Was that to be his fate? He could be in this position again next year. He had to move on. But it was impossible.

Someone was talking to him, not that he cared. The time for talking was over. He wanted to act, to be a King, but how? When, what to do next? That was his dilemma.

....“And so, Sire....” Sheriff Tofi of Somerset was speaking, a pompous little man, full of his own importance, he stood before the dais, his hand pressed to his chest, head raised to the rafters like some Roman orator:

“I hope the Exchequer will feel able to compensate the widows of the men of my County so recently lost to us in your service...”

“Yes, yes, of course,” he heard himself reply. *Lost in your service...damn the man. Is it not enough that I pay with my conscience? Is that not a greater currency than gold?*

Someone else was addressing him now; pointing to the crowd. A messenger from Morcar had arrived. He was pushing through the crowd, the press of men anxious to hear his news. The man ignored them as his eyes searched for the dais, for himself. Harold absently noted his gaunt features, the haunted look in his eyes as he looked around and then hurried forward, anxious to deliver his message. He bowed in obeisance then spoke in a flat voice that was entirely devoid of emotion:

"Hardraada has landed. He is marching on York..........your brother is with him."

He sat alone in the gloom of his private chamber, head in his hands warming himself beside the hearth. The wind continued to whistle outside as though deliberately mocking him. He stared into the firegrate, lost in a world of his own. Logs crackled and sparked, devoured by the consuming flames. The warmth comforted him as he felt the heat on his face, the flames casting giant shadows against the wall. *I should have killed him, my brother, when I had the chance. Now I must fight him again.* He rose from his chair, and in the act of doing so hurled it to the far side of the room where it broke, like a twig, into so many pieces. *Damn him! Damn Hardraada; damn them all!* He paced about the room like a condemned man in a cell, measuring its width, its depth, the totality of his being. *I am the King. I must act like one. What to do? What to do?*

They were all outside waiting; waiting for his command. They took their lead from him; no one else. If he could not give them leadership who could? He applied his mind to the problem as he had done to so many problems over the past few months. This time it was for real; the enemy was real, not some imagined foe on the far side of the Channel. He had wasted enough time on William.

William would not come. Not now. Perhaps not ever. *Damn him. Damn him to hell.* He reached a decision. March north, to York. Take Hardraada. Take him first. And the man who was once his brother. Then back to London....*How far is it...to York? Two hundred miles. How long? say five days; then back. It can be done. I will do it. Harold Godwineson, the King of England will do it.*

He walked to the door of his chamber and opened it. No one there, but he knew they were waiting for him. He looked around and saw his brothers standing together in the corridor. Raising his voice he called to them:

"Gyrth! Leo! Fetch Ranulf and bring him to me. We have matters to discuss. All of us. Quickly now!"

CHAPTER TWENTY-FOUR

LONDON.

19TH SEPTEMBER 1066.

He stole furtively through the dark streets, one lost soul in the midst of thousands who lived their lives never knowing, or aspiring to anything better than the squalid existence that fate had handed to them. His face shone deathly white in the moonlight, beads of sweat pricked his brow, his eyes were opaque and dulled by days and weeks of self-inflicted abuse, his only refuge from the enmity of his colleagues in the regiment.

At last he came to the door – his befuddled brain recognised it as such – and he hammered hard on the knocker for entry. He closed his eyes and for a second he was back in the canvas tent with the parasites eating his flesh, devouring his arm, chewing their way through his chest and then into his eyes, blinding him, driving him crazy. He shook his head to clear it and now he was in the shield-circle with Eiric Mac Eirann coming at him. He stabbed Eiric through the chest as he had done that day so many weeks ago, but now Eiric kept coming, swinging his axe about his head, coming for him, coming for him… He stabbed again and rivers of blood poured from Eiric's chest, his eyes, his mouth; but he kept on coming; coming for him. He slumped against the door and nearly fell as it suddenly swung inwards, causing him to stumble across the threshold.

He looked up and saw her standing over him, the woman who had both saved his life, and taken it at the same time. He struggled to his feet and attempted to put a measure of authority into his voice:

"The King marches north tomorrow to fight Hardraada; I go with him. But I need the powder; I must have some more." Ceilwyc ignored the demand.

"Look at you!" she said, and he felt the scorn in her voice, "my disciple; my student; and yet you have learned nothing save how to indulge your own pleasures, your own *gratification.*" She spat out the last word with such venom that he involuntarily took a step backwards. But she was in full flow:

"I should have known better than to try to teach a soldier the mystic arts; the ways of our forebears; but I am old and time is short and there was no-one else but you. And so decided to teach a young puppy some new tricks, to try to teach a soldier to save lives rather than take them. And I chose you. I had hoped that you would give up soldiering to study with me, to learn something useful. Pah! How wrong can you be? Look at you – save others? You cannot even save yourself!"

"But you tricked me!" Cnut blurted out his response, his eyes wild, burning into his skull. "If you had not given me the powder, the books..." he tailed off as the realisation hit him that it had been her test and he had failed; failed her, and failed himself.

"Yes," she said, reading his mind, "It was a test. A test of your willpower; for if you cannot control yourself how can you hope to control others? Followers of the truth must be above such temptations. We must be prepared to forgo earthly pleasures in order that we may help others. Self-denial and self-belief. These are the watchwords of my people." She opened the door, inviting him to leave. The audience was over, her use for him at an end.

"Go fight Hardrdaada," she said. "Get yourself killed. You should be good at that. You are of no use to me."

Cnut sank to his knees, tears welling in his eyes. "But the powder!" he cried. "I need the powder! I cannot live without it now. You know that. You must know it! Would you deny me that?" He clutched her skirt in an entreaty but she pulled away, fixing him with her one good eye.

"But you deny me," she said softly. "You deny me the right, the chance, to pass onto future generations the secrets entrusted to me. Those secrets will die with me now; have you considered that? The secrets of generations painstakingly acquired over thousands of years will end with me. Because of you. Because of your weakness. Have you considered that Cnut?"

She looked at him with a look of pity and scorn, a look of sadness that spoke of their collective failure and Cnut had to avert his eyes.

"I thought not. Go now and do not bother to return. I have no wish to gaze on your face again."

The open door beckoned. And suddenly he felt anger, mixed with despair. The anger that had caused him to fight Eiric; the despair that brought him here tonight. And then he felt shame, and a knife in his hand.

"Then you shall gaze on nothing!" He slashed wildly; right to left, then back. A sigh, and there was a body on the floor. He looked quickly around, and then at Ceilwyc sprawled on the bloodstained rushes. She could have been asleep but he knew that she was not asleep for blood was pouring from the terrible neck wounds that he had inflicted. He looked at his knife, the blade stained with her blood and felt a sudden pain in his chest. The enormity of his offence hit him like a blow from a hammer and for a moment he contemplated fleeing this place of death. But his need was too great, his desire unquenched, and stepping over the prone figure on the floor he walked to the door and gently closed it. He moved to the shelves lining the wall of the room and began to rummage through the jars arrayed along them. He checked the contents carefully at first, but soon with total abandon, wrenching off lids, spilling the contents, until he found what he was looking for.

He dipped a finger into the white powder and put it to his lips. Satisfied, he tucked the jar inside his cloak and headed out into the night, a lost soul amidst thousands, but one with guilt carved across his heart and murder to his name...

CHAPTER TWENTY- FIVE

THE TAVERN, LONDON.

19TH SEPTEMBER 1066.

They sat together, naked on the bed, the feeble glow of a small tallow candle casting its light over them. His arm was around her shoulders, holding her close. Her head was against his chest and he could smell the sweet fragrance of her dark, lustrous hair, a counterpoint to the acrid smoke of the candle. He looked bleakly ahead, pondering their future, whether they had a future. In a few days he could be dead and all this would be as nothing.

They had sat thus for several minutes, neither knowing what to say, neither wanting to break this last embrace before he must leave to join his comrades. In truth he should not have come at all for there was much to do, much to prepare, before he marched north at dawn. But he could not leave without seeing Alice, and the child growing in her womb one final time.

They had made love but there had not been the usual joy in it. Ranulf had not been himself and Alice had taken the lead, guiding and encouraging him. And now they sat naked in the damp night air neither noticing the chill for both were engrossed in their thoughts of the morning, and what it might bring. Finally he said:

"I should go, or I will be missed. God knows that I could stay for ever but the King needs me as never before and…." She silenced him by putting her finger to his lips.

"Hush, my love," she said, "I know; I have always known. You are a soldier. No need for further explanation. Were you not a soldier you would not have rescued me that night and we would never have met. Have no regrets, my love, for what we cannot change."

Ranulf considered her words; he knew that she was right, but it was still not easy to accept.

"But you, the child….my son. I could be killed…"

"Then I would remind him every day of his father, who he was, what he was. I will not forget; I will not *let him* forget."

He looked at Alice and could see tears welling in her eyes. No words could make things any different, or change them one jot. He would have given anything to stay a little longer, to hold her in his arms forever, but he had to go. He pulled her to him, hugging her, kissing her tenderly on the forehead then down, to kiss the unborn child in her swelling belly.

He picked up his breeches and jerkin and pulled them on. Outside, across the river the bells of Westminster Cathedral were calling the people to evening prayer. *They should say a prayer for England,* he thought; for deliverance from Hardraada; *and for me.* It occurred to him that the wind had finally dropped; the peal of the bells resonated clearly through the cold night air. It was time to go.

"I love you," he said. "I love you both."

"I know," she replied. "And we love you."

He embraced her quickly, crushing her to him, and she was like a tiny sparrow in his arms. He kissed her again, released her and made for the door.

"Pray for me," he said, and then he was through the door, down the stairs and out into the street. He did not look back; he dare not look back for he knew that if he did he would see her face at the window and he would be lost.

For now it was time for war.

CHAPTER TWENTY- SIX

THE ROYAL HOUSECARLS CAMP

LONDON.

20TH SEPTEMBER 1066

Two hours before dawn, and the men of the regiment were preparing for the long march north. Some had lain awake all night, huddled in their blanket rolls, unable to sleep, their minds fighting over and over imaginary battles that had yet to be fought, whilst others had passed the time honing the blades of their weapons on the whetstone until they were satisfied with the keenness of the edge. Still others had spent the night gathered around their camp-fires, conversing with their comrades, reliving earlier battles, great deeds that they had performed, mighty enemies slain. Each one of them realised however that this time there was a difference; that there was more at stake than merely the outcome of a battle. This time a nation would stand, or fall, depending upon the outcome, depending upon *them.* The knowledge that so great a prize was at stake affected them all in one way or another, but the overwhelming feeling was that this time was a watershed in the affairs of their nation and the mood of the men was subdued.

An eerie silence pervaded the camp as the housecarls quietly prepared themselves for the day ahead, the long march north, and for the battle that would decide a nation's future.

They would march in full battle armour. For the men of the Royal housecarls this meant a march of two hundred miles – forty miles a day – in leather jerkin or doublet, over which they would wear their heavy suit of chain-mail whilst carrying sword or axe, a short stabbing knife, and their shield of linden wood and burnished leather. What their King had demanded of them was no more than they had expected for when they entered his service they swore an oath to give their lives to him. Yet even so it was a great deal to ask of them, to march two hundred miles and then fight a battle at the end of it. It was a venture fraught with risk; tired men make poor soldiers. Yet not one of them would have traded places to be anywhere else. They loved their King and they knew that he loved them.

Gradually, in the east, almost imperceptibly at first, it began to grow lighter; the deep coal black of the night slowly giving way to dawn's grey light. It would soon be time to march. Those men of the regiment that had learned the first rudiments of grammar hastily scribbled notes to their loved ones; their wives, children, or their mistresses; then helped their comrades to do the same. They were all brothers this day; now, more so than ever. They could sense that somehow or other if they lived through the next few days and weeks they would have a tale to tell that would thrill their children, and their children's children.

And then suddenly, like a shadow, the King was amongst them, his grey charger picking its way around the camp fires, the groups of men, some large, others small, all of them preparing for the march. He acknowledged with a nod of his head, a smile, or a few chosen words their cheers as they stopped to look at him as he passed by them. The King had come to join the march and they knew that with his steady hand to command them they were invincible.

Harold slowly picked his way into the centre of the camp, his mount sure-footed and solid beneath him, *Requitur* tight and reassuring against his thigh. He was wearing his best mail armour and behind him, held in the mighty fists of Ranulf and Guthrum, casting their own dark shadows over the ground, were his two great Standards. *The Golden Fighting Man* glowed in the light of a hundred camp fires and at times it seemed as though he were imbued with life as the flames from the camp fires caught some movement of the Standard, illuminating the warrior picked out in golden thread before the Standard passed once more into shadow.

And by the great camp-fire, glowing bright and golden in the early morning mist Harold reined to a halt. Still mounted he addressed his men, the men who would give their lives for him. He started softly, slowly, choosing his words with care, as though each word was a pearl, a treasured prize.

"Soldiers!" He cried. "Today we march north. We march because we must. Because if we do not do this England will fall to the Northern invaders; to Hardraada, and to Tostig, who is no longer my brother but my enemy. And if England falls then we shall have failed. Failed in our God given duty, you and I, all of us, to preserve this nation, to keep it safe for Englishmen and women, Saxon men and women." He paused to gauge the effect on his men. They were listening to him, the numbers around the campfire growing larger each minute.

"When I came to my Coronation," he said, "I swore an Oath in the sight of God, in the Cathedral dedicated to him. Some of you were there that day; others were not. To all of you I remind you, and myself, of that Oath: *To guard the Church of God; to forbid violence and wrong; to keep Justice, Judgement and Mercy.* These are words; just words. But they are also the promises that I made to God, and to the people of England. And I intend to keep them. And why must I do this? Why do I ask you to follow me - perhaps to our deaths? I will tell you: Because I am the King, and if a King cannot be true to his vows then what worth his Crown but a handful of dust? And what worth his realm but a lawless land for men to fight over like packs of marauding dogs. And what worth the man himself? Nought but a straw that will bend with each wind. That is why I fight. That is why I ask you to fight with me." He looked around. "Are you with me?"

"We are with you Sire!" a voice called from the rear. It was echoed and repeated by the hundreds of men gathered about him. He drew Requitur from its scabbard and the blade rang as it left the sheath. He waved it aloft so that it caught the first rays of the sun.

"Then north with me to York!"

The men loved it; they surged forward, surrounding him, mobbing him, crying his name, and then streaming forward like a tidal wave; a tidal wave of armed menace that would sweep the invader back into sea. Harold was swept along with them for he had created a momentum that was unstoppable, a momentum that would carry him to the very gates of York, and beyond, to a date with destiny. At last, after months of waiting, of frustration and despair, he could at last, be a King.

And two hundred miles north, that very day, his Kingdom was in the balance.

CHAPTER TWENTY-SEVEN

FULFORD GATE,
TWO MILES SOUTH OF YORK

20TH SEPTEMBER 1066.

Dawn, and through the mist the English army of Earls Morcar and Edwin watched the Norwegian host steadily advance towards them. There was no faltering or hesitation in their footsteps as the Scandinavian troops of King Harald Hardraada inexorably closed upon the ranks of the English nervously awaiting them. Edwin held the right of the English line, his brother, Morcar, the left. After much debate the two young Earls had deployed with the river Ouse protecting their right flank whilst on their left lay a water filled dyke with marshland beyond. This was their first battle and the young Earls, inexperienced, but hopeful of success had chosen what they hoped would be a strong defensive position to stand against the Thunderbolt of the North and his treacherous ally Tostig Godwineson. They stood directly in the path of Hardraada's march upon York and knew that if they could somehow prevail one of the greatest threats to the realm would be eliminated forever.

But Hardraada, the old campaigner, had seen what the English Earls, for all their careful planning had missed. When his army reached the ridge that ran across the battlefield, sloping gently down to the dyke on the English left, he suddenly halted his advance and deployed across the ridge, giving his army the advantage of the high ground. He concentrated his strength on his own left, the English right, leaving his own right wing under the command of Tostig Godwineson thinly stretched across the ridge and down to the dyke, inviting attack.

In the English lines Earl Morcar watched the Norwegian host manoeuvre along the ridge, the thousands of men in their ranks appearing to move as one body, as if a single mind was controlling their movement. No orders were given that he could discern, no Captains on horseback were shouting out instructions to their men and yet, almost as if the multitude in front of him had but one giant body, the component parts slowly swung into place along the ridge as if to a pre-arranged signal. It was impressive, and unnerving, and Morcar's bowels, which had already turned to liquid, churned again, causing him to grimace with the pain. He knew he could not let the men see his discomfort for the slightest show of weakness, or fear, on his part would have a disastrous effect upon morale. He must be strong and lead from the front like any good commander. He cursed under his breath. Why could they not have stayed safe and secure behind the City walls until Harold arrived? He had urged the City fathers to do just that, but fearful of what might happen to their precious City if Hardraada attacked they had persuaded him – against his better judgement – to take the field well away from the very walls that offered him what he most needed – shelter from the men now determined upon his destruction. Well, it was too late now. He was here, and there, on the ridge was the enemy. So he must fight.

He studied the faces of the men gathered about him, most of them familiar, all of them frozen into masks of concentration as they stood motionless, like himself, watching the Norwegian devils manoeuvre into position. What were they thinking? Were they as fearful as he? Would they stand? He would soon find out.

He turned again to study the enemy arrayed now along the whole length of the ridge, their steel helmets and weapons glinting in the watery sunlight that was at last casting its benign light upon the land. It seemed to Morcar that for some reason Hardraada had exposed the flank directly in front of him for the numbers of the enemy gathered along that section of the ridge were clearly fewer than the men under his own command. Over to his right, on the highest point of the ridge he could see Hardraada's banner, *Land Waster,* hanging limply in the calm, damp air. Surrounding it was the cream of Hardraada's force, over two thousand heavily armoured housecarls. That was undoubtedly where his strength lay.

On this flank however the men bestriding the ridge were not so well armoured, many wearing just their leather doublets and steel helmets. And there were gaps in their ranks; not many, but enough. Perhaps Hardraada had made a mistake. Perhaps he had underestimated the strength of the English army and did not have the numbers to hold the whole length of the ridge. There was only one way to test this theory. His mouth was as dry as he could ever recall but drawing his sword he turned to Earl Waltheof, who on receiving news of the invasion had hurried north with his men from Huntingdon to join him.

"Sound the advance," he said. Waltheof did not move; appeared not to have heard him. Morcar touched his elbow and Waltheof, no more than twenty years old himself, jerked violently as he was brought back to the present. His blue eyes registered his surprise.

"I was thinking of my late father, Earl Siward," he said. "He fought Macbeth you know. Fought him to a standstill. And then broke him." He looked at the Norwegian army arrayed across their front then back to Morcar.

"He held Northumbria once, like you. He could fight. God, we could do with him today." The words came out in a nervous staccato; he was as fearful as Morcar himself.

"Yes," he replied. "He was a great man your father. Fight well; make him proud of you." He smiled and Waltheof returned it. Platitudes, but all that he could think of at this moment. He paused, swallowed, and repeated the Order:

"Now sound the advance. Let us see how these fellows like the taste of our steel." His confident tone belied his fear. He raised his sword, held it aloft and took the first hesitant steps toward the ridge. His heart was in his mouth and his legs felt like lead but he forced them to go forward, one foot in front of the other. Behind him came the blast of a trumpet, the signal for the advance, and prayed that his men would respond. He closed his eyes and offered up a silent prayer. "Lord preserve me this day," he said. He whispered the words beneath his breath. He could taste salt on his tongue and realised that despite the damp he was sweating, rivulets running down his cheeks from beneath his metal helm. He opened his eyes and looked around. The English line was moving resolutely forward with him, toward the ridge, toward the enemy that waited for them. With a great yell, as much of relief as a battle cry he charged forward over the sodden grass, urging his men to follow.

Tostig Godwineson stood silent and impassive on the crest of the ridge watching the English army advance on his right flank along the line of the dyke. His thin lips parted in a smile when he saw that they had taken the bait as Hardraada had forecast they would. He had already issued orders to those holding the far right of their position to give ground only very slowly, to draw the English onto them, to commit them utterly and completely to the attack. Then, when the English were fully committed, Hardraada would strike with the full weight of his reserves, sweeping down from the ridge onto the English flank. With the dyke and the marshland beyond it at their rear they would be trapped. Those that survived the assault would perish in the marshes beyond. He smiled again, but there was no humour in his cold, flat eyes. Taking his eagle-winged helmet from his aide he pulled it hard down over his head. He looked to his left and saw two hundred yards away, on the brow of the ridge the massive presence of Harald Hardraada, all seven feet of him. With him were his personal bodyguard, formidable fighters, all of them. He looked calm and confident as well he might. After today Hardraada would be the next King of England, and he, Tostig Godwineson would be the King's right hand man; answerable to no one but the King himself. But first he had a battle to win.

"Follow me," he said to the men standing around him as he strode away down the ridge. "We have some English fish to gut."

The armies met with a bone shattering crash that rent the air. No quarter was asked; none given. Axe and sword cleaved through leather and chain-mail, then skin and bone as men began to die. And continued to die in their hundreds; English and Norwegian both. And the blood. So much blood, and death, and the stench of death; sickly, cloying, nauseating. It was a world of blood and death and hatred and waste. But slowly the Norwegians gave ground; inch by bloody inch, then foot by foot as the English poured more and more men into the attack.

Morcar's sword arm was numb, his head throbbed wildly from a blow he had taken on his helmet and he was exhausted to the point of collapse. But for all that he was exultant: the vaunted warriors of the North were being pushed back. He could feel it; could sense that they were struggling to hold their line. Not long now, he thought. One big push. Not long now. His thoughts were interrupted as the man beside him – he did not know his name – took an axe blow on his shoulder that bit deep into his chest through tendon and bone before lodging there, his assailant unable to free the blade. Without hesitation Morcar despatched him through the heart before he could wrench it clear. He dragged his own sword free and fancied that the man had smiled before he died but he could not be sure. There was no time for such things, no time for anything but to cut and hack and to block the blows that were aimed at him. *Where was Edwin?* The thought suddenly came to him, cutting through his maddened senses like an icicle. Edwin had to hold the right, and the centre, to prevent the Norwegians taking him in the flank. *Where was he?* Surely he would see what was needed? No time now to worry of such things. Just keep fighting. Edwin would not let him down.

The Norwegian retreat continued; but they did not break. Instead they just died; one by one, where they stood, crying to their God Wodin as they were cut down by axe or sword as the superior numbers of the English army began to tell.

Behind the Norwegian lines Tostig watched the English progress, the Norwegian sacrifice, with detached interest. It would soon be time, but first he must draw in more of the enemy. He wanted them all, but knew that was not possible. Still, the magnitude of the victory he had planned would shake his brother to the core. Sending boys to do a man's job. How typical of him. He sneered, and his aquiline features lit up with pleasure at the prospect of so much death to come. Yes, his brother would rue this day alright.

He looked up to the ridge, to where Hardraada awaited his signal. Patience, he told himself. Patience. Then the day will be yours.

The retreat was finally becoming a rout. One by one, and then in greater numbers the Norwegians began to break from the line. Morcar was beyond exhaustion, beyond rational thought save for the need to kill and to keep killing. Victory was within his grasp; he could almost taste it, and with a desperate cry he urged his men forward, to give the enemy no respite, no chance to regroup. He had lost all sense of where he was, or how much time had elapsed since dawn, or how many men he had cut down. His sword arm was bloody to the elbow. He looked to the sky, to find the sun but it was lost in a cloud. A trumpet blast dimly reached his ears and the Norwegians broke.

"After them!" he cried, and the English host raced forward, all discipline forgotten as they hurried to slaughter the defeated enemy.

"No quarter! No quarter!" he heard himself cry to the men racing forward with him, tripping over themselves in their haste to cut down the foreigners who had threatened their shores. Another blast of a distant trumpet registered in his subconscious but Morcar's thoughts were far away, concerned only with the butchery to come. His head was swimming from the blow he had taken, and the noise and the heat of the battle, but slowly, slowly, the realisation came that somehow, at some point in the past few moments, the battle had changed. The screams and shouts of the dying were also behind him; no longer just in front. *What was happening? Where was Edwin? Where was he?*

A man raced past, terror registering in his face. And then another, and another, and suddenly the whole English army were racing, not ahead, to slaughter the enemy, but to his right, towards the dyke, and the marshland beyond. He grabbed hold of a man, his weapons already discarded, ripping off his mail coat.

"What is it man?" he cried, his face no more than an inch from the others. "What the hell is happening?"

The man looked at him blankly, hardly recognised him, then the question seemed to register.

"Hardraada!" he said. "Hardaada is at our rear! We are lost! Lost!" He snatched Morcar's hand away and stumbled forward toward the marshes. Ahead of him the Norwegian flight had halted and now those same men were advancing again in a solid line, their shield wall locked together. Behind him, and over to his right, were the screams of men dying, but now they were his men dying, mercilessly cut down by the housecarls of Hardraada who had swept down onto their flank from the ridge beyond. He was trapped, his army doomed, and it was his fault. The utter despair of defeat overcame him and his vision blurred as tears came to his eyes. He snatched them away with the sleeve of his doublet. He must think. He must save himself. Only the marshes offered any hope of salvation. Desperately he tore off his helmet, wincing with the pain, and picked at the buckles of his mail coat. He must hurry. His fingers would not work. "Come on! Come on!" he said aloud in his anxiety to rid himself of the heavy mail armour that would inevitably seal his doom in the marshes beyond. Eventually the coat came loose, and he tore it off, discarding it on the ground. He looked about him. They were much closer now; he could see their helmets bobbing up and down as they cut and hacked their way through the pockets of English resistance. He must be quick. He stumbled towards the swamp, ripping off his doublet and breeches as best he could, anything that would bear him down beneath the treacherous miasma. Stark naked he hurled himself into the dyke as the Norwegian army finally broke through the last remnants of the English defence. Thank God he could swim. Desperately he clawed his way to the opposite bank and looked back. The Norwegians were pouring in their hundreds through the English lines and making for the dyke, intent on butchering anyone still alive. He held his breath as he headed into the marshes. He could be dead either way. Wading through the sucking, clawing, mud he spied a small islet, if one could call it that, surrounded by a sea of treacherous, shifting, swamp. He lunged for it, and for a moment thought he had missed, but his hand held fast to a small tuffock of tough marsh grass and he held on for dear life. Behind him he could hear the screams and cries of the dying as the Norwegians went about their grisly task, hacking to death those that could not cross the dyke. Everywhere was chaos and noise, and his ears were assaulted by the screams and cries of those about to die, as though they were calling to him personally. He caught his breath and forced himself to think: *Stay hidden, stay still.*

Do not move. Taking a deep breath he lowered himself into the swamp, one hand clutching precariously at the tuffock of grass, his lifeline to the world, while all about him his comrades died under the hand of the enemy, or had their lives snatched away by the sucking, cloying, mud.

He could not say how long he remained hidden beneath the swamp, barely able to breathe, choking silently on the mud that was all about him. After what seemed an eternity, as dusk began to fall and the noise of the battle abated he stirred from his self imposed grave and struggled towards the land. If he lived to a hundred he would never forget the sight that greeted him for there were literally thousands of his comrades littering the ground, some fully clothed in battle armour, others, their torsos naked, covered in the mud through which they had attempted to escape. All were dead, their throats slit from ear to ear, their blood staining the ground black as dusk finally fell. In his desolation he sank to the ground and burying his head in his arms sobbed out his heart.

CHAPTER TWENTY-EIGHT.

TADCASTER, YORKSHIRE.

24TH SEPTEMBER 1066

Dusk was falling as King Harold arrived in the village of Tadcaster with his bone weary troops. Just nine miles south of York, the army had marched one hundred and ninety miles by day and night over the past five days, barely stopping for food or rest. Some men could hardly stand, others barely walk, from the agonies of blistered feet and the desperate need for sleep. Upon arrival many simply lay down and slept where they could. But the condition of his men was as nothing to the wretched news he received from the handful of survivors of the carnage at Fulford Gate.

There were so few of them; pathetic, broken men, crushed physically and mentally by the atrocities they had witnessed. The tale they told of the slaughter of their comrades' defied belief. Many wept openly as they told of how, trapped against the marshes, the Englishmen had chosen to end their lives suffocating in the treacherous mud rather than be cut down by Hardraada's butchers. Those that did try to stand had been hacked to pieces unmercifully before Tostig, the King's own brother, had ensured that there would be no survivors by slitting the throats of the English fallen with his own sword. Edwin and Morcar were believed dead, killed with their men, and worse still, York had capitulated to Hardraada.

Harold's gorge rose as he listened to the litany of disasters that had occurred whilst he had been hastening northwards. Why the hell hadn't Morcar and Edwin waited for him? Their combined force would surely have given them the advantage. Why hadn't they waited? He shook his head in disbelief. And as for his brother, he was sickened to the core by what he heard. Tostig had now sealed his fate beyond any question. He was worse than Hardraada, worse than William the Bastard, for he had turned on his own people, a traitor to his family and to his Country.

Harold was filled with loathing and sadness at the thought of the bloodshed still to come, but he knew that there was no alternative. Perhaps there never had been; from the moment the Crown had been placed on his head. As ever, it all rested upon him. Upon him and his tired army. *So be it then.*

He closed his eyes to think, pushing the desire to sleep into the farthest recesses of his mind. He needed some answers, and quickly. He turned to one of the survivors, a young man, barely nineteen, his cheeks streaked with tears.

"Where is Hardraada now? Do you know? The questions were put gently but there was an edge to his voice that was unmistakable. The young man looked at the King for a moment, not comprehending, initially, that he was being spoken to. And then the question sunk in and Harold saw the spark in his eyes as he replied:

"He has returned to the fleet to rest his men."

"And York boy? Does he have a garrison in York?"

"I am not sure Sire," the boy replied. "I believe not."

Harold thought there was more to come, that the young man had more to offer, but perhaps he was mistaken for there was only silence from his thin pale lips. And then like a flood the words came, tumbling out in a torrent:

"He said you would come Sire! Morcar said you would come! He went down on bended knees, pleaded to be allowed to wait for you before giving battle! But they would not let him. The City fathers did not believe him; made him fight even though he did not want to. They were so scared themselves; scared of Hardraada, of what he might do!"

So that was it. Morcar, and no doubt Edwin also, had argued caution, advised against giving battle until he had arrived with his housecarls, but the good burghers of York had made him do otherwise. He might have known. Merchants and politicians, they were the same the world over. But Hardraada had not taken York; it was a mistake. A grave mistake. He spoke to the boy in the same careful tones:

"Listen, boy," he said. "Does Hardraada know? Does he know of my approach?"

"No Sire." The words were the sweetest he had heard since his arrival. "For all Hardraada knows you are still in London, awaiting his advance. Your presence here will be the last thing he expects." The boy was smiling now. It was a remarkable transformation.

"He is in for a surprise, lad." Harold said. "You have done more than you know. Go get some rest, join your comrades."

The boy stood silent and unmoving, reluctant for some reason to leave his presence.

"May I march with you Sire?" he asked suddenly. "I am still strong, and can wield a sword as well as any man." Harold doubted that but the boy deserved his chance.

"If you wish," he said. "You have earned it. Your name boy? How are you called?"

"Cadoc, Sire."

"Well Cadoc," he said, "I will find you a place amongst my fyrd. Fight well for me."

"I will fight," Cadoc said, "but not only for you. I fight for my two dead brothers, slain at Fulford Gate."

He left to join new comrades in the fyrd, to prepare again for battle. Harold watched him go and knew that the boy had found a new meaning to his life: plain and simple revenge.

Gyrth approached through the gathering gloom, his tunic dusty and sweat-stained from the long march north, his chain-mail temporarily discarded. He looked absolutely shattered as he dropped down onto a rock.

"The men are exhausted Hal," he said. "They need to rest." Harold considered this, the need for rest against his desire to get at Hardraada before he learned of his presence. Gyrth was right; tired soldiers make poor warriors.

"Tonight we rest," he said. "Tomorrow we advance on Hardraada."

CHAPTER TWENTY-NINE

YORK.

25TH SEPTEMBER 1066.

The cobbled streets of York were deserted as Harold marched his army through the Jubber Gate into the City in the early hours of the morning. First came the peasants; those who had joined him during his march north. Armed with pitchforks, scythes, or homemade clubs they marched with a swinging, infectious gait, setting the pace for those that followed. Next came the men of the fyrd, the regular army, armed with swords or spears, and carrying their familiar wooden shields. A few wore mail hauberks but most, unable to afford a coat of mail favoured the padded jerkin that was their standard issue. Finally came the housecarls; the King's personal guard, the rock upon which his army would stand; men loyal unto death.

For over a mile the procession stretched through the streets but not a soul turned out to greet their liberators or to cheer them on their way. The silence was immense as the citizens of York remained in their homes, behind closed doors, contemplating their collective guilt. They had surrendered to Hardraada only yesterday; had thrown open the gates of the city to welcome him; had promised him support, and men, and provisions, and now, incredibly, here was the King with his army, arrived from London to do battle for them. Fearing his wrath they stayed indoors.

Ranulf marched alongside Guthrum, his head turning this way and that, looking for signs of life but seeing only empty streets and shuttered windows; hearing only the regular tramp of feet on the ancient cobbles.

"The craven bastards," he said. "You would think we had the plague by the greeting they give us."

"Aye," Guthrum replied, "two hundred miles we march to save their worthless skins and they hide from us like rabbits. A pox on them I say." He spat a stream of saliva into the gutter, just as the King rode past, flanked by his brothers. The King looked to neither right nor left, but rode proudly upright, staring fixedly ahead, his face grim and set. Upon his shoulders he wore his finest mantle trimmed with ermine, and upon his head he wore the Crown of England. He was showing the people of York that he was their King, no matter what they, or Hardraada might think.

Almost as an afterthought Harold reined to a halt several yards in front of Ranulf and turned his horse skilfully, almost carelessly, to speak to him:

"When we depart through Walmgate Bar I want a guard set on every gate. No one is to leave, Ranulf, no one. I don't trust these bastards." He wheeled his mount again and was gone, galloping up the column, leaving his brothers trailing in his wake.

Ahead of the army the King's twin banners of the Fighting Man and the Red Dragon of Wessex fluttered bravely in the breeze, catching the sun as they dipped and turned with each breath of wind. And seeing them Ranulf's heart filled with pride; he was reminded of the man that Harold had once been, and had thought was lost to him for ever. But now he had found him again. Harold, the warrior; Harold Godwineson, the warrior King of England.

Seven miles east of York lay the village of Gate Helmsley and, one mile beyond that, a narrow bridge that crossed the river Derwent. Men called it the Stamford Bridge. And it was here that Harald Hardraada had chosen to accept a deputation from the City. Hostages, provisions, arms and men had all been promised to him by the terrified citizens of York and with the confidence borne of victory he had drawn up his army on the eastern bank, dispatching only two hundred men across the narrow bridge to await his supplicants. He would not deign to greet them himself. He was a warrior, the next King of England and it was not meet that he should parley with women.

It was unseasonally warm for the time of year and despite a slight breeze the sun burned brightly in a clear blue sky. A bead of sweat trickled down his cheek into his greying beard and Hardraada wiped it away with a huge fist. Like his men he had left his chain-mail with the fleet anchored upriver at Riccall where, he had no doubt, it was being polished until it shone. His wolfskin, stitched from the carcasses of eight wolves was too heavy for the balmy autumn weather and unfastening the shoulder clasp he threw it onto the grass. He looked at the men all around him. These were the men who had crossed the Poison Sea with him, the men who had fought and won a great battle; the men who would see him crowned King of England.

Their spirits were high after the crushing victory over the English earls and those involved in the fighting lay around enjoying the sunshine, laughing and joking, recovering their strength, tending their wounds. He surveyed the countryside and marvelled at the greenness of it all; the rich rolling hills, the cattle and sheep gently grazing, the sun sparkling on the river. It was all his; or soon would be once the Godwineson had been crushed. And then he must plan his Coronation. Spreading his wolfskin he lowered his corpulent frame onto it and lay on his back. He looked into the clear blue sky, the sun warm on his face, the smell of the long grass assaulting his senses. He had just begun to doze when a shadow fell across his face.

"Dust. To the west. See, they are coming." Tostig Godwineson stood over him like a great black crow, his eyes mere slits against the glare of the sun, his torso silhouetted against the brightness of the day. He was a hard man to like, Hardraada thought, so bitter and vengeful, but as an ally had proved indispensable. Rising from the ground Hardraada followed Tostig's outstretched arm. Yes, there in the distance he could see a cloud of dust, the expected delegation, anxious no doubt to have done with it all. Women and old fools. He lay back on the grass and closed his eyes.

"You go meet them," he said.

Tostig marched down to the bridge accompanied by two of his Flemish mercenaries. He trusted them rather more than Hardraada's own men; could speak his mind in front of them without fear of his words being reported back to the Norwegian King. He was not in the best of humour and Hardraada's decision to leave the handling of the delegation to him had soured his mood even further. Diplomacy was not his strong suit and, in any event, he felt that they were wasting time. Push on South, he had urged Hardraada; gather support and keep up the momentum. He knew his brother; knew that the only thing Harold understood was a knife at his throat. But Hardraada had chosen to wait; to wait for the delegation from York now approaching in the far distance. Tostig had not agreed with the decision. What were a few more men and horses against the need to move south, to seize the Capital? They had argued violently but he had had to give way.

Three hundred yards ahead was the bridge, an old wooden construction, wide enough only for two men to cross at a time. One man had been posted at either end and both appeared to be dozing in the midday heat, their chins resting on their chests, their steel helmets catching the sun as they breathed fitfully in and out.

"More like a Sunday bloody picnic than a campaign," he muttered to himself just loud enough for the two men flanking him to catch his words. They exchanged knowing glances and decided to ignore the comment. Tostig Godwineson was not a man to cross. He looked further west, beyond the bridge, at the column of dust growing ever larger. Half a mile, he estimated. He narrowed his eyes and shaded them against the sun, trying to pick out individual features, but could not do so. He stared at the column for a long time, and the longer he stared the more his unease grew. There was something about it that was not quite right. Something that set his nerve ends tingling. What was it? He looked again, but could not identify what it was that troubled him so. Turning to the younger of the two men he said:

"Your eyes are younger than mine. Over there. What do you see?"
The mercenary followed Tostig's gaze and shaded his eyes. He peered into the distance for what seemed like minutes before saying:
"A column of men; some mounted."
"How many?"
Again, the mercenary stared for what seemed like whole minutes before responding:
"Five, maybe six thousand; hard to tell."
Tostigs' breath caught in his mouth. *Five thousand! Who are they?* Once more he asked a question:
"What else? What else do you see? Hurry man!" The mercenary shot Tostig an anxious glance before resuming his scrutiny of the approaching column. When he turned back to face Tostig he also looked troubled.
"I could be mistaken, but see those two splashes of colour at the head of the column? Could they be banners?"
Tostig stared at the column of dust growing ever nearer and focussed his eyes intently at its head. Several feet above the ground, above the swirling dust he could indeed see two splashes of colour as the young soldier had said. Red....and yellow. No, not yellow. Gold. And as he stared at them recognition slowly dawned: The twin banners of the Dragon of Wessex and the Golden Fighting Man. The

banners of Harold, his brother. It was not possible, but it was true. A lump came to his throat and in a voice that was near to panic he said: "Get everyone back across the bridge. Now!"

And heart pounding in his breast he started to run back to Hardraada.

Hardrdaada's eyes blazed like fireballs from hell as, breathless and frightened, Tostig broke the news.

"You said the Crown of England was mine for the taking! You said Harold would not leave London! Now you tell me that he is here! What am I to do Godwineson? Tell me that!" His eyes, bulging from their sockets burned into those of his ally as he spat out the questions. And he wanted some answers. Quickly.

Tostig was not easily cowed but Hardraada's fury had unmanned him. He said meekly:

"I advise we retire on the fleet. Our mail armour is there and...."

"No!" Hardraada bellowed his reply. "Hardraada runs from no one. No one, do you hear!"

"I did not say run..."

"I *run* from no man. I shall tell you what we shall do. We shall fight. To the last man, we shall fight, do you hear me?"

Tostig had no doubt that he meant it. Hardraada's courage was legendary. He cast an anxious glance to the west. His brothers' army was now clearly visible; footsoldiers were hurrying forward, urged on by a solitary rider who Tostig could just about recognise as his brother Leofwine. More ominously a small detachment of cavalry had left the column intent on capturing the bridge. Tostig could see that Harold himself was at their head, his horse straining at the bit in his anxiety to reach the bridge before the enemy. It would be a close thing, but if Hardraada's men did not reach the bridge before Harold's cavalry they were doomed. And then Harold could cross unopposed. For months Tostig had felt nothing but hatred for his brother, the need for revenge, but now cold fear coursed through his veins. He turned back to Hardraada.

"For God's sake man!" he cried. "Why do this? It makes no sense! Retire on the fleet and then give battle. We haven't a chance if we try to stand!"

"Then I shall die," Hardraada said softly. "And you, my friend, shall die with me. But we shall die an honourable death shall we not? And I shall dine with Wodin this night!" He laughed, a huge bellow of a laugh that caused the pendulous flesh on his chest and arms to shake up and down. But then he stopped and looked at Tostig from the height of his full seven feet and the look that he gave him was one of pure contempt.

"Pray that your God is smiling on you," he said. "For no man here shall mourn your death." And Tostig could only stand and watch, ashen faced, as Hardraada turned his back on him and hurried away to do battle.

Down the grassy slope Harold hurled his cavalry towards the bridge, his face set in a grim rictus, his heart pounding, his stallion lathered in sweat. Ahead of him the first of the Norwegians were hurrying to cross the bridge, looking fearfully behind them every few paces to see how much time they had before the enemy were upon them. Behind them one man was attempting to create a shield-wall to protect their rear, its flanks bent back in a semi-circle against the river banks either side of the bridge. He was pushing and shoving men into position and from his frantic gesticulations Harold could tell that he was having difficulty in persuading them to stand, to face certain death whilst their comrades escaped across the bridge. Harold noticed that this man, obviously an officer of some kind was the only one to be wearing chain-mail. The flimsy shield-wall so hastily assembled was now only a hundred yards ahead. Either side of him mounted riders, his housecarls shouted oaths or curses as they surged past him, plunging at breakneck speed towards the shield-wall, intent on smashing it aside.

Suddenly Gyrth was beside him, his eyes beneath his helmet wild with blood lust, his features taut and strained as he leaned forward over his stallion's neck. He carried a huge lance with a wicked leaf shaped blade and which he had levelled at the frightened men in the shield-wall.

"Stay back Hal!" he cried, "these boys are mine!" And then he was gone, his words snatched away by the wind as he raced toward the bridge and the doomed men nervously awaiting him. The English cavalry, over a hundred heavily armed men crashed into the shield-wall with an impact that shook the earth and reverberated to the heavens. Their momentum was unstoppable and the shield-wall disintegrated, blown away like leaves in the wind. And then the butchery began. Harold, wielding Requitur, saw a Norwegian, dazed, bloodied, and scared running for the bridge, all thought of opposition gone. He rode him down and slashed at his face pausing only to see a river of blood erupt from the man's cheek before turning to find another victim. He knew that there could be no quarter, no mercy, nothing less than the total destruction of the Scandinavian forces under Hardraada for this was a fight for the Kingdom itself.

He looked for Gyrth amongst the mayhem of fallen bodies and continuing slaughter and at last saw him, crazed beyond recognition, skewering a man on the point of his lance, his helmet gone, his arms and chain-mail bloodied, his horse foaming and lathered with exhaustion.

"Gyrth!" he cried. "Gyrth! Over here!"

Gyrth looked around at the sound of his name and, seeing Harold, galloped over to him. His eyes had a madness about them that

Harold had not seen before. He took Gyrth's arm in his hand, stared him hard in the face.

"Gyrth!" he cried. "Look at me! Look at me!" Gyrth's eyes slowly lost their wildness, focussed upon his own.

"You can rest now," he said. "Rest. Now listen to me. Listen. I want you to bring Leo and Ranulf to me. Others can finish this. We have Hardraada to deal with."

He pointed to the east bank, across the river, to where, on the crest of the gentle slope Hardraada was gathering his men for the decisive battle. He could see Hardraada's Standard waving defiantly in the sunshine, his housecarls massed about him. Then, from across the river, from the men gathered on the far slopes, a growing crescendo of noise could be heard as the Scandinavians hammered out their war chant, a dreadful ululation of death, on their burnished shields. Turning his back on the noise he looked once more at Gyrth, seated motionless on his lathered mount, glaring with a look of pure hatred at the enemies ranks.

"I see them Hal," he said. "I see them. Hardraada. And Tostig. Look to the left of the Standard. The bastards." Harold followed Gyrth's gaze and thought that he could just about make out Tostig's eagle winged helmet but he could not be sure. They were wasting time.

"Go!" he said. "Get Ranulf and Leo. I want to get at Hardraada now." Gyrth nodded in acknowledgement, taking a final look across the river before he departed.

Harold turned his attention once more to the fight on this side of the river. Much of the Norwegian resistance had been swiftly and brutally ended but still, on the bridge, a pocket of Norwegians were making a final desperate stand. Around them lay the bodies of half a dozen Englishmen, cut down in a desperate attempt to storm the crossing. Harold noted that amongst this final pocket of die-hards was the same massive Norwegian who had hastily organised the shield-wall. He was wielding a large two handed axe, scything down his attackers with huge arcing blows whilst all about him his men were falling one by one; cut down by sword or axe or battered to death by the peasants with their clubs. But still the big Norwegian stood defiant and strong, continued to bar their passage.

Behind Harold the sound of hooves signalled the return of Gyrth with Leo and Ranulf, and the rest of the English infantry.

"That man," he said, pointing to the bridge, "is determined to sell himself dear. But we must have this bridge. We must have it." He tugged at his moustaches, deep in thought. Then he turned to Ranulf. "You have the honour," he said.

"Me, Lord?" Ranulf's pulse quickened.

"I can think of none better than my own Champion."

Ranulf looked at the bridge, at the desperate Norwegian barring their way. He was buying Hardraada valuable time; time that they could not afford. As he watched he saw yet another Englishman fall under his swinging blade, the man's torso almost severed in two by the ferocity of the blow. He looked at Gyrth.

"Your lance, Lord?" he asked. Gyrth gave him a quizzical look and handed it over; eight feet of hardened ash tipped with steel. It was heavy, the point and stock sticky with blood.

"Do it quickly," Gyrth said. "We need to get at those bastards." He looked across the river to where Hardraada had formed his army into a huge crescent atop the hill, waiting impatiently for the English advance. Their war chant had increased in volume; more and more men had gathered beneath Hardraada's Standard and the noise of their chanting boomed like distant thunder across the river.

Taking a last look at his King, the man who had assigned him the unenviable task, Ranulf approached the bridge, lance held firmly in both hands. He noticed that they were shaking. What had Alice said, that last night together? *Don't take risks my love.* Christ. What would she think if she could see him now? He tried to push all thoughts of her to the back of his mind, but it was impossible. Any moment now he could be dead and he would never see her again. Or the child. He crossed himself.

The Norwegian now stood alone on the bridge surrounded by the corpses of both sides. They littered it from end to end, staining its ancient timbers a dark crimson. As Ranulf stepped onto the bridge the Norwegian said something that he did not understand, but then beckoned him forward with a wave of his hand. Ranulf saw that his chain-mail was bloodied and torn, evidence of the ferocity of the fighting, but then he noticed the eyes. Pale blue, as cold as ice, as fathomless as the ocean. The eyes of a killer. A shudder went down his spine and he hoped that the King hadn't noticed. Steeling himself he accepted the challenge and stepped forward onto the bridge.

He had chosen Gyrth's lance for the advantage of reach that it gave him. He could thrust and probe at the Norwegian's defences from, he hoped, a safe distance, beyond the arc of the Norwegian's axe. But as he moved toward the man barring the bridge he soon realised that the Norwegian had no thought for defence for he suddenly came at him like a madman, his axe making the air sing with the ferocity of his attacks. It was all Ranulf could do to hold him at bay using the shaft of his spear to block the unremitting blows. He was forced further and further backwards as the axe sang in the hands of the Norwegian and the blows rained down. There was no respite, no chance to make a move of his own, no time to do anything but try to survive. His arms screamed with pain and his head swam; it was like facing a whirlwind. And then the inevitable happened: the shaft snapped under the weight of the blows, splintering like matchwood. He lost his balance, falling backwards, slipping on the timbers, slick with blood. He went down heavily, his head hitting the planking with a fearful crack that caused him to see stars. Dazed, he looked up, into the sky, but saw only the Norwegian filling his vision, axe raised for the downward blow. He closed his eyes; it had taken mere seconds. He suddenly felt ashamed. He should have done better, fought harder. He gritted his teeth. It would soon be over. He waited for the blow.

The blow never came. The Norwegian was about to deliver it, was anticipating the kill, when a spear was thrust upwards, from below the bridge, into his groin. He screamed with pain as the spear point entered then erupted from, his stomach. Viscera and entrails were wrapped around the bloodied shaft and the Norwegian stared in horror at the wreckage of his body. The blood drained from his face, his eyes glazed over. He fell to the timbers. The spear shaft was twisted inside his gut and he screamed again. He should have died but somehow he still lived. And now he lay clutching the spear shaft with bloodied hands, his mouth forming unintelligible words, his body rocking backwards and forwards with pain. Blood pumped from his stomach to mingle with the blood of those already dead.

Ranulf saw all this and could not help but feel pity. Whatever he was the Norwegian was a brave man. He got to his feet and walked over to him. The Norwegian looked up and somehow, through his agony, mouthed a few words. Ranulf did not understand the words but the message was clear enough. He picked up the axe that had fallen from the injured man's hands and in one swift movement struck off the head. The eyes, he saw, were still open, the mouth still moving...the head rolled from the timbers into the river.

He stood for a moment over the headless corpse, a warrior's tribute to another. A noise from below the bridge caught his attention and he saw Cnut scrambling up the bank side, muddied, bedraggled, but something else besides. In Cnut's face he saw the utter desolation of a man without hope, without a future. Alive, but somehow dead inside.

"Thanks," he said, not knowing what else to say.

Cnut shrugged. "Now we are even."

Neither man ventured anything further as they walked back to the English lines.

The bridge finally cleared of defenders Harold Godwineson hurled his men across the river, onto the eastern bank. Once across, their backs were to the river and for a while Harold was concerned that Hardraada would try the same tactic that had succeeded so brilliantly at Fulford Gate. To his relief Hardraada maintained his position at the top of the slope and simply waited for Harold to attack him. And all the while Hardraada's housecarls boomed out their deep rhythmical war chant, a haunting refrain of death and despair, designed to unnerve their opponents.

Harold threw everything at them; his archers peppered their shields with arrows then his cavalry charged up the gentle slope to be met by Hardraada's shield-wall, implacably standing its ground, their spear shafts set into the earth, pointing upwards, towards the riders' breasts. As the charge hit home the English cavalry found itself impaled upon a hedge of spears and battered by two handed axes that wreaked devastation upon horse and rider alike. To the awful din of men and horses dying the first charge broke, the cavalry streaming down the slope to gather itself for a further assault.

From his position in the English lines Ranulf watched the first futile attempt to sweep Hardraada from the ridge. He was grateful for the respite that the cavalry had given him for the fight with the Norwegian had sapped his energy and his confidence. Never before had he been bested in single combat and were it not for Cnut it would now be himself and not the Norwegian whose headless corpse lay rotting in the autumn sunshine to be picked over by the buzzards until the flies settled upon it. No one had said anything to him about his failure to overcome the Norwegian but Gyrth had given him an odd look as he apologised for the loss of the lance, and he wondered whether Gyrth had noticed his fear as he had gone forward to meet the Norwegian. He made a promise to himself that next time he would do better. If there was a next time...

But now the cavalry were thundering up the slope again, a second, desperate attempt to break Hardraada's shield-wall. Many of the horses were already blown, their eyes rolled back, the whites showing stark and bright in the sunshine, their riders feverishly whipping their flanks for the last ounce of speed. Even as he watched them breast the rise he knew they would never do it. They had not broken Hardraada the first time and Ranulf knew it was odds on they would not do so now. His thoughts were interrupted as Guthrum arrived at his side, his huge axe held easily in one giant fist.

"The King should support them with us. We'd show the buggers eh!" He slapped Ranulf on the back, apparently impervious to Ranulf's introspective discomfort.

"This is just a skirmish," he replied. "The King is testing them; their willingness to stand. You will see action soon enough old friend, I warrant you that."

As if he had read his mind Harold Godwineson rode across on his grey stallion.

"Feeling recovered?" he said. Ranulf nodded. "Good. Then clear those bastards off the ridge. Leo will support you with the fyrd. He needs some work."

Ranulf gazed up the slope. The cavalry had charged for a third time, but as he expected the shield-wall had held. The cavalry were now reduced to riding across the front of the wall in a half-hearted attempt to find a weak point. Their efforts were greeted with derision by the Norwegians whose jeering could clearly be heard even from this distance. Occasionally a defender would rush out from the wall of shields to impale a rider with his spear or cleave him in two with an axe before running back to the refuge of the shield-wall and with each success the Norwegians would give a great cheer. It was hopeless; their momentum spent the cavalry were riding around in circles achieving nothing. Eventually the order was given for them to retire. It was time for the infantry.

Turning to Guthrum Ranulf gave the order for the housecarls to advance and the word was spread excitedly along the line. In marked contrast to the Norwegians who were once again booming out their war chant the English housecarls advanced in near silence, their shields locked together, their spear points directed at the enemy awaiting them. Behind the shield wall, mounted on a magnificent white stallion, Leofwine was urging the fyrd forward, his sword flashing in the sun, waved aimlessly around his head. Ranulf saw that he had discarded his steel helmet and his blonde hair flowed freely over his shoulders. Guthrum had seen this also and remarked: "He should be careful. Some bastard might think we have women fighting for us." He paused to consider. "When it comes to Leo we probably have!" He laughed and the joke helped to cheer Ranulf as they approached the enemy shield-wall. But even Guthrum fell silent as the opposing armies came within fifty paces of each other. Fifty paces from death.

Sensing the tension in the English ranks and feeling it within himself Ranulf let rip a roar that started in the pit of his stomach and rose to emerge from his throat as a blood-curdling yell. It was a cry for Saxon England, a cry for his King, for Alice and her unborn child, a cry for himself. It was a cry echoed by thousands along the line. Hurling himself over the grassy slope he launched his housecarls at Hardraada's shield-wall and the battle of Stamford Bridge began.

Behind the Norwegian shield–wall, beneath Hardraada's Standard, Tostig Godwineson watched the battle unfold with concern and alarm. The charges of the English cavalry had been repulsed but he was under no illusion that those were just the preliminaries before the main assault on their position began. Now,

160

as he had feared, the English housecarls, the cream of his brothers' army, were advancing steadily up the slope towards them. He had no great confidence that Hardraada's men would stand. They had hurled their war chant, a dreadful wailing noise, at the English in an effort to disconcert them but Tostig knew that it would take more than that to stop the men that were marching determinedly up the slope. This was a very different prospect from Fulford Gate. For a start, they were fighting his brother, and for all Tostig's hatred of Harold he knew that his reputation as a tough and uncompromising Commander was not undeserved. Second, they were facing possibly the finest infantry in Europe, and third, the English were wearing their chain-mail whereas the Norwegians were not; theirs had been left with the fleet. And the Norwegians were tired, many having wounds from the fierce encounter at Fulford Gate just five days ago. No, he had no great confidence that they would stand, and if they didn't he was a dead man.

He looked over to his right, to where Hardraada stood beneath *Land Waster* just a few paces away. He was like an enraged bull, Tostig thought, as he swore and cursed, exhorting his men to stand and fight, to repulse the hated English down the slope. There was no question of retreat; no doubt either that Hardraada expected him to stand his ground and to die with the rest of them should it be necessary. And Tostig was sure that it would be. He shuddered involuntarily, and wondered not for the first time how he had come to be in this position. If only there were some way to extricate himself. But how? Hardraada was just a few yards away and the slightest hint of betrayal would surely bring swift retribution. Tostig could see out of the corner of his eye two of Hardraada's housecarls idly watching him and he guessed that they had already been given orders to slit his throat if he even so much as looked like running. No, he would have to await developments, be prepared to seize whatever opportunity came his way, if it did... His mind was still running along those lines when a blood-curdling yell erupted from the English housecarls and his thoughts became lost in the heat, the madness, of the battle.

There was no day, no night, no light, no dark; nothing but blood and death and pain and despair as the two armies met in the meadows above the Stamford Bridge to fight for a Kingdom. Axes rose and fell, swords thrust and clashed and finally shattered, spear points ran with blood as the English army strove with all their might to break the Norwegians, who clung to their sacred piece of English soil atop the gentle slope. For a bloody hour, then another, the armies slugged it out, brute force met with brute force as men from both sides killed, and died, for their King. But slowly, slowly, as dusk began to fall, the Norwegians, worn down beyond endurance began to give ground before the English housecarls. And then a great cry went up, audible even above the din of battle, and for a moment the battle changed; for Hardraada, enraged and desperate, had charged into the English shield-wall wielding in his two great fists a mighty axe that most ordinary men would struggle to lift. Shouting his battle cry he swung his great axe again and again, splitting shields' like matchwood, men's skulls like eggs, as he carved his way into the English lines and threatened to change the course of the battle.

Ranulf's sword arm was numb and his shield arm black with bruises, so many blows had he given and received for his King. He could not say, dare not think, how many men had fallen beneath his blade, crying and gasping their despair as huge wounds, mortal wounds, opened up in their chests as the point of his sword found its mark. His head swam from the noise of battle, the blows he had taken, the cut to his forehead that now ran with blood. Only the *nasal* had prevented the wound from being fatal. *When will it end!* His subconscious cried as he parried a blow aimed at his head before retaliating with a thrust of his own, opening up a wide cut in his opponents' throat which quickly filled with blood. The Norwegian clutched at the wound, an instinctive attempt to stem the flow of blood but it was in vain. The blood simply ran through his fingers, staining them, staining his jerkin and then his breeches scarlet as it continued to pump from his throat. He fell to the ground, already soaked with the blood of others and died where he fell. Ranulf hardly saw the man fall, felt nothing for his death; was sickened beyond reason by so much blood. He looked to the heavens and gulped in great mouthfuls of air, an attempt to clear his head. But it was impossible for all around him was the din, the chaos, the brutality of battle. *Why me?* He sobbed, *Why me?* But his only reply was the cry of men dying as the battle continued to rage…

The two housecarls assigned to watch Tostig had now been pressed into the Norwegian shield-wall so desperate were they to hold the English and for a few moments Tostig was alone, unwatched. Hardraada had gone completely crazy, careering into the English lines, all rational thought lost in the madness of the battle. So far he was carrying all before him but Tostig guessed it was only a matter of time before he was cut down like all the others. And once Hardraada fell that would signal the end. The Norwegian position was becoming desperate; they could barely hold the English who, fighting like madmen, had the advantage of their chain-mail. It could not last much longer, he thought. The shield-wall would break and then the English would pour through the gaps to butcher anyone alive. After what he had done at Fuford Gate he had no illusion as to the fate that awaited him. He looked about to see if anyone was

watching him but all attention was riveted upon the English
housecarls who were slowly but surely pushing the shield-wall
backwards, reducing its numbers steadily, man by man, minute by
minute. Heart pounding he took a few paces to his rear and then a
few more. If he could somehow gain some distance without being
noticed he might yet make good his escape.

But then, just as Tostig was about to slip away into the gathering
gloom Hardraada fell, an arrow catching him in the throat, spilling
his blood onto the ground. Hardraada yelled, a cry of agony and
despair, a cry for what might have been but now never would; the
cry of a dead man. He fell to the ground mortally wounded and even
as he fell the English rushed forward to hack at his defenceless body.
Seeing their great King fall some of his housecarls lost the will to
fight, throwing their weapons onto the ground in surrender. Others
looked instinctively for their ally, Tostig Godwineson, and spotting
him several yards to the rear of the shield-wall ran to surround him,
urging him to continue the fight in that strange, guttural tongue that
he had come to know so well.

He cursed his luck and hiding his fear urged them back into the
fray. He still hoped to escape but two men, massive and bearded,
part of Hardraada's personal bodyguard, took him by the arms and
led him to the Standard of their dead King. He guessed that they
intended to make a final stand beneath the fluttering banner but as
they drew their swords and stood either side of him the awful
realisation dawned that he was to die there with them.

But he did not wish to die. He wanted to live; he wanted to make
love to women, lots of them. He wanted to reach old age and die
contentedly in his bed, preferably in the arms of a beautiful young
girl, not cut to pieces on this bloody field.

He felt tears sting his eyes as the reality of his precarious hold on
life grabbed him by the throat. And then his bowels opened. He sank
to his knees, ignoring the housecarls who, seeing the abject figure

between them, spat on the ground in disgust. And he prayed. He prayed to a God he had long ago rejected; he prayed for salvation; he prayed for life. And as he prayed he became slowly aware that the sounds of battle were diminishing, the cries of the warriors ceasing, the field of battle falling silent. He rose to his feet hardly daring to believe, and saw to his astonishment, to his utter joy, a white flag carried aloft from the English lines; the white flag of truce.

"Godwineson!" a voice cried. "Tostig Godwineson!" Tostig recognised the voice of that of his brother, Gyrth.

"Hardraada is dead!" Gyrth called to him. "Swear allegiance to your brother the King and you shall live." He paused, "and the Earldom of Wessex shall be yours. What say you? I will have your answer!"

Wessex? Was Harold mad? He would gladly have settled for a patch of earth in Wales if his life were to be spared. *Yes! Oh, Yes!* He wanted to reply but with Hardraada's henchmen at each elbow ready to slit his throat how could he? How the hell could he? He walked forward a few yards so that he could see his brother, somehow explain his predicament. He was in view of Gyrth now, but the two Norwegians had followed him, not trusting him, were right behind him. As if to confirm his worst fears the man on the right hissed at him through bared teeth:

"Tell him we fight. Tell him stick Wessex up his arse! Tell him, you worm, or I slit your throat right now!"

He looked at Gyrth but Gyrth had not noticed, could not help, was completely unaware.

"Tell him!" The words were hissed again, and Tostig, a lump in his throat the size of an egg sadly complied, each word choking the life from him as he rejected his brother's terms in the scornful, mocking tones demanded.

Gyrth listened open mouthed, unable to believe what he was hearing. On the field of battle there was silence; nothing stirred, no one moved. It was as if the very Gods had been shaken by the audacity of his reply. Eventually, after what seemed a lifetime, Gyrth responded in the only way that he could, a voice thick with sorrow and regret:

"Then it will be a hard death for you my brother," he said. "A hard death indeed."

The white flag withdrew, and with it his brother, his last chance for life. And Tostig, broken in spirit and mind by the cruel twist of fate that would take his life collapsed to his knees and wept like a child.

As if to a prearranged signal the fighting began again, but the Norwegians had lost heart. No longer an even fight, it was now butchery. Those that had surrendered their weapons were cut down where they stood. The English housecarls gave no quarter; slaughtered like cattle anyone in their path. Those Norwegians that chose to fight took longer to die but they died just the same, crying to their God Wodin as they fell to the ground, their bodies hacked to pieces by the maddened, blood crazed Englishmen.

Beneath Hardraada's Standard Tostig watched through tear-misted eyes the ending of a dream, the unstoppable advance of the English as they cut their way through the remnants of the Norwegian resistance. A small band had gathered beneath *Land Waster,* the defiant emblem of their dead King. There was nothing left to fight for, save a glorious death, but this small band, resigned to their fate, stood toe to toe with the English and traded blows until one by one they fell, cut down by the sheer weight of numbers. And then, suddenly, like the bursting of a dam, the English were through them, were pouring through in their hundreds to slaughter the survivors. The battle was lost but instinctively the two Norwegian housecarls watching Tostig rushed forward to meet the enemy and as they did so, in less time than it takes for a heart to beat, Tostig bolted.

He ran for his life. Over the meadows he ran, through the fields of cattle and sheep, up hills and down into the valleys, away from the field of slaughter. He ran until his heart and lungs were bursting, until his legs would carry him no longer, until he was finally spent. Only then, panting and breathless did he look back. And saw that he was being pursued. Six men, young and strong, were relentlessly tracking him, their weapons carried easily in their hands as they ate up the ground, closing the gap between them.

Desperately he cast about for somewhere to hide. He had to lose them. He had to. About three quarters of a mile away he saw a forest of trees, a thicket. A slim chance, but he had no choice. Panting heavily he set off again, heading for the trees, but the pain in his chest was beyond description and he could not run. He looked back and saw that they were much closer now, much closer. Tears welled in his eyes, blinding him. He tripped over a tree root and went sprawling, face first, onto the ground. He got to his feet and tried again to run, but a wall of pain hit him in the chest. Then another, sharper pain, sent arrows of fire shooting through his leg. He looked down and saw that a spear point was protruding from his thigh. He fell once more, tried to scramble to his feet, but could not do so for the pain in his thigh. He raised himself to his knees, unable to stand, and saw that they were above him now, their faces hidden by the night sky. Strange, he thought, that he had not seen the sun go down. "Traitor!" A man thrust a fist at him. Pain lanced through his stomach for the fist was holding a knife. He doubled up in agony, curled into a ball, his blood staining the dew-damp grass.
"Murderer!" cried another, and he felt the searing fire of steel, another spear point, lancing through his shoulder, through tissue and muscle to lodge in his lungs. He shuddered with the pain, coughed blood, managed to whisper through bloodied lips:
"Mercy; please!"

And Cadoc showed him mercy; the same mercy that Tostig had shown at Fulford Gate. Whipping his knife from his belt he drew it quickly across Tostig's throat. He sighed a gentle sigh that could have been a sigh of regret and then he died, as he had lived, alone with his thoughts in an orgy of hatred and bitterness and blood.

CHAPTER THIRTY

NIGHTFALL

25TH SEPTEMBER 1066.

Like tiny stars the light from a thousand torches punctuated the night, casting their ephemeral glow over the field of slaughter as the task of clearing the corpses of the fallen began. Men searching for their comrades wandered amongst the dead like ghosts whilst monks from nearby St. Wilfrid's Minster could be heard whispering prayers over the fallen, their tonsured heads bent reverentially as they slowly and methodically checked for signs of life. There were pitifully few survivors amongst the Norwegian host. Hardraada's body was found near to where he fell, surrounded by the corpses of the English housecarls that he had hacked down, enemies finally embracing each other in death.

Tostig's corpse was discovered almost a mile away. Hastily covered in a woollen cloak, a makeshift shroud, his broken body was brought on a stretcher to Harold. A single tear fell onto his cheek as he pulled back the cloak to examine the face of his brother, his sworn enemy. What he had cost England was beyond counting and the full price was still not known.

Covering the face he directed that Tostig be buried beside the tomb of St. Cuthbert; a Christian burial for a man who had lived much of his life outside the teachings of the risen Christ. At least his soul would be spared, and Harold's conscience salved, for despite everything his brothers' death sat uneasily upon him. Why he had offered surrender, and Wessex, to Tostig at the height of the battle he still did not know; even more Tostig's refusal. Was Wessex not enough to satisfy even his unsated desire for power? He would never understand it; why Tostig had chosen death when he could have had his life and more besides. How his mother would weep for him; one more grieving mother amongst so many.

Harold's thoughts crowded in on him, one upon the other, and he looked around the field of battle, at the piles of corpses stretching from the gentle slope upon which Hardraada had made his stand, down to the ancient bridge straddling the river. It looked so peaceful now, in the moonlight, the thousands of fallen still and silent. But if he closed his eyes for a second, just for a moment, he could hear again the noise, the chaos of the battle, the clash of sword on sword, and sword through flesh, the screams, the cries of the dying, and the pathetic pleas of those about to die. Pray God that he should never see this days' slaughter again.

He suddenly felt old and tired. He sighed and rubbed his eyes. He needed sleep but he knew that he would not sleep for his mind was still racing. He heard a noise behind him and turned to see Gyrth approaching, his face drawn and pale in the moonlight, exhaustion etched in every line, but the madness now gone from his eyes. With him was a well-built young man that he did not recognise: blonde hair, blue eyes, Norwegian. His beard had not yet reached maturity and the soft hairs on his jaw and cheek were like down. His eyes sparkled in the flickering torchlight but Harold could see that they were rimmed with red.

"This is Olaf, Hardraada's son," Gyrth said. "He remained with the fleet. He begs permission to take his father for burial in Norway." Gyrth was almost pleading the boys' case, calm now after the ferocity of the afternoon. Perhaps even Gyrth had had enough of the slaughter. He looked at the forlorn young man, now an orphan. What great ambitions had he seen turn to ashes this day? It was idle to speculate.

"Your father died well," he said. "He was a brave man, even though my enemy. You have my consent."

Olaf nodded, turned to go. Then a thought occurred to him: "What are your losses boy?" Olaf paused before answering. "Seven thousand, this day."

There was a hint of shame in his voice as though it were somehow his fault.

"And survivors?" Harold pressed him.

"About a thousand, Sire," he said, "including the wounded. Those that stayed with the fleet." *Only a thousand. God in heaven.*

"Take your father, and your men," he said. "Return to Norway on the next tide. None here shall prevent you." There was no point visiting the fathers' sins upon the son. One day, he thought, it might be possible to rebuild bridges with Norway. He watched the young man walk away. He managed twenty paces before his broad shoulders heaved and tears, denied for so long, welled in his eyes, a son grieving for his father.

And on the field of battle the monks continued with their grisly task of clearing and burying the unclaimed English dead whilst the bodies of the Norwegians lay untended to rot; carrion for the birds of the air and beasts of the field until, bleached by the sun and blasted by the cold northern wind, their bones would finally turn to dust.

CHAPTER THIRTY-ONE

YORK.

26TH SEPTEMBER 1066.

Ranulf's head ached abysmally and it was not just as a result of the fearsome blow that he had taken during the height of the battle. Following their crushing victory over Hardraada, Harold's army – those that could still walk or limp – had returned to York to celebrate with a great feast. And there, in the Great Council Chamber normally reserved for matters of State he and the rest of his comrades had settled down to carouse away the night, jubilant in their victory which would surely now seal Harold's position as King of England. Moreover upon their return to York they had discovered to their absolute delight that contrary to what had been earlier believed, both Earls Morcar and Edwin were alive, and if not in the best of spirits after their shattering defeat were at least in one piece.

Harold had greeted them both as long lost brothers, hugging them to him and demanding that they sit on his right and left respectively whilst they recounted to him the tragic unfolding of events at Fulford Gate. Gyrth and Leofwine seemed to mind not at all and Leofwine had passed the night engaged in the gentle art of seduction, practising his nefarious charms on several of the young serving girls swarming around him whilst he told them of his heroic part in the battle.

One of the serving girls had looked remarkably like Alice with the same raven hair and lithe body. Thinking of her, and thankful that he had survived the most bloody battle in anyone's memory with just a cut to the forehead Ranulf settled down to carouse away the night, downing jug after jug of bitter English ale until he collapsed onto the floor rushes in an alcoholic stupor, impervious to everything around him.

But now it was dawn and the events of the previous day and night came flooding back in a painful reminder of the abuse that his body had taken. Stirring himself from the floor, which stank of ale and urine and God knew what else, his head pounded and his muscles rebelled as he slowly raised himself to his feet. And he almost wished that he hadn't as a wave of nausea swept over him. He took huge lungfuls of the foetid air in the Council Hall and looked around as he tried to clear his head. Men were sprawled everywhere; on the floor, on the long tables that ran the length of the hall, and upon each other. No one else was moving save for him, and seeing his comrades like this Ranulf was suddenly reminded of the gruesome scenes in the gentle meadows above Stamford Bridge and the terrible battle that had been fought less than a day ago. Only there was a difference. These men were not dead. At least he did not think so.

He took another breath of air and stumbled outside, his head beating like a hammer. The cold morning air hit him and he suddenly felt terribly ill. He retched and a stream of vomit erupted from his mouth as his stomach voided its contents. He decided to sit for a while to clear his head and after five minutes began to feel a little better. The sun was beginning to climb in the sky, the day brightening all the while. And with the sun his mood brightened. He decided to look for Guthrum. The Kingdom might have been saved but there was still work to be done. A head count was required to ascertain the number of their dead and wounded and that meant getting everyone to their feet.

Most of the fighting at Stamford Bridge had been borne by Harold's housecarls and their losses, although slight compared to that of Hardraada's Norwegians, was still high. He needed to know how high. Their numbers would have to be brought up to force as soon as men could be trained. Gyrth's words, *from dawn until dusk,* leaped immediately to mind. More work to be done, and, no doubt, he would have to do it; he and Guthrum. The main threat was now over, but there was always William the Bastard, probably next year, if he still wanted to chance his arm. And then there were the Welsh to keep an eye on; they could be troublesome bastards when they wanted, and of course Malcolm of Scotland had harboured Tostig for most of the summer whilst he had plotted his treacherous intrigues.

But for now the country was at peace, and he longed to see Alice once more, to hold her in his arms, and to feel his child growing in her belly. Another three months, God willing, and he would have a fine son. How he would cherish that day. His mind relived yet again the horrors of yesterday. Christ what a battle it had been. He could not go through that slaughter again. No man could. Thank God it was over. Thank God.

Taking a deep breath he stepped back inside the foul smelling Hall and began to search for Guthrum. He was to find him lying in a heap of insensate bodies, snoring loudly and stinking to high heaven.

It was the start of another day. And he had a head count to perform.

CHAPTER THIRTY-TWO

PEVENSEY, ENGLAND.

28TH SEPTEMBER 1066.

The boy threw the stick and saw it land with a splash in the shallow water at the edge of the shingle beach.

"Go on boy!" he cried, and Patch, his little black and white mongrel went tearing after it as though his life depended upon it. Plunging into the shallow water the dog paddled madly until it reached the stick and then, taking it in its mouth began to paddle just as enthusiastically back towards the shore. They both loved this game and the boy was conscious that he had been here too long already. His mother had shouted to him just as he had disappeared through the doorway to their tiny croft; something about collecting the eggs for their breakfast. He had not yet done so and he debated throwing the stick just one more time before returning home by way of the hen house. Chores always got in the way of having fun, but still, if he were getting hungry so too would his mother be, and his two little brothers.

The dog scampered up the shingle beach, his little legs slipping and sliding comically as he hurried to return to the boy, the stick held firmly between his jaws. His coat was soaking wet from the seawater, and as he obediently dropped the stick at the boys' feet his tail wagging with pleasure, he shook himself vigorously, spraying the boy with cold seawater.

"Hey, stop that!" The boy cried, but he didn't really mind, and bent to give him a hug. He decided to throw the stick one more time, just once more; but then, out of the corner of his eye he saw something far out to sea. At least he thought he did. He stared hard at the bank of fog that had not yet rolled away from the shore and strained his eyes to see through the mist. Yes! There it was again; something like a shadow, a deeper patch of grey within the grey mist itself. He stared at the shadow, unconscious that he was doing so, his little dog momentarily forgotten. And then, like a veil being lifted before his eyes, he saw it gliding silently out of the fog bank into clear, bright, daylight. A ship. A ship like nothing he had seen before; its huge dragon-head staring fixedly, angrily, ahead, its gaily coloured sail hardened like a shell before the wind. And on board he could see men; lots of men, their steel helmets and mail armour glinting dully in the grey light.

And horses; he could see horses too, skittery and nervous, their owners doing their best to quieten them in soft soothing tones. The boy stood transfixed before this sight, everything else forgotten, before he remembered where he was. He looked about for Patch and saw him investigating a starfish thrown onto the beach by the tide. He quickly picked him up and ran to the head of the beach where he hunkered down behind a sand dune, Patch held tightly under his arm. His heart was pounding with excitement as he watched the slow progress of the ship towards the shore. And then, through the mist he saw another, just as big if not bigger. He turned his attention to this new vessel, intending to study its progress towards the shore but even as he did so he realised that yet another had emerged from the fog bank, and then another, and another. And as the boy stared in amazement, struck dumb by the sight that assailed his eyes, the rest of the fleet hove into view. Ships; hundreds of ships, all packed tight with men and horses, and equipment and armour, and spears and shields and untold menace.

Breathlessly the boy continued to watch as the first ship reached the shore and the men on board began to disembark. They jumped eagerly over the side and into the shallows before encouraging the horses on board to leave their precarious berths and venture once

176

more onto *terra firma*. Whilst they were doing this, the boy had an opportunity to study the foreigners from his hidden vantage point. All of them were wearing heavy chain-mail suits and helmets with the familiar *nasal* that he had seen the King's housecarls wearing on their patrols along the south coast all summer long. Armed with huge double-edged swords and shields they were an awesome sight and the boy felt a twinge of fear as some of the foreigners scanned the beach for signs of life and at one point seemed to be looking directly towards him. After a while he decided that they could not have seen him and heart pounding rapidly resumed his survey of the beach.

More ships had now reached the shore – he could not count them all – and were being dragged up onto the shingle by a few men from each vessel whilst orders were being bellowed to them in a strange tongue he did not recognise. The panting seamen were obviously being exhorted to ensure that their vessels were well clear of the high water mark to avoid them being washed out to sea on the next tide.

The boy realised that these foreigners intended to stay. It did not look, did not feel, like simply a raiding party. This was on a much bigger scale and the boy realised that he was witnessing the invasion that had been expected all summer long. The King's army, he guessed, should have been here to greet them, to sweep them back into the sea but the days had turned into weeks, and the weeks into months, and the English had finally gone home. So there was no one here now, only him.

He looked along the sea shore, far, far, to his left, and as far as his young eye could see there was nothing but ships; ships and soldiers, hundreds of them, thousands of them, making their way slowly towards an assembly point. His gaze rested on the group of figures patiently waiting there, some sitting, others looking out to sea, watching the remainder of the fleet slowly pulling in towards the shore. He noticed that for some reason this small group were dressed rather differently to the remainder of the men pouring ashore. They wore the same mail hauberks and helmets as the other soldiers but over their chain-mail these men appeared to be wearing some kind of surcoat; bright tunics of red and gold and scarlet and yellow, and bearing fantastic designs such as he had never seen before although he recognised the Holy Rood well enough. This emblem was emblazoned on the surcoats of many of the men in this small group whom he guessed were the leaders of the invading army.

He had just decided to slip away, to warn his village of these titanic events when his eye settled on a man disembarking from one of the biggest ships in the fleet. He was a large man, a commanding figure, broad and tall and carried himself easily as he waded through the surf towards the shore. He was magnificently attired in scarlet and gold over his chain – mail and the boy could just make out the design of two golden lions emblazoned on his chest.

The other men in the small group rose to greet him but as he walked towards them he tripped, perhaps on a pebble but the boy could not be sure, and he fell forward onto his face. Instinctively the other men in the group ran forward, anxious to help him up, but the man dressed in scarlet and gold laughed, and waved away their concern. And then he did a strange thing: he held out his hand to them, spoke some words that the boy did not understand, and slowly opened his fingers. Sand trickled between them onto the beach. And then he raised his eyes to the heavens and dropped to his knees in an attitude of prayer. The others immediately copied him. For perhaps thirty seconds the man remained on his knees and then he rose, and marched determinedly up the beach followed by his entourage.

"William the Bastard!" the boy gasped in his excitement, remembering the name that been repeated by the English housecarls all summer long. He had intuitively picked out from the thousands of men on the beach the one man responsible for them being there.

"William the Bastard," he said again, as though he could not believe his eyes. Finally he tore his eyes away and stared once more at the shoreline. All he could see now was a forest of masts and soldiers and horses. More soldiers and horses than he could ever have imagined. And they were heading his way. He realised that it was time to go. Hastily he scrambled to his feet clutching Patch under his arm. Hoping that his little dog would not bark a protest and thus alert the foreigners he slipped quietly away towards his village, his mothers eggs, his breakfast, quite forgotten.

CHAPTER THIRTY-THREE

YORK

30TH SEPTEMBER 1066

He awoke with a jolt and was surprised to see that it was still dark. He rubbed his face with his hands and realised with a shock that it was covered with sweat. And it was not just his face. His upper torso, his legs, his arms; all were cold and damp. His cot beneath him was the same, as was the thin blanket in which he had been cocooned during sleep and which still clung to his body. He lay for a while, remembering and then rising, groped his way in the darkened room to the chamberpot at the foot of the cot. He urinated loudly into it and felt a little better. He would not sleep now.

Slipping on his breeches he walked barefoot on the cold stone slabs to the window and looked out. Dawn had not yet broken and the stars still twinkled brightly in the cold night sky. He guessed that it was four of the hour but he could not be sure. Outside, two housecarls stood motionless at the door to his chamber speaking in hushed tones to keep themselves awake during the night watch.

He gazed up to the sky and searched the heavens. It was gone now, the long tailed star. Gone, he knew not where, but its malign influence had been felt just the same. *The fall of a nation; the death of a King.* Hardraada had been the object of its prophetical doom; Hardraada, the King of Norway. Not him. Not Harold Godwineson. They had been wrong.

He turned away from the window and sat on his cot. The dampness reminded him of the reason for his waking. He had dreamed the dream again. He had not had the dream for months; he had almost forgotten about it, *almost;* but he had had it again last night and he felt wrung out; exhausted. He turned it over in his mind, tried to rationalize it, but found that he could not do so. He was the King, secure now that Hardraada was dead. *And your brother!* his subconscious whispered to him and he felt a stab of guilt. *I gave him a chance. He did not take it. Am I to be blamed for that?*

He rose from the cot and walked about the room, not noticing the chill on his bare feet. If only Edith were here. She would have an explanation. She always did. Practical, level-headed, beautiful, Edith. He found that he suddenly missed her and his mind wandered back to those days they had spent at Bosham before his return to London. He had felt like a child again then; the fact that he was King meant nothing when he lay in bed with her, naked and vulnerable, their bodies pressed against each other as though they might leave their imprints as a permanent reminder of the time they had spent together.

It was quite remarkable how she had managed to persuade him to forget his troubles when they were alone together. He would come home, weary and careworn from a day of intolerable strain, of watching and waiting for William and she would minister to him with those long, slender hands of hers and soothe away his cares. He must see her soon. And the children. He must. He had been in the north too long already; but there was so much to do, to put right after the damage caused by Hardraada and Tostig. Another week should do it; restore Morcar to the Earldom with a show of public support and castigate the bastards that had tried to betray him. They were keeping low at the moment, but he would seek them out. He knew who they were and he would find them, and punish them. He was not a vengeful man, but he was the King. And the King must be obeyed. A few more days should do it, he reflected. And then back to London. And Edith.

A smile crossed his lips as he concluded that life would be easier now. The hard work and uncertainty of the first few months were behind him. He had faced the crises of his reign and had come through unscathed. A miracle perhaps, but he had done it. Yes, he thought, life should be easier now. Then a thought struck him; a thought as chill as the night itself. If that was so, why was he awake at this ungodly hour, pacing the room, his sleep disturbed by a recurring dream? Why?
He found that he had no answer.

CHAPTER THIRTY-FOUR

YORK.

1ST OCTOBER 1066.

After hours of searching for him Ranulf finally located Cnut slumped in the dirtiest corner of the filthiest alehouse in York. The floor rushes could not have been changed in months and the whole place stank of neglect and decay. Ranulf reckoned that the shuttered windows had not been opened to allow daylight and fresh air into the place for years.

The landlord, whose appearance reflected the condition of the establishment that he ran gave Ranulf an inquisitorial stare as he made his way across the dimly lit room to where Cnut sat in isolation at a rough hewn table. The landlord did not attempt to sell Ranulf a drink and Ranulf didn't ask. He had other business here today. He looked around and confirmed his first impression, which was that save for Cnut and the indolent landlord the alehouse was empty. Cnut looked up as he approached and Ranulf saw that his eyes were red and glazed. His breath stank of stale beer and his doublet was stained a deep dark brown from the liquid unintentionally spilled down his front. For how long he had been drinking Ranulf could only guess.

"They said I would find you here," he said. Cnut made no reply. Only the slightest shrug of his shoulders showed that he had heard.

"The head count. You were missing, but Aelfric said you were alive. Said I might find you here."

"Well you found me." Cnut took another swig of beer from the flagon in front of him.

"Yes, and look at you. What's going on?" the question hung in the air between them. Cnut simply closed his eyes and leaned back against the wall. He could have been asleep.

"Still here?" he said after a minute, opening his eyes and giving Ranulf a baleful glare.

"Still here," Ranulf said. "And still waiting for an answer." Cnut looked at him in silence, gave him a world-weary smile.

"What do you want, Ranulf?" he said. "Why not leave me alone? Find another protégé to train." The word "protégé" came out slurred and indistinct; testimony to the amount of alcohol he had consumed. He picked up the flagon, took another pull and crashed it down.

"I can't leave you alone boy," Ranulf glared at him. "You are a housecarl remember; you swore an oath. You belong to the King. And that means you belong to me." He picked up the flagon and poured the contents onto the floor. "The first thing you are going to do is to stop drinking, and the second is to come back with me."

Cnut slumped against the wall, an attitude of defeat characterising his every movement.

"Damn you then," he finally muttered through pursed lips.

Ranulf studied the wreck of a boy slumped carelessly before him. Something had happened to bring about this change but he did not know what. Perhaps it had been the fight with Eiric, or perhaps it had been the butchery at Stamford Bridge. Whatever it was he needed to know. He studied Cnut's face. He had always been small and pale, but now he looked bone weary, as though some cancer were eating him from within. What was it? What had caused this? He decided upon a different approach.

"What are you hiding boy? What devils are tormenting your soul? I am still your friend. It will go no further, I promise."

Cnut eyed Ranulf in silence, and just when he seemed to make up his mind he would suddenly hesitate and fall into silence once more. Finally to Ranulf's relief he spoke at last:

"No further, you promise?"

"I promise."

Cnut turned his face away, studied the wall.

"Ceilwyc is dead," he said.

"She was old; her time was near."

"No. You do not understand. I killed her."

And slowly, with tears welling in his eyes Cnut at last spoke the awful truth. That he had murdered her; stabbed her with his knife and left her bleeding to death whilst he had fled with the powder that had saved his life and taken his soul. But now it was all gone; and the void it had left behind was unbearable for it was filled with a guilt so great he could not endure it. He simply could not.

When he had finished telling his tale he cried like a child, his body heaving with great racking sobs whilst Ranulf could only sit in silence and stare at him, this golden youth who had had so much and lost it all.

Guthrum stopped running and cursed under his breath. He was lost. He looked up and down the muddy lane and could see no sign of the place he was looking for. Ahead of him the lane petered out into a few small wood and thatched huts, and beyond that there were open fields.

"Damn!" he cursed under his breath and turned to retrace his steps, to run back the way he had come. There was not a moment to lose and beads of sweat pricked his forehead as he forced his tired body to respond to the exigencies of the situation.

He had never seen the King so enraged. Even at the height of the bloody encounter at Stamford Bridge the King had somehow maintained his composure whilst all about him were losing their sanity but this, this shocking news, had completely thrown him.

Find Ranulf! the King had demanded, the veins in his temple standing out like cord as he had flown into a tirade, cursing and swearing and sending messengers here there and everywhere. They had hastened to do his bidding, fearful of the terrible consequences of delay and Guthrum was no exception.

Sweat was running freely down his face now, mingling with the grease and other detritus in his thick beard. He hardly noticed. At last he found the turning he was looking for and quickened his pace even further. His sword slapped against his thigh, annoying the cut that he had taken on it just a few days ago. He had placed a rough bandage around the wound after the battle, to stem the flow of blood and after he had collapsed into drunken oblivion during the victory celebrations he had thought no more about it. But now, with every *slap, slap, slap,* against his thigh he could feel the wound opening up again; the warm, wet sensation of fresh blood seeping through the sodden bandage. He winced from the pain but did not slacken his pace. He had been ordered to find Ranulf and he bloody well would.

At last, gasping for breath he found the sign on the door that he was looking for. Without hesitation he pushed through it into the stench and the darkness beyond and cast about. There, in the corner, was the man he was looking, for seated in studied silence with Cnut. "Ranulf!" he said. "Ranulf - Thank God!"

Ranulf listened with a sinking heart whilst Guthrum recounted the dreadful news brought to the King by way of his relay system. Even Cnut appeared to awaken from his reverie as Guthrum told the tale of how two days ago, at dawn, William the Bastard had landed on the south coast with a vast army. Heavily armoured infantry, archers by the score, and vast amounts of cavalry had all been seen. The long awaited invasion had finally arrived. And Harold? Harold had been dragged away two hundred miles to the north to meet the threat from his brother Tostig.

William had been able to land unopposed, had been able to start reconnoitering the countryside, was building a fort, a secure base, all without the slightest threat from the King and his army. Because they were here, in York, licking their wounds and getting drunk.

After the bloodbath at Stamford Bridge Ranulf had thought that they could never go through such hell, such carnage again. Now, he realised, that they must. But with what? Three thousand housecarls had been in the shield – wall at Stamford Bridge, had given their all, in many cases their lives. Now there were barely eight hundred left and many of those, himself and Guthrum included, were wounded in one way or another. Is this what Harold would put up against William the Bastard? Of course there were his brothers' housecarls, their personal bodyguard, but many of those had perished along with the others at Stamford Bridge. The Wessex militia would support the King; as would the fyrd; but these were not professional soldiers; had neither the training nor the steel to stand as the housecarls would when the enemy was bearing down on them. No, whichever way he looked at it the King was in dire peril of losing his Crown. He had done everything possible and more to counter the threats that had come one after the other to plague the first year of his reign. He had planned and fought hard, so very hard, but for all that here he was, with his tired and broken army two hundred miles north of the capital with the enemy knocking at the door.

It was more than anyone could take. Ranulf sighed a bone weary sigh. He was tired and dispirited. He too, had gone through so much, and lived, but now he must do it all again.

"Let's go," he said to Cnut as he rose from the table to see what the King wanted, as if he could not guess. Cnut looked up.

"You still want me?" he asked.

"You're a housecarl, remember," Ranulf replied. "That's why I came for you."

"Where are we going?"

"Back to the regiment – what's left of it. Your life is the King's now," he said. "Yours, mine, Guthrum's, all of us. Do your duty boy. There's nothing left for you…. perhaps for any of us."

The three men left the tavern, their mood sombre, resigned. Quite unexpectedly a tear pricked Ranulf's eye as he made his way back to the regiment. A tear for Alice, a tear for the son he may never know. He did not wipe his eye or turn to face his comrades for he did not wish them to see.

CHAPTER THIRTY-FIVE

THE BLUE BOAR TAVERN,
SOUTHWARK, LONDON.

3RD OCTOBER 1066.

Outside in the street there was panic. Citizens who had lived all their lives in the cramped, filthy lodgings offered by the Southwark stews were moving out. News of the Norman invasion had spread like wildfire through the City and its inhabitants, terrified lest the foreign invader should appear on their doorstep had hurriedly collected up their few belongings to head north, to safety. The streets were thronged with people; anxious, frightened people; all of them hurrying in the same direction. All of them heading for the Westminster Bridge that would put a large stretch of water between themselves and the foreign army that were rumoured to be at the City gates this very moment.

Alice closed the shutter to her window and moved towards her bed that was pushed against the far wall. She believed none of the rumours that were spreading throughout the City and refused to be a part of the hysteria affecting everyone else. For two days now the cry had been the same: the enemy were at the Gates. If that were so, where were they? She lay down upon the damp, straw filled mattress and stared at the white washed ceiling, lost deep in thought. A spider was industriously spinning a web in the angle formed by the rafters and Alice watched its frenetic activity with a detached interest, her thoughts two hundred miles north of London, concerned with the welfare of one man, the man who had become the centre of her universe.

She sighed a deep sigh and restlessly pushed against the bed to sit up again. As she did so she felt the sharp pang of the child growing in her womb kick out as if in protest. It was a boy. She was sure it was. Only a man would protest so much.

"Hush my love," she said softly and gently stroked her swelling belly. "Your father will be home soon."

She rose from the bed and sat on its edge looking toward the shuttered window, a crack of light illuminating the gloom. Beyond the shutters, in the street below, she could hear the cries of the frightened inhabitants as they pushed and jostled their way northwards; a great migration of humanity anxious to be gone before the invaders arrived. She would not be going with them. That decision had already been made: had been made two weeks earlier when Ranulf had said his goodbyes that doom laden night before departing north with the army.

He had promised to return. He had kissed her and then the child in her belly and had said he would return. She could remember his words as though it were yesterday; could see again the look in his eyes, recall the timbre of his voice, his hands on her, gentle but insistent. She loved him so much, and she knew that he loved her. If he lived he would return to her. And so she would stay. The whole City could head north for all she cared; she would stay until Ranulf returned, or she learned of his death.

But he was not dead. Call it a woman's intuition; call it sixth sense, she just knew.

What Alice did not know, had no way of knowing, was that the King and his army had already embarked upon the long haul south. The King had gathered up his housecarls, what was left of them, and the rest of his men, and had set off for the Capital at dawn the day before. Prior to leaving York he had given orders to Morcar and

Edwin to gather the remains of their own hearth troop and to follow south at all speed. Even as Alice sat listening to the panic on the streets of London Harold was hastening southwards, urging his bone weary soldiers to march ever faster, ever further.

"One more mile my lads!" he would cry, before stretching it to two, then five, then ten, before he would call a halt; a brief respite before resuming the march again. They never complained, those men that had already given so much, suffered so much, but placed one blistered foot in front of another; one more step towards home and an uncertain date with their destiny.

Alice could not know of any of this, but still had faith that Ranulf would return. And so she sat in her room, waiting for him, while outside, on the streets below, the exodus continued, the streets slowly emptied.

CHAPTER THIRTY-SIX.

THE NORTH OF ENGLAND.

4TH OCTOBER 1066.

It would only be later that Ranulf would recall with any clarity the horrors of the march south to London. By then a far greater, a cataclysmic, horror would have occurred that would overshadow everything else in his life and haunt him for years to come. But that event had yet to occur; was still in the future. Even so the march south to the Capital was hard. More than hard, it was torture. The dark clouds that had hung menacingly over the hilltops the previous day finally disgorged their contents on the third morning of the march drenching the weary warriors of the regiment with cold, hard rain that froze their bodies and numbed their minds.

A strong wind added to the misery, driving the rain into the men's faces, blinding them, taking their breath away so that it became difficult to march, impossible to speak. Each step became a minor triumph as the housecarls, encumbered with sodden woollen cloaks, weapons, and leather jerkins that weighed them down and froze to their bodies struggled to get home.

Feet and toes froze on aching legs as the woollen socks worn under their leather boots turned to limp, damp rags by the rain. The northern roads, not repaired since the Romans departed the shores of England six hundred years earlier turned to mud under their feet and progress became impossible.

Ranulf, exhausted and frozen through to his skin did his best to encourage and cajole his comrades to keep going. For hour upon hour he marched up and down the muddied column to offer whatever he could to the weary and disconsolate warriors under his command. He could have ridden, like the King and his brothers, but Ranulf wanted to set an example. He still remembered the fight on the bridge and how he had failed for the first time in his life, and his decision to march with the troops was also an act of penitence.

But he could only do so much and eventually, at noon on the third day, he too succumbed to the torrential rain that sapped the body and froze the mind.

Unable to march any longer, the Kings housecarls were simply falling from the column to collapse in a heap at the roadside until helped to their feet by their equally desperate colleagues or left where they were to die in the freezing rain, beyond earthly help.

It had become hopeless and during the afternoon, with a heavy reluctance the King called a halt.

The army took refuge from the elements in a pine forest, the needles of which, though damp, provided a bed of sorts upon which the men gratefully collapsed in a state of exhaustion. Above their heads the canopy of the forest provided some shelter from the downpour. In the distance the sound of thunder rolled slowly across the sky. A smell of pine assaulted Ranulf's senses as he wearily flopped down against the trunk of a tree and rested his head against it. The bark was rough and damp but felt like the softest down and he was instantly transported to the bed in that tiny room in the Blue Boar inn where Alice was waiting for him. Despite the cold and the wet and the pain in his head from the cut taken at Stamford bridge which had started to throb again, he began to lose consciousness as the desperate need for sleep overwhelmed him.

"Where the hell are we?" His sleep was disturbed as Guthrum flopped down beside him. Ranulf saw the cut which had opened up in Guthrum's thigh during that desperate search for him and which had now, as a result of the rain, stained his leggings bright pink. Guthrum grimaced as he tightened the torniquet he had placed around it – a damp blood stained rag – in an attempt to stem the flow.

"Not sure," Ranulf replied. He almost said that he didn't care either, but of course that was not true. He cared very much.

"Damn leg!" Guthrum cursed out loud as he finished tightening the bandage and stood gingerly to test it.

"How much further do you reckon?" he asked.

"Not sure about that either," Ranulf replied. In truth he was in no mood to talk; not even to Guthrum. He recognised that that was unfair but he needed to rest; some sleep if it were possible.

"Another two days," he said. "I think."

Guthrum grunted in response but Ranulf hardly heard for unseen hands were already pulling him down into a deep unconsciousness: a world that was warm and dry and filled with love and laughter and the sound of a baby crying for its father.

After two hours that passed in a moment the King ordered the march to resume. The weary housecarls struggled to their feet and slowly, reluctantly, formed themselves into a column. For many of them even that was an effort. At least it had stopped raining, and the air was eerily still and quiet after the thunderous downpour of earlier. The men formed up on the road leading south. Harold gave the order and the bedraggled men at the head of the column forced tired and aching bodies to obey. The rest of the column followed. Harold drove them south. A man possessed, he rode up and down the column for the rest of the day, issuing orders, shouting encouragement, showing concern and compassion for the wounded and joking with them whenever he could.

To the men in the column he never seemed to tire although he must have been tired. He never seemed to despair although his precarious hold on his Crown must have driven him to it. Instead the men saw a look in his eye that had never been there before, not even during the madness of the battle at Stamford Bridge.

Ranulf tried to place that look, to identify it as the King rode past him, his clothes drenched and spattered with mud, his hair plastered to his head, but he could not do so. Exhaustion fogged his mind and he could not think. All that mattered to him, to any of them, was to get home, to reach London before William the Bastard. That, or die in the attempt.

Ranulf did not die, but many times on that terrible march south he thought that he had. Later he would recall how for the last two days, as the rich fields of southern England finally came into sight, he had virtually carried Guthrum, in pain and protesting, as blood ran unchecked from the open wound to stain them both with its bright scarlet blossom.

For mile after mile they had staggered along together, Guthrum limping awkwardly on one foot, his arm wrapped around Ranulf who struggled to bear his weight. Eventually, when Ranulf could not support him any longer, when every muscle and sinew screamed out in agony Cnut had helped him with the burden. Cnut the murderer, Cnut the golden boy, golden no longer, took the weight of Guthrum like Christ on the road to Calvary; atonement for his sins. He refused all offers of help until he too, cried out in his anguish, his slim, frail body protesting at the burden until he could bear it no longer.

And then Ranulf shared the load, taking Guthrum's other shoulder, their friendship reborn in the cauldron of the long march south.

And so the three of them covered the last day, the last forty miles together. Ranulf, Guthrum, and Cnut, arm in arm, struggling and gasping and cursing and praying until finally, blessedly, the spire of Westminster Abbey came into view.

They were home.

CHAPTER THIRTY-SEVEN.

THE HEIGHTS ABOVE HASTINGS TOWN.

7TH OCTOBER 1066.

Duke William watched with quiet satisfaction as the timber stockade that he had ordered to be built on the heights above Hastings town slowly took shape. His carpenters and labourers were busily, noisily, hammering away and the pallisade was slowly rising from the ground, a safe base from which he could launch his invasion. From the watchtower of the partially constructed fort he could see for miles, even on a cold, grey day, such as this. Below him, far below, was the harbour, sheltering his fleet; his dragon ships pulling at their anchors, their sails tightly furled to prevent unnecessary damage from the wind that now whipped about him as he stood motionless surveying the countryside.

Inland the green rolling hills stretched north as far as the eye could see and William studied the rich wooded countryside with a proprietorial air. All of this had been promised to him. And soon, God willing, it would be his.

He reluctantly turned his attention back to the fortress that was rising into the air, dominating the skyline. This was the second such fort that he had ordered to be built since landing on the shores of England, and the work was going well but he wanted it finished. Only when it was finished would he feel secure. Another, smaller fortress was being erected at Pevensey, further west, but he had decided for reasons of security and as part of his overall strategy to move his base camp to Hastings. There were sound reasons for doing so.

First, Hastings had a larger harbour, and a more prosperous and yielding, pliant, community than Pevensey. Those wealthy merchants that had not already fled to London had proved to be easy pickings for food and provisions. Second, and more importantly, Hastings could be easily defended. The town was located at the bottom corner of an inverted triangle about ten miles long and six miles wide. Duke William's quick tactical brain had immediately spotted the advantages of such a location; one road in and one road out; a prehistoric track that lead to London, his ultimate destination. From here he could bide his time, ravage the surrounding countryside in safety, and keep watch for the enemy. *Godwineson.*

When he had landed eight days ago he had no way of knowing who his opponent would be. But now news had reached him that Godwineson had won a great battle near York; had slain both Hardraada and his brother Tostig.

He had never liked Tostig. He had met him only briefly earlier in the year when he had come crawling to his Court demanding an Earldom. An Earldom! As if he would do that! Well, now he was dead, and God willing the rest of the Godwinesons' would soon be joining him in a private hell of their own.

Somehow he had always known that it would be Harold Godwineson that he would have to fight for the Throne. It was right that it should be so; it was appropriate and just. After all it had been Harold Godwineson who had sworn a Holy Oath, his hands outstretched, placed firmly on the Testaments, as he had promised the Throne of England to him. So it was his right, his *destiny*, to be King, and if destiny sometimes needed a helping hand so be it. He *would* be King…but he must be patient. He had a plan, and would shortly execute it. It carried a risk but he was used to taking risks. He had done so a hundred times, a *thousand* times before as he had climbed and intrigued and battled his way to the pinnacle of power in Normandy. He was sure it would work but he must be patient and control the faction that would have him march on London today.

He smiled to himself as he slowly worked his way down the companion ladder leaving the watchtower empty and silent save for the wind. Everything was going to plan. Now he must find a way to execute it.

As he reached the foot of the companion ladder he saw Fitz Osbern and his half brother, Bishop Odo hastening toward him. He walked forward to greet them. He had already guessed what news they brought, but to hear his suspicions confirmed by others was a pleasure he did not wish to deny himself. If he was right, and he was sure that he was, it would demonstrate what he already knew beyond any doubt: that in matters of warfare and strategy he had no equal. No equal at all.

CHAPTER THIRTY-EIGHT.

THE PALACE OF WESTMINSTER, LONDON.

8TH OCTOBER 1066.

The last rays of the late evening sun filtered through the windows of the Great Hall, casting long and silent shadows on the floor as Harold Godwineson tore open the sealed parchment, the latest message from William the Bastard. He quickly scanned the document, his cheeks colouring as he did so.

"Trial by Combat!" he hurled the document onto the flagstones where it lay, illuminated by the dying embers of the sun until it was picked up by his brother Gyrth. He also scanned the document before crumpling it in his fist, the great wax seal of the Norman Duke shattering into a thousand tiny shards as he did so.

"The bastard's toying with us, Hal," he said.

Since Harold's return to London, William the bastard had kept up a stream of desultory demands: that Harold renounce the Confessor's deathbed nomination in favour of himself; that Harold submit to litigation on the matter. Litigation! As though some blood-sucking lawyers could resolve the issue! And now this; single - handed combat between the two protagonists. The two earlier demands had been contemptuously rejected and this one would suffer the same fate.

Harold had not rested since returning to London. Exhausted both physically and mentally he had nevertheless not wasted a moment in organising the defence of the City against the expected assault. Such of his, and his brothers' housecarls who were still able to fight had been pressed into service and although the fyrd of London had been mustered prior to his return he had also issued summonses to the fyrd of Sussex and Kent to join him without delay. He needed all the men he could get.

Morcar and Edwin had not yet arrived from the north but that was not unexpected. Their armies had been virtually annihilated at Fulford Gate and now they were having to recruit new armies; something that would obviously take time. But not, he hoped, too much time.

The strain that he was under was plain for all to see. His face, now thin and gaunt from the tremendous exertions of the past few weeks would twitch every so often as he tried to control his increasingly fragile temperament. Outbursts of temper would flare up for the lightest reason; would arrive suddenly, unannounced, and just as suddenly disappear. It was evident too, in the way that he carried himself, as though the weight of the world were on his shoulders.

Gyrth was struck by the fact that Harold no longer seemed to *see* anyone when he looked at them. He looked at them, certainly, but he appeared to be looking *through* them as though searching for something beyond the face that he was addressing. He had first noticed it during that terrible march south. Somewhere, something had happened to his brother, but he knew not what. There was a haunted look about Harold's eyes which reminded Gyrth of something; something which sparked a recent memory but he could not place it. It would come. But now Harold was speaking again and his train of thought was lost.

"He burns my towns, ravages the land, and now this!" Harold was gesticulating wildly, flinging his arms about him, punctuating his words with sweeping gestures. His frustration was obvious. The latest insult had obviously upset Harold more than he had realised. It could, of course, have been worse. William could have been here, in London, already. And what price his brother's Throne then? But he kept such thoughts to himself. Things were bad enough without him adding to them.

"Is he mad?" Harold cried, continuing in the same vein, his voice echoing in the vastness of the Great Hall.

The sun had disappeared below the horizon now and the land was in darkness. Torches were being lit in their wall beckets. Acrid smoke drifted upwards, staining the roof timbers and assaulting the senses.

"Gyrth!" Harold cried again, "Is he mad? Why do this? Why play these games?"

He considered his brother's questions, but in truth he had no more idea than Harold why William the Bastard was delaying his march on the Capital; simply resorting to insults. It was clear that William was indeed playing some sort of game. But why? That was the question.

"He is baiting you Hal," he said decisively. "I think he hopes to persuade you to make a rash move, to draw you onto him before we are ready. Why else would he burn and devastate the south? He must be hoping that we will not stand back and let that continue..."

"Damn right we won't!" back came the retort, much as Gyrth had expected. He could not talk to his brother in this mood. But Harold was in full flow:

"We march on the Bastard as soon as possible. If he has not the guts to come to me, then I will go to him. And then we shall see who shall do the *baiting."* His eyes flashed in the torchlight, the anger clearly visible on his face.

...."We shall march as soon as we are rested. Morcar and Edwin can follow later."

Gyrth did not like the sound of this; not at all.

"But Hal," he said, reasonably, "surely this is what he wants? Why give him what he is hoping for? Time is now his enemy. While we grow stronger, he must grow weaker. Why give him this chance? Why?" He paused to emphasise the point, hoping his brother would see it. He must see it. Harold's reply destroyed such hope.

"We march when *I say,* brother. *When I say.* And I tell you this: I will not allow this Norman bastard, this *Duke William* to remain on English soil for one day, for one minute, longer than I need." He looked at Gyrth and his voice was thick with anger. "I will not, Gyrth," he said, quieter now, "God help me, but I will not."

Gyrth could see that further argument was hopeless. When Harold was like this one may as well argue with the moon.

"At least I can lead the army," he said. "No point risking your life. I can manage with Leo and Ranulf. Stay here until I send word." On this point at least he hoped persuasion would prevail but again his argument was to founder on the rock of Harold's will.

"No, brother," Harold said decisively. "I cannot allow that." Gyrth tried again.

"Why not Hal? It makes no sense to risk you!" His own voice was now raised; in frustration rather than anger, but again he was to be denied.

"I am the King. And whilst I am King the duty is mine." Harold jabbed his chest with his finger, underlining his point. "The army expects me to lead them. What would they think if I were not there? That I were afraid? That I had no confidence in the outcome? No, brother," he said finally, "I must be there when we face William on the field of battle. You know that don't you?"

And in truth he did. For what was an army without its King? As ever Harold had had his way. It had always been so. Perhaps that was why Harold was King and he was just his brother.

"Very well, Hal," he conceded. "Whatever you say." He had tried. Lord knows he had tried.

"Be careful, though," he said finally. "I have the feeling that William is no Hardraada."

"Don't worry, brother," Harold said. "I will. In any event," he added, "you will be there to look after me." He gave Gyrth a smile with his dark, haunted, eyes. And as he did so Gyrth suddenly remembered where he had seen that look before: on the face of his brother, Tostig, as he had proudly rejected their peace terms at Stamford Bridge. Although the words were proudly spoken, the same fear, the same uncertainty, was mirrored in the eyes staring back at him. But it was not Tostig's face that was here, before him, but his eldest brother, the King. As the realisation hit him a shiver went down his spine and just for a moment he had to look away.

CHAPTER THIRTY-NINE

THE BLUE BOAR TAVERN, SOUTHWARK

9TH OCTOBER 1066.

Three days. Three days it had been since the King had returned to the capital with the shattered remnants of his army. They had been greeted with tumultuous applause by the relieved citizens of London who could still not believe that their King had made the long journey back before William of Normandy had arrived. The public lined the streets and shouted themselves hoarse.

But Alice did not share their joy. She might have done had she been there to watch Ranulf and his comrades hobble the last final mile to Westminster Palace, but heavy with child, and confident that he would soon be with her, she had waited patiently in her tiny room for him to appear.

But now it had been three days since the King's return – three days that had dragged like three months – and there was still no sign of him. At first she had not been unduly concerned. She made excuses for him, telling herself that he had important duties to perform; urgent tasks to undertake for the King. After all he had responsibilities other than to her. She told herself that she was just being silly. But still Ranulf had not appeared and the doubts were beginning to creep in.

For the first time she questioned whether or not he was still alive. She had been so certain that he was that she had not even attempted to struggle the few miles necessary to watch the King's approach to the City. How she wished that she had. Then everything would be clear. But she had stayed in her lodgings, foolishly expecting him to come running to her immediately he was free of his duties, and now she was paying the price.

Then the thought occurred to her that he might be wounded and unable to reach her. She agonised with herself, imagining Ranulf lying wounded and neglected on some stinking hospital cot, his mind and life blood slipping away as he struggled to leave a message, some last despairing words for her She tried to close her mind to such thoughts but could not do so. She told herself that if Ranulf were wounded one of his comrades, Guthrum, or Cnut perhaps, would get a message to her, but she was not sure whether they knew where to find her or, indeed whether they knew about her at all. Wives and mistresses were not common amongst the housecarl regiments: life was often short and brutal and there was no way of knowing whether Ranulf had opened his soul and told them about her. In any event, both Guthrum and Cnut could be dead.

She paced the room, round and round, restlessly searching for an answer, for some explanation for his absence, torturing herself with scenarios that usually involved his death or fearful maiming.

Occasionally footsteps would be heard in the street below and then she would run to the tiny window hoping against hope that it would be him, only to have her hopes dashed as some stranger would walk by, or occasionally leer up at her with the offer of his company for the night. Then she would throw herself onto the bed in tears and cry herself to sleep clutching at the child, *his child,* growing inside her belly. And when she awoke the nightmare would begin again.

He does not love you. The thought cut across her misery like a knife. *He cannot care otherwise he would be here.* Voices were speaking to her now. Her voice, but somehow not hers. Who's then?

She rose from the bed and felt the child kick again. A strong kick, it made her wince with the pain.

"Be quiet!" she snapped irritably. She started once more to pace the room, round and round, torturing herself with his absence until she thought she would go crazy. And then she stopped. And reached a decision.

Pulling on her winter cloak, a heavy woollen mantle given to her by the object of her misery she opened the door to her room and carefully made her way down the narrow stairs. She hesitated only briefly before stepping out into the street. The wind was bitingly cold but she did not care. Wrapping the mantle tightly around her she started walking towards the river.

If he would not come to her, she would go to him.

As Alice headed north for the river, three riders spurred tired horses south. For two days they had searched the rolling hills south of London for some sign of William the Bastard's army, but all they had encountered was frightened villagers heading north, their meagre belongings loaded onto carts or simply carried upon their backs. Not one of them had seen the Norman army but rumours of rape and pillage and burning of villages were rife and they were not prepared to be next. They sought safety in London. And so the three men continued to ride south, through the open country of the North Downs then deep into the Andredsweald, the great dark forest that lay north of Hastings. They followed barely trodden tracks and boggy streams until they emerged, tired and tense into the cold sunlight on the far side.

It was a bright day, but the wind whipped through Ranulf's beard as he squinted into the low sun for some sign that would betray the enemy presence. Instinctively his right hand went to the hilt of his sword and closed tightly around it as he scanned the horizon for activity. His mare was nervous and he gave her a gentle pat as she fretted at the bit.

"Easy girl," he said. Like his comrades beside him he was tired and anxious to return to London. He had not wanted this mission in the first place but the King had insisted. He had tried to persuade Harold to choose another housecarl, someone who did not have a loved one anxiously waiting for word of him, but the King was in no mood for argument. He had to do as the King wanted. And the King wanted him to scout south for some sign of the Norman army. He had no choice; he was bound by his oath. He cursed his luck and wondered not for the first time how Alice was faring, what she must be thinking, alone in her room whilst he was here, deep in enemy country when he should be with her. He cursed his luck again and turned to his companions. Cnut, their friendship reborn, and Leofwine, the King's brother accompanied him; Cnut because Ranulf had suggested it and Leofwine because the King had ordered him to come. All three sat uneasily on their mounts, their eyes screwed against the low sun, looking for some sign of the enemy.

Directly ahead of them lay the town of Hastings, where, they knew, William had set up his Command headquarters. Further west lay Pevensey and the marshy countryside where William had first landed. All was quiet; nothing stirred save for the rustle of leaves in the cold autumn breeze and the nervous snickering of their horses that had somehow caught the tension of the moment from their riders.

Cautiously they edged their mounts forward, their senses alert for the slightest sound, or glint of steel in the sunlight that would betray the presence of the enemy. They rode down into a dip in the rolling hills, following a barely discernible track and for a fleeting moment Ranulf was aware that his line of sight was lost. It was an ideal place for an ambush if anyone had seen their approach. His heartbeat quickened as he realised his mistake and urgently spurred his mare to the top of the rise and to safety. He was quickly joined by

Leofwine and Cnut, who, realising the danger, hastened to follow him out of the gully. Leofwine gave an audible sigh of relief as he crested the rise to find the horizon empty and Cnut, for the first time in months actually grinned to see the proud Earl's discomfort. Leofwine was more than happy to give Ranulf the lead on this enterprise and so he gave the order to move forward with a nod of his head. He silently rebuked himself for his mistake and vowed not to make another; the next one could be his last. Nervously the three men gently spurred their horses forward, acutely aware that with every step they were closing with the enemy.

And then Ranulf saw what they had been searching for. Over to the east a thick pall of black smoke suddenly arose from behind a copse of trees, staining the steel blue sky a dirty grey before being whipped away by the wind. The faint smell of burning reached his nostrils and, from the same direction, carried on the wind he could hear the excited yapping of a small dog.

"Over there!" he whispered to his comrades, turning his mare towards the smoke. It took five minutes for them to reach the outer edge of the copse and now the smoke was thicker than ever, tinged with orange, as flames leaped greedily up the side of a wood and thatched cottage.

Tethering their horses to the fallen bough of an old oak they moved in single file through the copse, careful not to tread upon any fallen twigs or branches that would betray their presence. Ranulf could feel his heart pounding, his breathing tight in his chest, as he cautiously moved through the trees towards the clearing on the other side. Careful not to trip over his sword he hunkered down behind a huge fern and, spreading the leaves peered through them towards the clearing. Leofwine and Cnut soon joined him, sprawled carelessly on the damp ground and grimly followed his gaze.

The cottage was now engulfed in fire, a roaring inferno, as the breeze fanned the flames up to the thatched roof and whipped them ever higher into the air. Sparks crackled and leaped to join the pall of smoke which was now spreading thick and black across the countryside. On the ground Ranulf saw there were two bodies lying silent and inert, their torsos twisted into macabre shapes as red stains slowly spread across their chests.

He could just about make out that they were a man and a woman; husband and wife perhaps, for tied to a tree, naked and dishevelled, tears staining her once pretty face was a young girl who could have been their daughter. He guessed she was about fifteen, but she could have been younger. She was plainly terrified, and with good reason.

Around her neck was a noose, the end of which had been slung over the branch of the tree to which she was tied. On the other end of the rope were two burly soldiers dressed in mail armour, and they were amusing themselves by occasionally tugging on the rope to snap the girl's neck violently upward, causing her to moan with pain.

Milling around her were another twelve soldiers, similarly attired in mail armour, and all carrying long, keen edged swords. Save for one other they were laughing and joking in a strange nasal tongue that Ranulf had not heard before. The cause of their laughter was their colleague, a swarthy, dark skinned man, whose breeches were around his knees as he thrust into the young girl, giving great grunts of pleasure as he did so.

For how long this had been going on Ranulf did not know, but it was clear that the girl was almost beyond consciousness, beyond caring. He could only hope that she was. He had seen many things in his time, many act of brutality, many violent deaths, indeed he had been the cause of many himself, but that was in warfare, between professional soldiers. This sickening spectacle was a world removed from that. His face flushed with blood as anger welled up inside him.

"Bastards!" he hissed between bared teeth and looked to his left to see that Leofwine was equally appalled, his handsome face suffused with anger at the barbarity of the Norman soldiers.

"We must do something!" he whispered, his blue eyes flashing, reflecting the flames from the burning cottage.

"There's nothing we can do," Ranulf replied, "there's too many of them."

"They're just animals!" Even Cnut joined in the condemnation, spitting out the words with such vehemence that he almost startled his colleagues. It was the first expression of any feeling that Ranulf had heard in weeks. He was about to respond when his attention was drawn again to the clearing.

The dog that he had heard yapping minutes earlier had appeared, and was sniffing around the corpses on the ground, pathetically nudging and pawing at them to provoke some reaction. Getting none it ran towards the tree, to the young girl tethered to it like an oxen to the yoke and started to bark at the man brutalising her. The man turned to face the animal and with a curse took a swipe at it with his hand but missed as the little dog backed away from the blow. He shouted something to the others and then returned his attention to the girl, who, mercifully, appeared to have blacked out. One of the other men now stepped forward and drawing his sword from its scabbard thrust violently at the dog but he too missed as the dog, sensing danger ran away through the crowd of soldiers and headed for the trio hidden in the copse.

Ranulf saw the little dog, a scruffy tan mongrel, coming towards them and prayed that the soldiers would not follow it. As the dog reached them, it slowed and cautiously sniffed the air. Ranulf cast an anxious glance toward the foreigners, concerned lest they pursue the animal further, but fortunately they had now forgotten the dog and their full attention was focussed upon the young girl tied to the tree. He saw that the brute that had been pleasuring himself was now pulling up his breeches, his sated face flushed with blood. He cracked some kind of a joke as he wandered over to them and a burst of laughter greeted his words.

The girl, conscious once more, was sobbing and whimpering softly through lips that were cracked and swollen. Her body, frail and thin was red and sore from the treatment she had received and Ranulf guessed that were it not for the ropes that bound her to the tree she would simply have collapsed. And then he saw one of the other men, obviously the leader, point to their horses tethered on the far side of the clearing. The soldiers started to move away in that direction and, as they did so, the leader of these men, if such they were, pulled a dagger from his belt. Ranulf thought for a moment that he intended to use it on the girl but he did not do so. Instead with a swift slashing action he severed the rope binding her to the tree. She instantly slumped to her knees but the halter around her neck prevented her from collapsing any further. Instead she remained on her knees, her body swaying backwards and forwards, the halter holding her up whilst her swollen eyes closed, she mouthed something that Ranulf could not hear; a silent prayer perhaps.

With a nod to the men on the end of the rope the leader turned his back on the girl and walked quickly away toward his horse. And Ranulf realised with a sickening certainty what they now intended.

Struck dumb the three men watched in silence as the two soldiers on the end of the rope now tugged violently in unison, hoisting the girl up to the branch of the tree. She gave a shriek, a sob of despair, but then the sob was cut off as the rope bit deep into her neck, choking the breath in her throat. She struggled for a few moments, her torso kicking and dancing on the end of the rope in a desperate struggle for air until one of the men leaped up, grabbing her feet, pulling on them as hard as he could. The girl's neck was instantly broken. Her body stopped kicking and hung limp and silent, swaying to and fro on the rope's end.

"Jesus Christ!" Cnut swore under his breath. The two Norman soldiers were securing the end of the rope around the tree trunk to leave the dead girl dangling from the branch. Having done so, and without another glance at her, they left the clearing to join their comrades.

Ranulf could not say for how long he lay hidden in the undergrowth while the body hung from the tree like a side of meat. Time ceased to have meaning for him as he considered the atrocities that he had just witnessed, struggling to understand why such cruelty was necessary. Eventually, much later, when he judged it safe to make a move, he rose cautiously from the undergrowth and walked toward the tree. He looked at the young girl hanging there. She was beyond earthly suffering now, her body stiff and cold. He studied her for a few moments, the naked torso pale in the moonlight, her face battered and swollen. What had she done to deserve such an end? Savagely he cut the rope that held her and as she fell he caught her and tenderly took her in his arms.

They buried the girl beside her parents in a shallow grave marked with a rough cross.

"Remember this day's work," he said as they stood over the grave, "when we face these bastards on the field of battle. Show them no mercy, for Lord knows they deserve none." He needed no reply to know that his words were unnecessary. They all felt the same; moved beyond words by the spectacle they had been forced to witness.

As he remounted his mare for the journey back to London Ranulf saw that the sky to the south had turned a deep blood red as though a summer sun were sinking below the horizon, suffusing the land with its warm glow. But it was no longer summer and it was not the sun.

It was fire. The Normans were burning the villages along the south coast. It looked like the whole of the country was in flames. Perhaps, he thought, God truly had deserted England.

"My brother will hear of this," Leofwine hissed between gritted teeth as they turned their mounts toward London, "and he will exact a terrible revenge." Ranulf was about to ask where the warriors would be found to achieve this, but there seemed little point. There seemed little point to anything after what he had witnessed and his mood was dark and angry.

To his left he heard the yap of a small dog. Turning toward the sound he saw to his surprise that Cnut had managed to befriend the mongrel that had once, perhaps, belonged to the girl. Its scruffy little face was peeping out from beneath Cnut's jerkin, its eyes like shiny black buttons as it eagerly looked around, taking in everything around it, oblivious to the awful events of the day. Cnut carelessly stroked its chin with his free hand and the dog rewarded him by licking his cheek with a long, wet, pink tongue before it settled down within the bosom of its new master. It seemed that Cnut had found a new friend, another lost soul, and Ranulf was suddenly glad for them both. It was little enough on this terrible day, but it would have to suffice.

He did not know it then, but he would fight many battles over the coming years, bloody battles that would chill the soul and numb the mind. The battles would fade, eventually, the details lost in the mists of time; but he would never forget the image of the young girl hanging from the tree. Not until he drew his last breath would that memory fade, the anger finally gone from his heart.

CHAPTER FORTY

LONDON.

10TH OCTOBER 1066.

It was getting dark, and Alice was tired. Her back ached from the strain of carrying her unborn child and she was cold and hungry. And very close to tears. Yesterday she had set out with such high hopes of finding Ranulf, but as the day wore on and her enquiries came to nothing her spirits began to sink. She had reluctantly returned to her lodgings at the Blue Boar Inn determined that in the morning she would find him, but despite searching again all day she had not done so. The problem was that although she had received numerous reports of his being alive and well no one seemed to know where he might be.

And so, in her desperation she was heading for the last place she could think of: Westminster Palace. If anyone knew where he was it would be the King.

At least he is alive, she told herself as she nervously approached the guards on duty at the entrance to the outer gatehouse. They were eyeing her with interest. All day they had received visitors to the Palace but for the most part these had been men summoned to attend by the King; the Thanes of Wessex, Sussex and East Anglia; the Commanders of the London and local fyrd; members of the Witan, who, for the most part had behaved like frightened children. But no women. Until now. They rose to bar her path, spears levelled.

"I have business with the King," she said as confidently as she could but felt very small, very insignificant, compared to these two massive men. She also felt quite frightened. The two housecarls looked at each other and smiled. The younger one, a tall, well built man with massive shoulders and quite a pleasant face behind his brown beard said:

"And what business would that be?" He cast an appraising eye over her swollen belly and Alice instinctively pulled her mantle closer around her.

"That is a matter for the King himself," she said defensively, not knowing what to say, her mind racing for some excuse that would persuade these formidable men to allow her entry to the Palace for an audience with the King. *I must have been mad to come here.*

"The King's business is our business lady," the younger man said, a hint of steel in his voice, "and we must know your business with the King." He raised an eyebrow at her, a challenge; she must tell him. And suddenly it came to her, the key to the door of the Palace.

"You are a housecarl?" she asked, knowing the answer.

"Yes, lady," the younger man said, surprised at the question.

"Then you will know my husband?"

"Your husband, lady?" he said, interested now.

"Ranulf Redbeard, the King's Champion. I am his wife." A lie, but it came easily to her lips.

"You are Ranulf's wife? The young housecarl turned to his elder comrade, a puzzled expression crossing his face.

"Did I not just say so?" Alice felt more confident now.

"Ranulf never mentioned any wife." The older housecarl now spoke, "and we still do not know your business with the King." There was the hint of menace in his voice and her confidence evaporated like a summer mist. She decided to bluff it out.

"I have a message for the King from my husband," she said with as much authority as she could muster, "and unless you want Ranulf to remove your head from its shoulders I suggest you allow me to deliver it." The older man now looked at the younger, also unsure of himself in the face of this determined young woman.

"What do you reckon?" he said. The younger man, obviously the senior of the two despite his lack of years, stroked his beard.

"Your message is from Ranulf you say?"

"That's right."

"Then why can't Ranulf deliver it himself?" he asked, not unkindly. She had to think quickly, but her worst fears of the past two days came to her aid:

"Ranulf lies wounded, and cannot come himself. He has sent me in his place and I *must* see the King... It concerns the Norman Duke." How easily the lies came to her lips. The young housecarl looked at her, weighing the matter in his mind and then appeared to make a decision.

"Wait here," he said. He turned on his heels to disappear through a heavy studded door. Alice stood and watched him depart, her heart pounding as she contemplated what she had just done. How on earth would she explain this to the King? He would probably clap her in irons when he discovered the truth. Why, oh why had she said those things? She began to regret her decision and sat down on a low wall by the Palace gatehouse aware that all the time the older housecarl was watching her from under his heavy, knitted brows. She shivered but whether it was from the cold or from nerves she was not sure.

"Cold night," the houscarl said, observing her discomfort, an attempt to engage her in conversation.

"Yes." Her thoughts were not on the weather but on what she would say to the King, if he deigned to see her. The minutes dragged by. Eventually, after what seemed like an hour, the young housecarl returned and spoke to her:

"Follow me."

Alice rose stiffly from the wall and followed the housecarl through the studded door into the candlelight beyond.

"The battlefield is no place for a woman!" Harold did not intend to raise his voice but he was losing this argument and he was not used to it, especially not to a woman. But this was not any woman. This was Edith Swanneshals and if there was anyone in the whole of the realm who could bend him to their will it was her.

"My place is with you." So easily put and so hard to refute.

"Edith, my love," he said, in what he hoped was a conciliatory tone, "I am sorry, I truly am, but the horrors of war are not for such as you; believe me."

"Such as me?" she mocked him in the way that only she could. "What do you mean, Harold, "such as me?" What am I then that I cannot be with my King when he goes to war, to fight for his Kingdom? Am I a rose that wilts in the heat, a grape that withers on the vine? No, I am your woman, Harold, your woman who would be your wife, and my place is with you – wherever that might be."

There was no reasoning with her, he thought, and if he was honest with himself he loved her for it.

He decided to take a walk; he needed time to compose himself, to consider his reply. He rose from the Throne that stood in the centre of the dais and began to pace the length of the Great Hall with his familiar measured gait. He knew every flagstone, every crack in the floor, having paced it endlessly, night after night, sometimes for hours on end during his period of tenure as King, and he subconsciously avoided the cracks, the joins between the flagstones.

They had made love earlier that evening. Reunited again after his return to London they had given themselves to each other with an abandon that had afterwards surprised them both; it was as if it had been the first time for them, or, perhaps, the last. But he had closed his mind to that possibility. Until she had announced that she intended to accompany him to battle. And that had lead to this present argument. And everything he had said to dissuade her, to force a change of mind had fallen on deaf ears or been turned against him. She was a formidable advocate when the mood took her, would put many of his Council members to shame. And now she was using her talents on him.

And why? Because she loved him. She loved him. It was as simple as that. Why else would she risk her life for him? He knew he ought to be glad, grateful that after all these years she still loved him enough to accompany him to war, to witness with her own eyes the horror and the bloodshed and the slaughter. And, perhaps, his broken body. But he was not glad. The field of battle was no place for her, whatever she might say. He would be worrying about her when he should have his mind on the battle. Christ knows he would have his hands full with that. It was not a good idea. Not at all.

But he was proud of her all the same. He turned around and saw that she had seated herself on the settle, watching him, waiting for his reply. She knew him so well, his moods, his fears, knew him better than he knew himself.

"Well?" she said, and he thought he could detect the shadow of a smile creasing her lips.

"I could be killed; worse, you could be killed."

"If you fall I shall kill myself. I will not live without you. You think that I could bear the yoke of slavery under the Normans?" She hurled back her response, proud, fearless. He looked at her, digesting what she had said, and when the words sank in he surrendered.

"Why you're a lion!" he cried, "I chose a lion for my woman." He crossed the floor and took her in his arms. He pressed her to him, her slender body a reed against his chest.

"Very well, my love," he whispered, his mouth stroking her ear, "come with me if that is your wish. We shall go together. And neither war, nor death, nor William the Bastard shall separate us."

And hearing his words she found herself praying that that was so. For last night, in the privacy of her own quarters she had cast the runes and read her fate.

And Fate, she knew, was immutable.

Across a wide courtyard and then down long torchlit corridors the young housecarl led Alice until she was quite lost, bewildered. She had never, in her short life seen anything to compare with the splendour of this building that was Westminster Palace and she found herself wondering whether the heavens themselves could be so vast.

Eventually they reached what seemed to be some kind of ante-chamber leading to the Great Hall itself. She realised this because beyond the great studded door at the end of the room she could hear voices in animated conversation. The voices, though raised – she corrected herself – one of the voices was raised, and seemed to be coming from far off, as if the speaker were in a valley and his voice carried to her on the wind. *The King,* she thought, *and he sounds angry.*

"Sit there," the young housecarl said, and pointed to an elaborately carved chair by the wall. Alice sat and the housecarl took up a position opposite her against the far wall. He stared across, at a point on the wall a foot above her head.

"Ranulf, how is he?" he asked.

"What?" she said, her thoughts far away, on the audience to come.

"Ranulf's wound? How is he?" The housecarl looked at her in earnest, as though he really cared. Perhaps he did. She searched for an answer.

"His leg," she said quickly, "but it will heal." More lies, but what could she do? It seemed that with every word, every minute that passed, she dug herself into an ever-deeper hole.

"Good, good," the housecarl replied thoughtfully, and they fell silent again, an uneasy silence that hung over them both. The housecarl returned to studying the wall and Alice her lap. How would she explain all this to the King? Her mind raced to find some excuse, anything that would explain her presence here tonight when the King had so many other worries to attend to. Perhaps, she thought, she should tell the truth. She was about to speak again, to tell the young housecarl it was all a mistake when he pre – empted her.

"It took courage to come here alone, " he said. "Ranulf must be proud of you.

"Thank you," she said, surprised, not knowing what else to say. She could not tell him the truth now. She fell silent again. Suddenly the young housecarl moved toward her, not menacingly so that she felt afraid, but instinctively, as though he could not help himself.

"Lady," he said, "men call me Aelfgar. I would have you know that I respect and admire your husband as a great warrior." He paused then, choosing his words with obvious care. "But even great warriors can die. Enemies seek them out, anxious to gain honour for themselves; or a chance blow, a moment of madness in the heat of the battle......any of these things could happen." He paused again, perhaps wondering if he had said too much, but nevertheless he pressed ahead.

"If your husband should fall in battle, and I should be fortunate to survive, I would have you know, Lady, that I would be honoured to care for you....and the child."

These last words were spoken as though they burned his tongue. In three days Aelfgar would be dead, a Norman lance piercing his heart as he fell, one of a last desperate knot of warriors gathered about their King as dusk fell over the bloody field of Senlac Hill. But he was not to know this when he spoke these words to the beautiful, nervous girl, another man's wife, who was seated opposite him and beneath his beard his cheeks flushed scarlet.

"Thank you," Alice said. "Those are fine words, and I shall not forget them." She was genuinely touched by his offer and was about to say more but at that moment the door swung open and another housecarl spoke to her.

"The King will see you now," he said.

CHAPTER FORTY-ONE

LONDON.

10TH OCTOBER 1066.

It was late when three riders spurred their tired mounts across Westminster Bridge, iron shod hooves striking sparks on the cobbles as they rode hard for the Palace. Ranulf was cold and tired, and the melancholy that had touched him earlier in the day had not yet dispelled. He wanted to see Alice, to know that all was well, but first he must see the King, to report upon the day's events.

And then what? He asked himself. From what Leofwine had said it seemed that the King was hell bent on facing William on the field of battle without delay, to drive him and his army into the sea. Whilst he applauded the intention he could not help but question the wisdom of it.

The King was tired, his army, the professionals left after the bloodbath of Stamford Bridge were exhausted, and as far as Ranulf could tell they would be seriously outnumbered. William was estimated to have almost eight thousand heavily armed men, including Cavalry. Harold now had barely twelve hundred.

Further, it was clear that William was taunting them, drawing them onto him before they were ready, forcing Harold to act by burning and wasting the land and by murdering his people. He had seen a graphic example of it earlier that day. Why else commit such atrocities? It was naked provocation. *Here I am,* William was saying, *come and stop me.*

And there was no doubt that Harold would take up the challenge for he was the King and he had sworn to protect his people. He had heard Harold's speech before Stamford Bridge.

Riding through the darkened streets Ranulf could sense that the City was buzzing with people and noise, men who had flocked to the King's Standards, the call to arms. They were everywhere, groups of men gathered together, eagerly awaiting the instructions for the march south. Many of them were old friends, often from the same county or town, sometimes from the same farm. These were hard men, men of the land, men with strong hearts and backs, their hands like leather from the turning of the soil; and they had come to fight for their King, or for their land, or both. Yes, he thought, they were hard men alright, and he was glad to have them, but they were not warriors.

The three riders clattered over the drawbridge that lead to the outer gatehouse of the Palace and here Ranulf saw that the volunteer army was gathered in its hundreds; more eager young men ready to fight under the King's banner. A few were laughing and joking and trying to impress their comrades but many also sat in contemplative silence wondering, like Ranulf himself, what the next few days would bring.

There would be a fight, of that he was certain, for the two adversaries were set on a collision course. Looking at the young men gathered about their cooking fires he could not help but recall the events of earlier that day; the naked brutality displayed by the Norman soldiers; their utter disregard for life. Compassion was a word that was quite alien to them; indeed they appeared to revel in their work, the slaughter of the innocent. He asked himself whether these young volunteers so eager now to give battle would be quite so eager if they knew what awaited them. And he was afraid of the answer.

The Normans that he had witnessed earlier in the day had all worn heavy mail armour the craftsmanship of which surpassed anything that he had seen before. It made his own mail suit seem clumsy by comparison although it had been specially made for him at the Royal smithy as befitted the King's Champion. But that was not all; every one of the Norman soldiers had ridden heavy, perfectly matched, faultlessly groomed mounts; heavy mounts that stood at least eighteen hands and carried a man as though he were a small child. And in full armour at that. *Destriers,* Leofwine had called them. The word was not known to Ranulf but it did not take much imagination to guess the destruction that they could wreak upon a shield – wall.

And their weapons too, were to be feared: lances that gleamed in the sunlight, their wicked razor edges gradually tapering down to a point that would pierce a man's chest – through his hauberk or jerkin should he be wearing one – as easily as though it were thin air.

And what did the Saxon volunteers have to counter all of this? Clubs and pitchforks; the lucky ones a sword, often old and rusty, a relic from earlier years, a hand me down from father to son, the edge worn away years ago.

The Saxons would fight hard, of that he had no doubt; fight with valour borne of pride and desperation borne of necessity; but a match for the Norman host? No. Once again it would be on his shoulders, his and his eight hundred housecarls, and the four hundred Gyrth and Leofwine had brought with them. Twelve hundred men against eight thousand; for if they broke the rest would break too. *Then God help us* he thought as they finally reached the inner bailey of the Palace, their horses flecked with sweat as they reined to a halt in a shower of dust that choked and blinded the livery boys who hurried to attend to them.

Dismounting, the three men quickly made their way through the inner gate and headed for the Great Hall, to give their report to the King.

CHAPTER FORTY-TWO

THE GREAT HALL

PALACE OF WESTMINSTER
LONDON.

10TH OCTOBER 1066.

Alice's heart was in her mouth as Aelfgar led her through the door into the cavernous chamber that was the Great Hall. Her footsteps echoed loudly on the flagstones as she approached the dais at the far end. It felt like a mile, but she stiffened her resolve as she remembered why she had come here this night. The acrid smoke from the pitch pine torches in their wall beckets caught the back of her throat and she coughed to clear it. She felt her son turn in her belly and suddenly envied him his warm, dark, sanctuary.

Ahead of her, in the centre of the dais, was the throne and seated easily upon it was the King, Harold Godwineson, King of England.

She had never seen the King before, not in the flesh, although she had heard Ranulf talk of him often enough. They were friends, he had said, and she found herself staring at this man who was the King, studying his features, wondering how it was that Ranulf could be both a friend to the King of England and the lover of herself, a woman who but a short while ago had been waiting on tables just to live.

He looked older than she had imagined, although she guessed that he was in his mid forties. His shoulder length hair and moustaches were going to grey, and his eyes were red and lined, exhaustion deeply etched there. But for all that she could almost feel the power in the man, the ambition that still burned bright within him. And also, she thought, anger. He was angry, but whether it was directed at her or at someone else she knew not.

Without warning a wave of nausea washed over her and she felt a little light headed. It was quite unexpected, although she was very tired and for a moment she swayed slightly on her feet. It did not go unnoticed.

"Would you like a seat child?" The question came not from the King but from another, to his right. She inclined her head and looked toward the sound of the voice and for a moment she was lost for words. For the voice belonged to the most beautiful woman she had ever seen. The woman who had spoken to her was seated on a settle, but even so Alice could tell that she was impossibly tall and slender, with long graceful limbs like the branches of a willow.

The speaker was older than herself. Alice judged her to be about thirty, an age at which most women's beauty has long faded, but in this woman her age seemed to enhance the whole. Her blonde hair was held in place by a circlet of gold and azure blue, which accentuated the blue of her eyes, which were soft, and kind. The whole effect was completed by a brilliant white gown set with sapphire stones that sparkled in the torchlight.

Alice realised that this must be the King's mistress, Edith Swanneshals, the mother of his children. She took to her immediately.

"Thank you," she said. "I am a little tired." Edith snapped her slender fingers and within moments a Palace servant appeared from nowhere with a sturdy looking chair and large satin cushion which he decorously placed beside her. Alice collapsed gratefully onto it. She had not realised that she was quite as tired as she was.

She turned to face the dais and saw that the King was studying her. His eyes roamed over her, from her face down to her swollen belly.

"The bairn," he said softly, "when is it due?"

"In two months, Sire," she said, "God willing."

"Then I pray he knows more peace than I have known these past months," the King said, not a little sourly. He exchanged a glance with his mistress. It was obviously some private matter between them. She began to feel like an intruder, allowed a privileged glimpse of a private, unattainable world.

"You have news for me of the Bastard?" the King asked suddenly, catching her off guard. He emphasised the last word. Before she could answer he spoke again.

"And Leofwine, my brother? You have word of him also?"

"Leofwine, Sire?" she asked, nonplussed by this latest remark.

"Yes, I sent him with Ranulf. He is well? Not harmed?" The Kings eyes bored into hers, seeking an answer, his concern clearly apparent.

This was so confusing. She had come to the Palace in the hope that the King could help her find Ranulf but instead he was the one seeking answers, reassurance that his brother was well. But how could she give this? What made the King think that she had the answers he was seeking? And where had Ranulf been sent?

Her mind began to fog; she was so tired after her efforts of the past two days and now she must deal with this. Why, oh why, had she come? The wave of nausea that had swept over her earlier now crashed over her again but this time much, much stronger than before. She felt herself sway and was about to steady herself by grabbing the chair arm when the pain hit her; a sharp pain like a knife in her groin, a sharp, warm and wet pain that started between her thighs then spread like a fire, an unbearable fire, through her belly and down her legs. She doubled forward in agony and was vaguely aware of someone hurrying towards her, arms outstretched, before a wall of blackness hit her and she knew no more.

CHAPTER FORTY-THREE

PALACE OF WESTMINSTER

11TH OCTOBER 1066.

She awoke from a fitful sleep feeling totally wrung out, exhausted. She had had such dreams, strange, vivid dreams, that she wondered for a moment whether they had been dreams at all or whether they were reality. The fog slowly cleared from her mind and she dimly realised that she was lying in a large bed in a strange and elaborately decorated room. She saw it was now dawn, for a soft grey light was slanting through the half shuttered window high to her right.

Her thoughts fled back to the evening before, to the awful trauma of her audience with the King, and the unbearable pain that had brought it suddenly, unexpectedly, to an abrupt halt. It dawned upon her that mercifully the pain was no longer present, but then a terrifying thought pushed all others aside.

Panic stricken, she tore away the richly embroidered bed sheets that someone, at some stage had placed over her and anxiously ran her hands over her swollen belly. Backwards and forwards, up and down, her hands moved over her navel seeking some sign that her unborn child still lived, that life still flickered within. Beads of sweat pricked her forehead as she searched for the familiar tell – tale signs that she had come to know so well, but for long seconds, seconds that seemed like minutes, nothing stirred under her urgent ministrations. And then, when she had almost resigned herself to the inevitable, to utter, unbearable relief she felt her child stir within her womb. It was a minute movement only, barely a twitch, but it was a distinct and voluntary movement that she blessedly recognised as such.

Suddenly, and without warning tears were rolling down her cheeks to stain the rich bed linen. She hardly noticed and would not have cared anyway; her child was alive, he was alive, and nothing else mattered. Almost nothing. For one other thing mattered to her very much and that was the reason for her coming to the Palace in the first place. She had come to find Ranulf, and she had failed.

Her mind turned to the events of the previous night and to the strange dreams that she had experienced after her loss of consciousness. She remembered first the pain, a pain such as she had never known; then strong arms bearing her swiftly upwards like a child. And the voices, distant and concerned; the cool breath of the wind on her face, but whence and where she was borne she knew not. And then what? She tried desperately to recall but could not do so. She could remember nothing until... until Ranulf himself was above her, looking down on her with eyes full of hurt and remorse.

In her dream he had spoken to her, questioned her; she had tried to answer him, to pull herself from the bed and into his arms but she could not move for unseen hands held her down. What had he said? What had he said? She knew it was important to remember but the memory of it all was fading so fast and soon, she knew, it would be gone altogether. And then, unexpectedly, it came. Not every word, but he had told her he loved her. That he would never, could never, love another. *Why did you doubt me?* He had cried, and in her dream he had buried his head in the folds of her cloak and wept whilst she had stroked the fiery mane of his hair and told him that all would be well.

After that things were a blur, other faces appeared above her, faces that were strange, distorted, and beyond that she could remember nothing, until she had awoken, emotionally and physically drained, alone in this bedchamber.

She slowly surveyed the room, taking in her surroundings. It was part of Westminster Palace; that much was clear, because the walls were of massive dressed stone. No other building in the realm was of such sturdy construction: the Confessor had built it to last.

But this was obviously not a man's bedchamber. The signs were everywhere, from the polished metal mirror hanging beside an effigy of the Crucified Lord on the far wall to the array of perfumes gathered together indiscriminately on the beautifully carved oak dresser.

Beside the bed was placed a leather bound volume that, although she could not read, she supposed to be a Bible, whilst hanging over the bed itself was yet a further effigy of the crucifixion. On the floor was an earthernware chamberpot and when she examined it more closely she saw that the water was stained with blood, her blood. She looked quickly away.

She raised herself onto her elbows and tried to peer out of the window set high in the wall. She was, however, still unable to see anything save for the tops of a few trees, bare now, with the approach of winter. With an enormous effort she forced herself to sit up. She immediately winced with the pain that lanced through her abdomen and the thought that she might be harming her child frightened her more than she could ever have imagined. She slowly sank back into the bed, careful not to move quickly, and then lay in quiet contemplation considering what to do next.

It occurred to her that everywhere seemed very quiet. Outside, in the Palace courtyard there was only silence, where last night men had been gathering in their hundreds to await orders from the King. Beyond the confines of her room however she could hear nothing, save for the occasional gust of wind stirring the fallen leaves. Equally here, inside the Palace all was still and quiet. Surely, she thought, the Palace servants would be up and about, attending to their many duties; the kitchen staff, busy preparing breakfast, the hand and maid servants attending their master or mistress; any number of other duties that were required to keep a place such as this running smoothly. But nevertheless the Palace too, was quiet, as silent, indeed, as the grave.

She lay still, staring into space, her mind now fully alert. Something was wrong. Something....her thoughts were interrupted by the sound of distant laughter. The laughter of a young child. Footsteps sounded, pattering unsteadily on the flagstones and Alice turned expectantly to face the door. Even that small movement was an effort. The footsteps grew louder and then, almost angrily, the door swung open. And Alice saw framed in the doorway a young child. A little boy of tender years, of no more, perhaps, than nine or ten years of age. He stood open mouthed, eyes wide with surprise. Alice recognised him at once even though she had never seen the child until this moment. There could be no doubt of his parentage for his eyes, the colour of his hair, his very manner, proclaimed that he was the son of the proud Edith Swanneshals. And his first words confirmed this to be the case.

"You are not my mother!" he said in a tone that belied his age. A reply was demanded, and given.

"No," said Alice. "I am not. But this is your mother's room isn't it?" The young child quickly nodded in affirmation. So she was right. Somehow or other she had been brought to Edith's chamber whilst unconscious and tended throughout the night. Whoever was responsible, she owed them a great debt of gratitude.

"Who are you then?" the question was fired at her peremptorily, reminding her that he was also the son of the King.

"A friend," she said, of your mother and father, who have been kind to me." The boy studied her doubtfully, weighing her answer.

"Are you ill?" he asked, after a few moments' pause, "and why are you still in bed?" The directness of the child was almost unnerving. And his capacity to pose questions seemed almost endless.

"I have been ill, " she said, "but I am getting better. And as to why I am still in bed, it is surely not yet late?"

"It is gone noon!" the child exploded with laughter, a great smile creasing his features, "and it is time for my lessons, but Gertrude cannot find me!" He laughed again, an infectious laugh, and Alice found herself warming to this little boy. If she had not been told that the hour was past noon she may very well have joined him in his laughter, but as it was she did not feel much like laughing. She had clearly been unconscious or asleep for much longer than she had thought, indeed for well over twelve hours, but if the hour was so late where was everyone?

She heard further footsteps now approaching her room: purposeful; adult. The child dived under the bed, narrowly avoiding the chamberpot with its less than wholesome contents. His feet disappeared in a tangle of bedding just as a large, round woman well into her middle years entered the bedchamber. The sight of Alice awake and alert obviously delighted her.

"So, my child," she said, a smile creasing her otherwise troubled features, "you have finally awoken from your slumbers. I had begun to wonder whether you would sleep for eternity." She stepped over to Alice and sat beside her on the bed.

"Who are you?" Alice asked. "How did I get here? Who tended me through the night?" the questions were fired one after the other in her anxiety.

"Hush, child," the older woman said, and with a show of tenderness that surprised her, she stroked Alice's bed tousled hair. "I will tell all in a moment, but first," she said, "war or no war, there is a young man who has lessons awaiting him!" She actually winked at Alice as she moved with surprising speed to quickly reach under the bed and, grabbing a scrawny limb, pulled the boy, legs first from his hiding place beneath the bed. His appearance was accompanied by squeals of laughter and pretended pain.

"Now then Godwine," the older woman admonished him, "you know what your father said. One day you may sit on his Throne, dispensing judgement and wisdom. But to dispense wisdom you must first acquire it. Is your father not right when he says this?"

"Yes, Madam," Godwine acknowledged, head bowed, eyes cast down.

"Then run along child," she said gently, "and do your fathers bidding; for if you do not I will be answerable to him when he returns......and do not tease your sisters!" she called after him as the boy scurried along the corridor, his legs hurrying now to do his fathers bidding.

"That child!" Gertrude said, with more than a hint of exasperation. "More trouble than a parcel of Normans!" She became suddenly serious again, the smile disappearing as though it had never been. Seating herself onto the bed once more she looked earnestly at Alice.

"Now, my child, " she said. "You deserve some answers. Be patient and I will tell you everything." She took Alice's hands and placed them between her own.

"After you collapsed the King himself, seeing your distress, caught you in his arms before you hit the floor. That was very lucky, my child, if you had fallen, well...we won't dwell on that. The Mistress asked that he bear you directly to her private chamber, the chamber in which you now find yourself. The Mistress, with my poor aid prepared you for bed and tended you herself. She is such a kind woman, my Mistress. So very kind...there was some bleeding, but thank the Lord we were able to staunch that before too much blood was lost. They say that a child born after the appearance of Christ's tears will be the stronger for it – an old wives tale - and I don't know about that. But I do know that you must now rest for all this hurrying and scurrying about will serve no good."

Alice nodded her acquiescence but otherwise said nothing.

"In any event," the older woman continued, "whilst we were tending you, the King's youngest brother, Leofwine, and his comrades arrived with news of the Norman army who seem hell bent on burning the whole Country, Lord help us. The King, hearing the grim news, directed that his army prepare to march at first light this morning. After that there was much coming and going, and Gyrth, the King's oldest brother begged and pleaded with him to wait, or to let him lead the army in his place. But the King would have none of it. *"I am the King,"* he kept repeating, *"I am the King, the responsibility is mine."*

"In vain did Earl Gyrth try to change the King's mind, but just like his father, the old Earl Godwine, Harold always did what he pleased, and now that he is the King, well...." She gave a little sigh that might have signalled her disapproval, but Alice could not be sure.

"But to return to you, my child. After we cleaned you up you fell into a deep and troubled sleep. My Mistress was greatly concerned for you and hearing that your... man... was one of Earl Leofwine's companions, she persuaded the King to allow him a few moments with you."

"Ranulf here? With me? Last night?" Alice could barely believe what she had just heard. She sat bolt upright in bed, for once heedless of the pain and stared at the older woman.

"Yes child, he was," Gertrude admitted. "He was with the King's brother when he returned to the Palace late last night. But he was much distressed to see you in such a plight, and not knowing whether his child would live or die. What made it worse was the fact that the King had already ordered him to lead the vanguard of the army through the City gates at dawn. He was only able to spend a few moments with you before leaving for the south. It was hard to bear, his distress at seeing you as you were. I think he would have given almost anything to have stayed by your bedside if he could; to have some last words with you. But he is a soldier and he had his orders."

Gertrude shook her head as she recalled the events of the previous night: Ranulf's obvious reluctance to tear himself away; his calloused, battle hardened hand lingering on that of this young girl as he stood to leave; his painful retreat to the door until only his fingertips were touching, and then, swiftly, like a shadow, gone into the night. She did not tell Alice this for fear that it might upset her. Instead she said:

"Sometimes it is better to have loved such a man for a moment than to spend a lifetime with another."

"A moment!" Alice cried. "What is a moment? It is nothing. Less than nothing; it is death."

"Then may the Lord bless you, my child, and keep him safe. For the Good Lord knows he will need his blessing where he goes."

But Alice was not listening. Her thoughts were racing, full of the events of the previous night.

"I dreamed he came to me last night," she said. Perhaps it was no dream after all. Perhaps some tiny part of me, my soul or my spirit recalls his presence, his words..." She looked at Gertrude, anxiety written in every line of her face.

"What did he say?" she asked. "You must tell me."

"He said that he loved you."

"Loved me?"

"Yes child, of course."

"And that he forgave me?"

"Forgive you child! Whatever for?"

His words, his dream–words came flooding back to her; a floodtide of emotion. *Why did you doubt me?* He had asked in her dream. *I love you; why doubt me?* The words echoed in her head, insistent, demanding an answer.

"For this!" she cried. "For being here when I should have waited for him! For doubting him when I should not!

"These things are not your fault, child," Gertrude said. "They are simply the foolish things we all do in our uncertainty. Only the Good Lord has the wisdom to set us on our proper course. We should pray to him for guidance."

"If I lose this child I shall never forgive myself," Alice whispered softly. Whether Gertrude heard or not did not matter; she was speaking to herself. And once more there were tears, but this time not of joy for the life that beat inside her, but of sorrow, that the life might yet be extinguished, and that she would have caused it. And there were yet more tears. Tears of guilt, mingling with the others, staining the beautiful silken sheets; tears which she would have been hard pressed to explain, for the reasons were many and her distress was great, but amounted to only one thing in her troubled mind: That she had failed him; failed his love, failed his trust. And now he had gone to war, to face an implacable enemy who had never known defeat. An enemy who would not, could not, be beaten.

Seeing the girl's distress, so deep, so unexpected, the older woman put an arm around her and embraced her close as though to cocoon her from the world, from her sorrow, from her guilt. And so they sat in silence; an old woman and a young girl, in the bedchamber of the King's Mistress, whilst a late autumn sun cast the last of its golden rays upon them. But they were in darkness, their minds troubled and sore, for the King had gone to fight.

In determined mood and with banners flying he had marched at first light to seek out William the Bastard, to bring him to battle. The King, his woman, his brothers, and all the Saxon host. And Alice, bedridden and weary, could only wait and pray, an island in a whole ocean of troubles.

CHAPTER FORTY-FOUR

CALDBEC HILL, SUSSEX.

13TH OCTOBER 1066.

Caldbec Hill: a lonely, windswept ridge eight miles north of Hastings. It was here, after a forced march of fifty miles that King Harold Godwineson finally brought his weary army to a halt. It was early evening and they had marched all day. The featureless terrain was broken only by an old hoar apple tree, standing alone one mile south of the Andredsweald. And it was around the hoar apple that Harold assembled his army, the army that would sweep William the Bastard back into the sea.

The London road to Hastings swept south from here and in the morning he would march down that road and catch the invader unawares. He had done it before, at Stamford Bridge; he would do it again. And there would be no escape for the Norman usurper: he had already despatched a fleet of 700 ships to prevent any prospect of a retreat by water. Even now they waited off the English coast, prepared to run down upon any vessel put to sea by William lest he seek to slip away unharmed.

And so it was that with spirits high, the Saxon army camped along the ridge of Caldbec Hill, lit their cooking fires and raised their voices to the heavens in song. They sang songs of valour, of great deeds, and of Beowulf, the greatest Saxon of them all. And they dreamed of victory in the morning.

Seated a few yards away from the main body of the army, his back resting against the hoar apple was the King. His face was a study in concentration as, cloak wrapped tightly around him he stared with deep-set eyes into the flames of a hastily constructed fire. Fanned by the northerly wind it crackled and sparked and blue smoke spiralled up into the clear night sky.

Opposite him, occasionally feeding the fire between mouthfuls of stew were his brothers and, nestling tight against him, as though the wind might snatch her away was Edith. This was still no place for a woman, but he had agreed, given his word, and the matter was settled.

By contrast to the raucous song of their men the quartet gathered under the hoar apple were quiet, lost in their thoughts of the morning, wanting to sleep, but knowing that sleep was impossible.

Harold turned his gaze away from the fire to the woman whose arms were tight about him. How pale she looked, in the moonlight, as if death had already taken her and frozen her face into a mask. But she had always looked pale, and when she blinked and turned smiling eyes upon his own he silently rebuked himself for his morbid thoughts and pulled her even closer to him. This was no time to think of death. In the morning he must be strong, stronger than he had ever been before. One last time. Just once, and the final victory would be his. And England, his England, would have peace at last.

He looked up and studied the stars. It was a clear, cold night and a waning moon, twenty-two days old, hung in the sky. No threat of rain. So tomorrow he could march unhindered down the road that lay before him, and with surprise on his side strike at the heart of the enemy.

He looked around, at the myriad camp-fires littering the ridge, at the men huddled about them against the cold. They were obviously in good heart, despite the wind and the cold and yet another forced march – their raised voices were testimony to that – and he was sure they would fight well. If only he had a few more housecarls to stiffen the new recruits. *And some of William's cavalry.* The thought came unbidden to his mind and he tried to shut it out but he could not. His thoughts flew back ten long months to the night of the

Confessor's death, to a conversation he had had with Ranulf. Can we win, he had asked, against William's cavalry? And he remembered Ranulf's hesitation before committing himself to the answer he had wanted to hear.

But that was before Stamford Bridge, before two thousand of the finest warriors in the world had bled the ground red in that terrible encounter just three weeks ago. Now he would face William without them. It was his decision. His alone. He could have waited in London, waited for Morcar and Edwin, but he had chosen not to. It was his decision and he must make the best of it. Battles were won in the mind as much as by anything else, and his men were determined. He would win. He must.

His thoughts of that long ago conversation with Ranulf reminded Harold of the personal crisis that the Captain of his housecarls was facing. It was regrettable, and he felt the genuine sorrow for the plight of the young girl left behind at the Palace, but he needed Ranulf to have his mind clear and focussed in the morning, and not clouded by such matters. He must speak to him, soon, before they march on William.

He looked across at his brothers, their faces glowing amber in the firelight, their thoughts, like his, on the morning. They had been through so much together, the three of them, ten long months that seemed like years. But tomorrow it would all be over; at last.

"Come with me," he said, " and show yourselves to the men. Show them we are of good heart." He looked pointedly at Gyrth with whom he had quarrelled more than he would have wished over his decision to lead the army. He knew that he had been right. What was an army without its King? Gyrth returned the look with equanimity. Rising, both he and Leofwine left the relative comfort of the fire and followed Harold along the ridge. Edith wrapped her cloak even tighter and huddled against the fire.

The three brothers walked along the ridge, picking their way from camp-fire to camp-fire. The men were in good heart, the warmth of their greeting more than compensating for the loss of the fire. As they walked along the ridge cheering broke out from a few camp-fires and was soon echoing along the ridge. Then the cheering became a chant; it was the King's name, repeated over and over. Harold! Harold! went the chant, rolling back and forward along the ridge and down, down into the valley below.

And in the valley, cloaked in darkness, for no Saxon camp-fires burned here, two shadowy, silent observers cautiously raised themselves from the marshy grassland. Their muscles ached with the cold and cramp, the result of silent watching and waiting, but that was a small price to pay for the information they had gathered. Taking great care to avoid being seen they crept stealthily back to their restless mounts, and leading them by the reins quietly slipped away into the night.

CHAPTER FORTY-FIVE

SATURDAY, 14TH OCTOBER 1066.

CALDBEC HILL.

The sun rose at 6.48 am, suffusing the gentle landscape with a golden glow. To the south the road curved away down Caldbec Hill, then wound its way through the marshy grassland of the valley before swinging south-east, rising again to climb distant Telham Hill.

From his vantage point on the ridge of Caldbec Hill Ranulf stood silently looking south as he studied the road. Save for Guthrum and Cnut, to whom he formed a close attachment since their return from Stamford Bridge he eschewed other men's company, preferring time alone, to think, to put his problems into perspective. He was a man torn in two; the twin obligations of duty to his King and loyalty to the mother of his unborn child chafing at him, eating at his soul until he could stand it no longer. Now he stood apart from his comrades, trying to concentrate upon the task in hand, which was to ensure that the road was safe from ambush.

He studied the road, which was little more than a dirt track, for the hundredth time. In one hour Harold would storm down this road, and on to Hastings, to take the Bastard by surprise. It was his task to ensure that the road was safe for that great enterprise. He looked south yet again. All seemed quiet; no movement could be observed to disturb the tranquil scene save for the branches of bushes and trees rustling in the gentle breeze. The wind had dropped; the land was slowly waking to another day.

"Quiet as the bloody grave." Ranulf turned to see Guthrum standing at his shoulder, his thigh tightly bandaged, proof of his continuing problems. It would not prevent him fighting today. Only death itself could do that.

"Almost too quiet," Ranulf said, "I think I will take a closer look." With barely a pause he strode away down the grassy slope, Guthrum limping along behind in a vain attempt to keep up. As ever these days Ranulf was lost in a world of his own, preoccupied with thoughts that excluded everyone and everything else. Guthrum finally caught up with him at the foot of the slope, just beyond the point where the marsh grass began, for as he strode forward, intent on scrutinising the landscape he stepped into a deep pool of mud that threatened to remove his boot as he attempted to extricate himself from the miasma.

Finally, after much cursing and swearing he found his way onto firmer ground and this time accompanied by Guthrum, the pair made their way towards Telham Hill. By now they were a good half-mile away from their own lines, from the Saxon army camped on Caldbec Hill and Ranulf was acutely aware of the time that had elapsed. The sun had climbed a little higher in the sky to the east and he estimated it was close to seven o' clock. It was time to be getting back. He indicated as much to Guthrum and was about to head back when, far ahead, from the crest of Telham Hill a movement caught his eye. He stared hard and saw it again. And this time recognised it immediately. Almost in shadow, but quite unmistakable was the figure of a man carrying spear and shield. And he was running.

Rooted to the spot Ranulf studied the man as he grew closer, growing larger until he could pick out the detail, his English style hauberk; the urgency of his gait; the way he turned his head every so often to look back; the rise and fall of his heaving chest.

And as Ranulf watched his heart slowly sank, for even as the man hastened toward him he knew that this was the news that he had dreaded, had hoped and prayed to avoid: that William was on the march; was even now heading their way, and that it would be Harold and not William forced to fight a desperate rearguard action. The gamble had failed and now, with a whole day ahead to decide the outcome they must stand shoulder to shoulder and take whatever the Bastard would throw at them.

"Bad news, old friend," he said, turning to Guthrum. "Return to our lines and warn the King. Tell him to prepare for battle – and tell him the land is very marshy down here. Not good ground for cavalry. He will know what to do."

"William?"

"Yes."

Guthrum looked at him and his eyes spoke volumes. They both knew what this meant.

"And you?" he asked eventually.

"I will be back soon. Go quickly now and warn the King!"

Guthrum motioned to go but then paused to grip Ranulf's arms in his mighty fists.

"See you in the shield-wall," he said, and then was gone, his limp forgotten as he hurried to convey the news. Ranulf watched him go then walked forward to greet the exhausted harbinger.

CHAPTER FORTY- SIX

THE BATTLEFIELD.

14TH OCTOBER 1066.

It took only a few moments to establish that Ranulf's worst fears were true. A half a mile away, and closing fast was the Bastard's army; vast numbers of heavy cavalry, archers by the score and company upon company of heavily armed infantry. The sentinel, having almost burst his lungs to bring news of the enemy approach was close to collapse, his breathing hard and laboured.

"How long do we have?" Ranulf asked his panting comrade who was now bent double, trying to get his breath.

"They will crest the hill at any moment," he said, his voice deep with resignation. He seemed almost too weary to look up. Ranulf cast his gaze in the direction of Telham Hill and watched, this time in awe struck fascination as the enemy at last appeared.

At first all he could see were lance points twinkling in the sun, some displaying brightly coloured pennants, others bare. Then the rider would appear over the rise, steel helmet pulled low, the nasal covering the face, the sun glinting off the mail armour. And then their mounts; the same beautiful, terrifyingly large horses that he had witnessed just a few days ago. He could hear the jingle of harness and bit, the shouts of the commanders as they sorted the squadrons into order as they slowly poured down Telham Hill, great rivers of silver and brown, a mass of horse and humanity all heading his way, to gather in the valley at the foot of Telham Hill.

And there they waited, this great tide of mounted chivalry, for now the infantry appeared over the crest, marching in step to the beat of a hundred drums. Down the hill they came, thousand upon thousand of them, until the very slope seemed alive with men.

At first came the archers, the crossbowmen and the slingers, the Norman light foot, moving swiftly and easily down the hill, their scarlet and blue jerkins bright spots of colour against the green of the Sussex hillside. And then came the heavy infantry, the backbone of the army, huge blocks of chain-mailed armour glittering and sparkling in the sunshine, wave after wave of them, an unending sea of metal, all being drummed forward into the valley by the drummer boys hidden in their midst. They were magnificent. Magnificent and terrifying.

"We had better get back – whilst there is still time." The weary housecarl made the point that Ranulf, transfixed by the awesome spectacle before him had momentarily forgotten. He looked again at the foot of Telham Hill, at the mass of horses and men growing ever larger before his eyes. The stream of infantry pouring down the hill seemed unending and still more were cresting the brow of the hill. The housecarl was right; he should be getting back; he should be preparing for battle with Guthrum and Cnut and all the others. But he did not wish to leave just yet; was oddly reluctant to tear himself away from the spectacle.

"You go," he said, eyes riveted upon the glittering array before him.

"Take care then." Without further bidding the housecarl picked up his sword and spear and, his breath now returned to his lungs, jogged back towards Caldbec Hill and relative safety.

Ranulf did not notice him go, saw nothing but the spectacular scene arresting his sight. For now they were moving forward; this great tide of infantry and cavalry, with banners flying and trumpets sounding and drums beating them forward and the whole, awesome, panoply of war. And still Ranulf stood and watched, almost a detached observer, for despite himself he could not tear himself away. He simply could not.

And then, even as he watched, a solitary figure broke from the main body of the army and galloped hard, excitedly, towards him. Ranulf felt the hairs at the nape of his neck rise as the rider approached, his destrier eating the ground, tearing it with heavy iron shod hooves, the man's arms pumping as he urged it through the marshy land at the foot of the hill.

Here was trouble; he could almost smell it. And he was badly exposed, his comrades a half mile distant. He had waited too long. He cursed himself for a fool and stood motionless, waiting until the rider was almost upon him. There was nothing else he could do. The man carried a lance and Ranulf knew that one should never, never show one's back to a lancer. To do so was to invite death.

The rider was almost up to him now, and Ranulf could see the wildness, the elation in the eyes. Barely a yard from him, just when Ranulf thought the Norman would ride him down, he suddenly stopped, reining to a halt in a spray of mud and water that spattered Ranulf's mail armour.

The Norman controlled his destrier with a practised ease, one leather gloved fist holding the reins whilst the other carried the lance, the point of which was now aimed unwaveringly at Ranulf's chest. There was a sneer on his dark face, a smile that chilled the bones.

"You serve the Godwineson?" his words were spoken with the same arrogant insouicance that had characterized his every movement thus far.

"You serve Godwineson?" He repeated the question, demanding an answer.

"I serve the King of England." Ranulf replied evenly. The Norman sneered again, his eyes cold, bleak as winter.

"Know then, that I am Hugh de Bohar, Knight Templar, and soldier of Christ," he said in a nasal voice, "and that I shall stain the ground with your blood." His dark, handsome, cruel face glared down at Ranulf from beneath his steel helm.

"The ground shall be stained, but the blood shall be yours."

De Bohar laughed.

"Mine is a holy crusade, Saxon," he said. "I bring God's justice to this fallen land."

"By burning its villages and murdering its people?"

De Bohar shrugged.

"I also bring retribution," he said. "The cancer of evil must be removed before God's word can be restored."

"Then I piss on your God. For he cannot also be mine."

"Hah! The heretic reveals himself!" De Bohar sneered and looked down at Ranulf through dark, hooded eyes. When he spoke again his voice was softer but the menace was unmistakable:

"Then know this also, Saxon," he said, "by sunset you, your heretic King and all his hellish legions will litter this ground. Their limbs shall be severed from their bodies and the crows will pick out their eyes." And he smiled, a mocking smile that revealed his perfect white teeth. It was a mistake. This preening, arrogant Norman aroused emotions in Ranulf that he had almost forgotten existed. Deep inside something primordial stirred, and rose within him like a fire, an angry flame that could not be contained, but must feed and feed, until it burned itself out.

"That may be so," he said, looking de Bohar in the face, "but you shall not see it Norman, for I shall tear out your heart and feed it to my hounds."

De Bohar blinked, shocked beyond reason by the Saxon's retort. Who did this peasant think he was? Without warning he spurred his destrier at Ranulf, his lance still couched, still aimed at Ranulf's heart. The movement was quick, the horse eager to respond, but for all that Ranulf had been expecting it, indeed had deliberately provoked it by his insulting reply. And now, his senses raised to a bestial height by this sneering, confident, Norman he reacted instantly. As the lance point leaped for his heart, Ranulf whipped to his right so that the point of the lance flicked past his ribcage, glancing off his mail, and into the void beyond. As de Bohar's mount plunged forward he swung his own sword, held in his right hand, in a great sweeping arc that caught the destrier on its left flank, cleaving through flesh and bone and bringing both horse and rider crashing to the ground. The force of the blow jarred Ranulf's arm to the elbow but he did not care; he needed this man's death like a drowning man needs air. Moving quickly past the thrashing animal he stood over de Bohar who lay dazed and unmoving on the ground. He took just a few seconds to study the man, savouring the moment, the anticipation of the kill. De Bohar's chain-mail held him fast in the mud. He could not rise for his right arm was badly broken, a jagged bone protruding from his shoulder at a wicked angle. Beneath his steel helmet blood poured from a head wound, running unchecked down his face to stain his dark features red.

De Bohar lay on his back, glazed eyes staring upwards, his last view of the world. Slowly, deliberately, Ranulf bent towards him, his face over the others, blotting out the sky. For a moment their eyes locked; the Saxon warrior and the Knight Templar, before de Bohar looked away.

"Your heart, Norman." Ranulf almost whispered the words. He paused for a moment, a last look, before the sun flashed on steel and the point of his sword was brought swiftly down, ending the conflict.

He could not be sure but he thought he had seen a flicker of fear, just the hint of it, on that cold, arrogant face before de Bohar had died.

And God forgive him, but he wished that it were so.

The death of de Bohar brought a loud cheer from the watching army on Caldbec Hill. Hearing the acclamation of victory from his still distant comrades Ranulf hastened to return to their lines lest another Norman decided to challenge him, to attempt to avenge de Bohar's death.

Ahead of him lay almost half a mile of open ground, almost all of it uphill and the Norman cavalry had him in their sights. If they decided to break rank, to pursue him, he would be fortunate to make good his escape for the Norman cavalry would soon overhaul him and if there were any number of them it would then be a foregone conclusion.

He paused for a moment to catch his breath and studied their line of advance. It was clear that their general approach to Caldbec Hill was to the left of the London – Hastings road, to take up position for a frontal assault on the saddle of land that lay between the marshy ground. He decided to go right, to the east, away from the immediate danger. His course of action clear in his mind he set off again, hoping against hope that he would not be followed.

At the head of the Norman army, bestride a black stallion, sat Duke William. Around his neck, over his chain-mail, hung the relics of St. Peter and above his head fluttered the Papal banner, given him by the Pope for this was a Holy Crusade. Watching the encounter between the unknown Saxon and one of his knights' templar, a side show only, he had sat silent and impassive. Even when Ranulf had driven the point of his sword, two handed, through the broken body of de Bohar he had said nothing, displaying no emotion, no weakness, for this was not a day for the faint hearted. De Bohar was a fool, seeking glory for himself, and he had underestimated his opponent. But what was one life when so many would die here today? He must not underestimate the Godwineson as de Bohar had underestimated his opponent. Even as he thought it he knew that he would not do so. Today could have only one outcome and that was the total annihilation of the English. And soon he would be ready to start.

He turned to his cousin, the loquacious Bishop Odo, given pride of place at the head of the army, a mark of his respect for the Church, an acknowledgement that this was a holy crusade.

"The Saxons clearly intend to fight," he said. His eyes were focussed upon the crest of the distant Caldbec Hill, upon the twin banners of Harold Godwineson. The scarlet Dragon of Wessex and the Golden Fighting Man, they fluttered defiantly over the heads of the Saxon warriors lining the hill. "But then they have no choice...do they?" This much was true, for he had forced the battle by provoking Harold to march on him and had then broken camp at six am to confront him here, at Caldbec Hill. And his strategy had worked to perfection. Now all he needed was the coup de grace, the total destruction of the Saxon army, which, even as he watched, were forming their vaunted shield–wall across the crest of the hill. It was, he saw, a strong defensive position, but one which he was confident he could break.

His cousin, Bishop Odo, magnificently accoutred in chain-mail lined with gold at collar and cuffs was riding a grey destrier the equal of the Duke's own mount and now he turned his destrier towards the hill, gazing at the men lining its crest.

"No cavalry, no archers, just a few hundred professionals.... I wager that noon shall see your Standard on yonder hill, cousin." William nodded thoughtfully, considering Odo's words.

"That may be," he said." That may be...but I warrant this day will see much slaughter before the sun sets." He paused again, to reflect upon what he had said and now looked earnestly at his cousin, his face grim and set beneath his steel helm.

"Make no mistake," he said, "these Saxons will fight. The Godwineson expects it. They have sworn an oath to die...to the last man if needs be."

"We should not disappoint them then!" Odo laughed at his joke but the Duke's face remained impassive. He looked again at Caldbec Hill, at the Standards fluttering on its crest, at the shield-wall growing ever larger as more and more men were pressed into its ranks.

"So many men," he said. "So many. But we must prevail today...whatever the cost."

Odo was about to respond, to assure the Duke that it was only a matter of time before the Saxon shield – wall would break before the onslaught of their cavalry when far to his right a movement caught his eye. The lone Saxon was breaking cover, heading back to his heathen comrades.

"The coward that slew de Bohar has not yet made the Saxon lines!" he exclaimed, and pointed to the east, to the figure of Ranulf clawing his way uphill.

"I would grant absolution to any man who slays him in revenge for de Bohar," he said. "The life of a knight templar is no small matter cousin."

William the Bastard followed his cousin's outstretched arm and looked away to his right, into the sun. There, framed against the hill was the Saxon. But he was well away to the east and heading still further away from his line of advance.

"Let him go," he said dismissively. "Plenty of time for him later." He looked up and studied the sun. Still low in the eastern sky, it stained Caldbec Hill blood red. Soon, he knew, it would be stained with the blood of the dead. And it was barely eight am. His eyes returned to the Saxon army swarming over Caldbec Hill, to their hastily forming shield-wall, its bristling hedge of spears.

"Plenty of time for them all," he said.

251

On Caldbec Hill King Harold Godwineson watched through narrowed eyes the squadrons of cavalry and massed ranks of infantry closing upon his position. They now filled the valley, a sea of colour, a sea of silver and brown. Behind him his twin banners, planted firmly into the ground with his own hands fluttered bravely in the breeze shouting their defiance.

Below him, across the slope of the hill his shield-wall was forming in time honoured fashion, an impenetrable wall of mail-clad warriors standing shoulder to shoulder behind their shields of wood and leather. And from behind their shields, steel-tipped spears glinted in the sunlight, pointing menacingly toward the enemy. It made a brave sight but Harold knew better.

He had been outmanoeuvred and he knew it. Retreat impossible, for there was nowhere to retreat to, he must stand and fight. Here, on this hill. It was as good a place as many, and better than most, but for all that he would have wished to avoid it.

The hill was cramped; eight ranks deep stood his shield-wall, but only the front two ranks would be engaged when the enemy came to close quarters. There was no room to manoeuvre; no room for his housecarls to swing their mighty axes – to do so would mean that they would have to break the shield formation that held them, bonded them, together. And once the shield formation was breached the Bastard's cavalry could pour though the gaps and butcher them all. It would take careful planning, and iron discipline to hold this army in place all day.

But that was what he must now do; until the Bastard was beaten, or night, or Morcar, came to his rescue. Ten hours, more or less. Ten long, bloody, hours. An eternity. There was no room for error, none at all. For the hundredth time he cursed himself for his impetuosity and for the hundredth time thought of that other battle, fought just three weeks ago, two hundred miles north of here, at Stamford Bridge. The comparison between the position in which he now found himself and that of Hardraada the dead Norwegian King was both inevitable and unavoidable for they had both been caught unprepared. Hardraada had fought and Hardraada had lost – both the battle and his life. God grant that he would succeed where Hardraada had failed.

He looked beyond his shield-wall into the distance. The Norman cavalry were much closer now, the leading group of horsemen almost at the foot of the hill. Not long now. Not long. A lump rose in his throat and he swallowed hard. The Norman cavalry was beyond counting. Two thousand horse, he estimated; at least.

Gyrth appeared from nowhere, his face serious, concerned. It was not out of place today.

"Look there, Hal," he said, and Harold followed his brothers' gaze down the slope of the hill. Picking their way over the marshy ground, splashing carelessly through the pools of mud that lay in the valley came a group of horsemen. Six of them, and now Harold saw what he had not seen before. Above the heads of this leading group flew a banner as white as virgin snow. But it was the cross that was blazoned in gold across its centre that caught his eye and held it fast.

"The bastard fights under the holy cross," Gyrth said, his jaw set firm, his cheeks flushed with anger. And as Harold studied the six horsemen cantering forward over the broken ground he finally recognised him. Two years it had been since their last encounter, since he had fallen victim to this man whose ambitions knew no bounds. Two long years, but he would recognise him anywhere. The familiar set of his head on those broad shoulders, the easy, almost careless way he sat in the saddle, the way he handled his lance as though it were a toy. And the contemptuous way he had of barking out orders to his subordinates. There was no mistaking him,

William, Duke of Normandy. William, called the Bastard, who would be King of England.

For a moment Harold was seized with an uncontrollable urge to hurl himself and his men down the hill and into this small isolated group and butcher them all; but even as the thought entered his head he knew it was impossible. The distance was too great and the Norman cavalry too close. They would barely make half the ground before they themselves were cut to pieces. And the Bastard knew it. It slowly dawned upon him that William had deliberately ridden ahead of his army to tempt him to some foolish, perhaps fatal venture in the hope of a quick and unexpected victory. But he would not be tempted. He would not. This hill was his citadel, the key to the battle. The Bastard must take the hill, or face defeat. As long as he could cling to it, hold his shield-wall intact, he could win. He would win.

He looked down into the valley again. Duke William had now reined to a halt, his small entourage closely, protectively, gathered about him. And there he sat, motionless on his warhorse looking neither right nor left, but staring fixedly uphill. Perhaps he was studying the Saxon shield-wall, searching for a weak point to exploit; perhaps he was seeking a glimpse of himself, a last look at his great adversary before the horror of the battle began.

He could not be sure, but whatever the reason, William the Bastard sat silent and unmoving whilst behind him his vast army slowly manoeuvred into position. And still he sat; the Papal banner with its golden cross flapping above his head as he stared uphill toward the Saxon lines. And then, suddenly, across the battlefield came the ringing, defiant tones of a solitary voice. Harold could not see, would never know, whose voice it was that shattered the calm of the autumn day but it was unmistakably Saxon for the chant was heard loud and clear across Caldbec Hill:

"Out! Out! Holy Cross!" The lone cry echoed along the ridge and down into the valley to where the Bastard sat bestride his destrier and Harold fancied that just for a moment his opponent's calm implacability was shaken for he saw the Bastard's hands go to his mounts reins; his knees to its flank. The cry was taken up by the Saxon's comrades, adding their voice to his, and within moments it had spread the length of   the densely packed army, eight thousand voices, acting in unison, hurling their collective defiance down Caldbec Hill so that the air sang with the sound.

"Out! Out Holy Cross!" The cry resounded along Caldbec Hill and now it was punctuated by the beat of eight thousand weapons on eight thousand shields as the Saxon army took up the chant with enthusiasm; a great crash of sound punctuating every word as the chant rolled backwards and forwards across the hill and down, down, into the valley below.

"Out! Out! Holy Cross! Out! Out Holy Cross!" On and on it went until their ears rang with the sound and every voice was hoarse with the effort. Up to the heavens it soared, the battle cry of a warrior nation that had never tasted defeat.

At the foot of Caldbec Hill Duke William sat impassively watching and listening. Occasionally he would turn to his cousin and make some remark, some comment upon the Saxon's dispositions, but for the main part he just sat and watched and listened. There was plenty of time; let them exhaust themselves beating their own shields. Rather theirs than his.

Eventually, when he had seen and heard enough he turned his destrier around and trotted back, through the bog of the valley floor to the main body of the army. There, in the saddle of land that lay between two streams it was drawn up in three massive divisions. Archers, infantry, and behind them, their mail coats sparkling in the sunshine, row upon row, squadron upon squadron, of his vaunted heavy cavalry.

The Saxon cry still rang in his ears and the beat of the sword upon shield still shook the ground, but now the ground would shake to his command. For it was time to test these Saxons. With a wave of his hand he gave the order for the advance and a terrifying blast of trumpets filled the air, their shrill cry drowning out all other sound as a hundred trumpeters filled their lungs and blew until they were fit to burst. It was 9 am and hell was about to come to Caldbec Hill.

Mud spattered and exhausted from fatigue Ranulf finally won through to the Saxon lines, gasping and stumbling the last few yards as he fell into the arms of Guthrum who had hurried forward to greet his friend. Men cheered his return wildly for Ranulf had given them what they most needed; the first blood of the day. And if one Saxon warrior could best a mounted Norman knight, the flower of Norman chivalry, surely they could prevail.

"Welcome back," Guthrum said. "I thought that bastard was going to skewer you on his point."

"Beat the point and they're a dead man," Ranulf said softly. "Works every time." He was about to grin, but what he saw froze his features into a mask.

Down the hill the Normans were preparing for an attack, dozens of archers hurrying forward to take up a position in two long lines forward of the main army.

"Looks like you were just in time," Guthrum said. "The buggers are ready at last."

On his right Cnut looked down the hill from behind his wooden shield. Strangely he appeared to be quite calm, almost, Ranulf thought, serene, as though what they were about to face was nothing more than a minor irritation.

"So," he said, "Here we are then." He turned his face from Ranulf to look at the Norman archers who were now making their way up the grassy slope. A lapwing passed overhead, heading for the trees as though it could sense the danger.

"Looks like they mean business," he spoke again in that quiet, enigmatic voice that Ranulf had come to know so well. "Ever faced archers?" he directed the question to Ranulf who was still staring down the slope, trying to count the men in the two long lines that were getting ever closer. Fifteen hundred; near as damn it. Too damned many.

"Llewellyn's Welsh bowmen," Ranulf replied without turning his head. "And those boys were good. Could take a man's eye out at a hundred paces."

"Here they come!" Guthrum's words interrupted his thoughts. "Shields' up boys!" To the awful din of trumpets the Norman archers and crossbowmen finally came to a halt, planting their arrows into the soft earth at their feet. For a moment there was silence, and then, to a single command arrows were notched to bowstrings and bows were raised heavenwards. Ranulf judged the distance at a hundred paces, perhaps less. Too damned many and too damned close.

"Loose!" the air hummed with noise as fifteen hundred arrows hissed up the hill. Into the Saxon shield-wall they thudded, fifteen hundred iron-tipped heads hammering like driving rain upon the wooden shields of the Saxon housecarls. For a moment the shield-wall buckled but when Ranulf looked around he saw that casualties were mercifully few for the vast majority of the clothyard shafts were either taken upon the shields of his comrades or else had passed harmlessly overhead for the steep angle of the slope meant that any arrow aimed too high would miss altogether.

But once more fifteen hundred bows were aimed skywards and Ranulf buried his head behind his shield, all further thought forgotten, as he prepared himself for the second volley.

"Loose!" Again the sky was black with arrows as the Norman archers released their second shafts as they sought to break the Saxon's resolve. Once more the dull thud of clothyard shafts striking wood could be heard as the shield-wall buckled beneath a second withering volley of iron-tipped death. But again, bent and bowed though it was, the shield-wall stood firm, the warriors in the front rank slowly gaining their feet as the last arrow landed in the earth forty feet beyond their heads. The angle of the slope was proving too great.

"Loose!" Once more the order was given, and again the housecarls had to bury themselves behind their shields to weather the storm. And now an attempt was made in earnest to break them: "Loose!...loose!....loose!" Volley after volley was sent thrumming up the hill to hammer the Saxon shield-wall into submission, a final withering barrage of iron that numbed the senses and sapped the resolve to stand before it. But it could not last forever, and as quivers began to empty the barrage began to abate. It ceased altogether when the dejected archers were given the order to withdraw. Hoots of derision accompanied their withdrawal down the hill as the Saxons, able at last to poke their heads above the burnished leather and wood of their shields hurled abuse and derision and battle-axes and slung stones after them. The shield-wall had held, and with hardly any casualties, but many men's shields now resembled the quill of the porcupine, studded as they were with countless arrows.

A great cheer arose as the Norman archers finally withdrew, hurrying beyond their own lines to rest, and, no doubt, replenish their stock of arrow-heads for later in the day. The first phase of the battle had ended but not one man on that hill deluded himself that this was the end. On the contrary it was just about to begin for now, to the deafening blast of trumpets, the Normans were coming again.

This time it would be the heavy infantry, split into three massive divisions that Duke William would send toiling up the hill in an attempt to smash aside the stubborn Saxons and their heretic King. And it was barely ten am.

"Ha Rou! Ha Rou! Notre Dame et Dex aide!" the Norman infantry gave voice as they laboured up the hill toward the Saxon shield-wall. Four thousand heavy infantry were committed to this assault, well armed and armoured, all aching for a fight. In the centre was Duke William with his own Norman infantry, the cream of this vast host. On his right were the Franco-Flemish contingent under the command of William Fitz Osbern and Count Eustace of Bolougne. To his left came the Bretons under Alan Fergant of Brittany.

Up the hill they came, chain-mail glinting behind their kite-shaped shields, steel swords flashing in the sun, a formidable host that would sweep away this rag-tag army of the false King Godwineson. And then on to London.

On the far right of the Saxon line Leofwine stood and watched dry mouthed as the Breton division, over a thousand steel-clad warriors came remorselessly on. Beside him his brother Gyrth stood ready, armed to the teeth with spear and sword and scaramax, his helm pulled low over baleful eyes, shield locked over his left forearm. With them stood the men of their own hearth troop, veterans of Stamford Bridge. They had seen all this before. But before, of course, matters were reversed. At Stamford Bridge it was they, crazy with blood-lust who had assaulted Hardraada's position whilst he could merely stand and watch and wait. Then there had been no time, no room, for fear; one minute they were marching, the next they were tearing headlong into the enemy, screaming and shouting and wild with hatred. And it was the waiting that was the hardest part, Leofwine reasoned, for whilst the enemy could whip up their courage as they swept up the hill, he could merely stand and wait, and show discipline in the teeth of this assault.

Not for the first time a shiver went down his spine and he had to steel himself to hide it from his men lest they notice. He looked across at Gyrth, all hatred and burning anger, his shield peppered with broken arrow shafts, hastily snapped off after the Norman archers had retired. How he wished he could be like him, he thought; or Ranulf, the King's Champion, or his brother the King, or any of the many others who lined this hill today facing death. Where did they find the courage to stand like this, motionless, vulnerable in the face of such overwhelming odds and not show fear? Or perhaps they did. Perhaps, like he, they also knew fear, but somehow managed to hide it.

"Gyrth?" he turned to speak to his brother.

"What?" his brother's answer came hotly, discouraging any further thought that he had of raising the subject.

"What is it?" Gyrth said again; eyes still locked on his front, upon the front rank of the Bretons who were about to charge. Less than one hundred yards now, they would soon be upon them.

"Give them hell," Leofwine said lamely.

"And you, brother," Gyrth said, turning away just for a second to study his little brother. And to Leofwine's joy he smiled then, the last smile that would cross Gyrth's face. Leofwine would remember that smile for the rest of his short life.

"Shoulder to shoulder eh," Gyrth said before turning again to face his front for now the menace was real and immediate: the Bretons were charging the shield-wall and all else was forgotten as he prepared for the slaughter to come.

At the same moment that the Bretons charged the right of the Saxon line, the Normans charged the centre and the Franco-Flemish the left so that simultaneously the whole of the Saxon shield-wall was engaged. Over four thousand men Duke William committed to this first assault upon the shield-wall in an effort to break it. The Saxons locked their shields together like the scales of a serpent, gritted their teeth, and prepared for the attack. And like a wave pounding the shore the Frenchmen hurled themselves upon it as they sought to sweep the Saxons aside. The ground shook with the violence of the impact as shield met shield in a resounding crash of noise that could be heard for over a mile. And for the third time in as many weeks the fields of England wept tears of blood as its destiny was disputed to the ring of steel on steel and the cries of the wounded and dying.

In the centre of the line Ranulf, flanked by Guthrum and Cnut fought like a man possessed. None could stand before him as first with spear and then, its bloodied shaft broken, with his sword, he scythed down the enemy like so much ripe corn. This time there was no fear, no thought for tomorrow, but merely a burning anger and a hatred in his heart and the need to kill. To kill, and to keep on killing until there was no strength left in his arm, no breath in his body.

Two more Normans came at him, eyes dark behind their nasals, their shields raised, covering their left sides. Before either could strike a blow at him Ranulf dealt them both tremendous blows of his own, his sword a blur in his hand as he struck with the ferocity of a madman. The Normans retreated, to take stock of the situation, but came on again. This time Ranulf feinted to go high, to the left, and as the Frenchman's shield came up to take the anticipated blow he suddenly struck low, to the right, bringing the man to his knees, his leg shattered. A second, even more savage blow crushed the man's skull like an egg. His comrade, momentarily shocked, lowered his guard, and from Ranulf's right a spear point flashed in the sun, taking the man in the chest. Surprise registered in his eyes before they glazed over and he too slumped to the ground beside his dead comrade. Eyes wild with triumph Cnut savagely pulled the dripping point from the dead man's chest and in the midst of this carnage turned to look at Ranulf. And to Ranulf's astonishment he could see that behind the wild eyes Cnut was laughing. He was *laughing*. With death but a sword-thrust away. As though redemption were, at last, at hand. Perhaps it was. But there was no time to dwell on such thoughts for now another wave of Normans were coming and Ranulf steeled himself to take their charge, to bend his arm once more to the slaughter.

For long minutes the outcome was in the balance. But the shield-wall had held and this first assault was beginning to lose momentum as the attackers laboured to make headway against the slope, against the Saxon housecarls who simply refused to yield so much as an inch. Bodies, butchered and bloody, began to pile up at the foot of the shield-wall and added to the attackers difficulties for they had to force their way over their fallen comrades to reach the enemy. The attack ground to a halt, headway impossible. Slowly at first, in one's and two's and then like a flood as more and more men joined them, the first assault broke and Duke William's army streamed back down the hill, no order to their flight, but sheer blind panic, for they had been broken. Broken by the Godwineson's twelve hundred housecarls. And William the Bastard's fury would know no bounds.

"Cowards! Women! Is that what I have for soldiers?" William was beside himself, his face flushed scarlet with anger. How could twelve hundred of the Saxon rabble repulse the cream of his infantry? His Captains shrank before his tirade, eyes downcast, unable to look him in the eye.

"To horse then!" he cried beneath darkened brows. "We shall ride the bastards down! You want this land? *You want this land?* Then fight for it! Fight! I will have this Godwineson! By God I will have him!"

He stormed off, grabbed his stallions' bridle, and leaped into the saddle. His Captains exchanged glances as the Duke raked his spurs into his mount's flank and rode towards Caldbec Hill, arms and legs pumping as he urged his mount through the mud. Not wishing to be seen as laggards they hurried to follow him.

Moments later, to the urging of their squadron commanders the whole vast host of Duke William's mounted chivalry, two thousand heavy horse, trotted forward. The sun reflected off lance points and chain-mail, bridles and steel helms as the long lines of cavalry organised themselves into their divisions. That done they paused for a moment to gather themselves before the ground erupted, eight thousand hooves pounding the earth to mud. The flower of Norman chivalry, Counts, Barons, Earls and Knights, hurled themselves and their snorting, spume covered mounts up the slope to where the twin banners of Harold Godwineson fluttered in the late morning sunlight. It was the third hour of the battle and they were determined it would be the last.

Up the slope the French cavalry surged, a tidal wave of horse and humanity, imperious and magnificent, unstoppable in their momentum as they breasted the rise of the hill. Lance points flashed in the sun as they were lowered to the horizontal and kite-shields raised as the shield-wall loomed into view just fifty paces ahead. The riders raked their spurs back, urging the last ounce of speed from their mounts, going full tilt now to sweep away this peasant horde that had defied them for so long. The Saxons, rooted to the ground behind their wooden wall waited grim-faced and silent, and braced themselves for the shock.

When it came it was like a thunderbolt from heaven. The serpent's scales that were the Saxon shield-wall rippled wildly back and forth as the housecarls in the front rank reeled from the savagery of the impact. The breath burst from their lungs, the muscles in their arms and backs screaming with pain as they locked their shields, clenched their teeth and attempted to stop the French cavalry from sweeping them aside.

And, miraculously they did. For as the impact hit home spear points were thrust wildly, desperately, into the horses' flanks bringing both horse and rider crashing to the ground in a whirl of arms and legs and blood. Great axes were swung, cleaving through horse and human flesh alike, and knives were savagely drawn across fallen riders' throats. To the whinnying cry of thrashing horses and the despairing scream of their riders the cavalry charge was broken, ended in bloodied rout.

On the right of the shield-wall Gyrth removed his helm and, bare headed, wiped an aching, almost numb, hand across his sweat covered brow; a moments pause amidst the chaos. They had held; God alone knew how, for he had never known anything like the shock of that first cavalry charge. He was strong, had always been the physical superior of his brothers, but that last assault, the unbelievable shock of the impact had taken his breath away. His shield, of hardened linden wood, had split apart like parchment as he bent his back to hold the Breton cavalry. Men against horses, infantry against mounted chivalry; it was an uneven contest, but they had held – this time. How many times they could take a pounding like that last one he could only guess.

Looking around at his comrades, all men of his own hearth troop, tough, experienced, he could see the fatigue, mixed with concern, etched deeply across their faces. This was warfare such as they had never known. Stamford Bridge had been hell, but this was worse, far worse, for all they could do with so much cavalry milling about was to stand and take whatever the Bastard chose to throw at them. The cavalry, which for the moment were retreating chaotically down the hill with the intention, no doubt, of regrouping for the next murderous assault held the key to this conflict.

He was about to tell his men to prepare themselves for the next inevitable assault when to his right a cry rang out, clear and sharp, and instantly recognisable. And hearing it Gyrth's heart, big and strong though it was, missed a beat for the voice was that of his brother:

"See! They run! They run!....after them boys! No quarter! No quarter!"

And to his unutterable despair he watched impotently as Leofwine led the charge down the hill after the retreating Bretons, his sword flashing in the sun as he exhorted his men to follow him.

"Leofwine! Leofwine! No!" he cried, a sob catching in his voice, but already it was too late, far too late, for his brother was hurtling wildly down the slope, no thought beyond the need to kill.

"Back!....come back!" Gyrth cried after the charging Saxons but his despairing words were caught by the wind and snatched away unheeded, unheard.

Down the slope, over the corpse-strewn ground Leofwine hurtled, heart pumping, adrenalin coursing wildly through his veins as he pursued the Breton cavalry with one thought only in his mind. Fleet-footed and sure, he flew over the ground as though his feet were wings. In no time at all he caught up with a straggling rider, the rear flank of his destrier thickly matted with blood. Instinctively he slashed hard with his sword at the surprised Breton's face and paused only long enough to see him tumble from the saddle, a river of blood erupting from his cheek, before hurrying past to find another victim.

"Kill them! Kill them all!" he cried in his excitement to the Saxons' following him down the slope, almost a thousand wild, yelling warriors, men driven beyond reason by the sheer hell of the battle. On and on they went, down the hill, slashing and hacking and thrusting until the ground was stained red with the blood of the enemy.

But now the momentum of their mad rush was beginning to ebb, their legs to tire as the ground levelled out and sheer weariness set in as they tried to force the pace through the marshland of the valley. The Bretons, preferring to face the Saxon charge than die a choking death in the marshes beyond formed a small pocket of resistance on a hillock of slightly raised ground. And it was here, tired and weary, that the Saxon counter attack faltered, then ground to a halt as the impetus was lost.

Leofwine, his head ringing from a chance blow taken on his helm, his heart heaving from his exertions, was only dully aware of the change in the tide of the battle. His sword ran red with blood and great droplets flew from it as he desperately parried the thrust of a spear aimed at his heart. His Breton assailant, no longer on horseback, for his horse had been killed, was fighting on foot, fighting for his life, as the Saxons desperately tried to claw their way onto the hillock, to wrest it from the Bretons. To both Saxon and Breton it had become a rallying point, a sanctuary for whoever could hold it in the midst of the slaughter. But for every Breton cut down, more and more were hurrying to join the small band that had made this hill their stand. All too soon the Saxons were becoming outnumbered, and badly so.

Leofwine cast about him. His men were struggling hard to hold the Bretons, their greater numbers beginning to tell. Beside him a Saxon was cut down unmercilessly as, weaponless he pleaded for mercy. But now his attention was drawn to his front as the Breton made another thrust at him, this time aimed at his face. Leofwine swung quickly to avoid it and hammered his own weapon into the Breton's thigh, a slashing blow that brought him to his knees. But even as he swung again to finish the prostrate Frenchman he could see others heading his way, swords drawn, eyes wild, keen for the kill. And beyond them, to his left, the Norman cavalry had rallied in the centre and were galloping over to join the fray. It was hopeless. He looked quickly about again. All around his hearth troop were fighting hard, but giving their lives in this uneven struggle. Within moments the Norman cavalry would arrive and then it would become a slaughter.

Hatred was replaced by cold fear as the gravity of his situation came crushingly home to him. All he had wanted to do was to prove to his brothers that he could win battles as much as they, but the enormity of his folly was now all too apparent. He had led them into a trap. He looked back, up Caldbec Hill, to the Saxon shield-wall, to his brother's banners flying in the breeze. His only hope was to get back to them now, before the chance was gone forever. Without further hesitation he started to run...

In the shield-wall Gyrth watched events unfolding with an awful sense of foreboding. Their only chance of victory had been to stand solid, unyielding, to present an impenetrable barrier against which the overwhelming superiority of the enemy could be matched. He knew this, as did Harold. As, he thought, did Leofwine. No army in Europe had as much experience of this type of fighting as did Harold's housecarls. Lock shields, present a hedge of spears and let the enemy break their backs on it.

But Leofwine had forgotten this lesson when he went tearing down the hill with an eighth of the army. And now they were paying the price. All around the foot of the hillock the Saxons, though still fighting manfully, were gradually being cut down as the overwhelming numbers of the French infantry and cavalry began to tell on them. One by one slashing, hacking swords and deadly lances with razor edges were taking a steady toll. The fight was no longer even; it was becoming a slaughter. The Saxons, try as they might, could not hold them. Finally, and inevitably, the pressure ceaseless and unremitting, they broke and ran.

William saw them break and now, at last, he smiled. For there is no better target for a lancer than broken infantry. God created lancers for just this work and to his cavalry it was like training ground practice. Choose a victim, line him up, a little to the right, couch the lance, pick a spot, preferably in the centre of his back where the needle-like point can find the spinal cord, then thrust just as you pass him on his left.

And now they went about their business with a ruthless efficiency. Almost to a man the Saxons were hunted down and killed, bloody lances thrusting, twisting, thrusting again and then on to the next man. There was no question of surrender for this was a fight to the finish. Neither side expected it. Neither would give it.

Gyrth looked on, aghast at the scene that met his eyes. He knew many of the men that had followed Leofwine in that suicidal charge down the hill. Many of them were friends of his, and though he was not one to shed tears he could hardly bear to watch as those same men, all brave fighters, were butchered like cattle. The Norman cavalry were relentless, remorseless in their pursuit of their victims.

He looked hard for some sight of his brother, but try as he might he could not see him amidst the mass of fleeing men and pursuing horses until, suddenly, his familiar figure came into view, panting hard as he laboured up the slope of Caldbec Hill, running for his life. "Leo!" he cried urgently, his voice catching with emotion. "Leo! Run!" At the sound of his name Leofwine looked up and quickened his pace. But it was hard going; he was tired and the Norman cavalry were gaining on him, their huge mounts eating up the ground. And they were still going about their business in a ruthlessly efficient manner, picking off the Saxons one by one, their dextrous use of the lance making it a one sided contest.

Barely fifty yards now, fifty yards from safety, but four of the Normans had Leofwine in their sights, lances couched beneath their arms as they swung towards him, great clods of earth flung high into the air as iron shod hooves pounded the hillside.

"Run Leo! Run!" Gyrth shouted again, desperation in his voice for they were almost upon his brother. Once more Leofwine quickened his pace, urged weary legs to go faster; but Gyrth could see, in that instant, that he would not make it. There were still forty yards to go; forty yards but it could have been a mile. The leading Norman was lowering his lance, head bowed low over his destrier's neck as he prepared for the kill, just seconds away.

"No!" Gyrth cried, "Oh God No!" and before he knew what he was doing he was hurling himself out of the shield-wall and down the slope towards his doomed brother. Hands clutched at him, tried to pull him back, but he was too strong, and they were too late. Down the hill he hurtled, no thought for himself as he threw himself into the fray.

"Fight me!" he cried desperately, "Fight me!"

But even as the words ripped from his throat he could see that he was too late. The lance point, a foot of hardened steel, took Leofwine in the small of his back, slicing through chain-mail as though it were not there. A cry of anguish erupted from his lips and Gyrth watched, horror-struck as Leofwine fell. Down he went, heavily, to the ground, a great crimson patch spreading across his back. Brutally the lance was twisted and Leo's body twitched and jerked like a fish on a hook.

"Leo! Leo!" he cried as tears stung his eyes and he felt his stomach turn. Over the grass he sprinted, toward his fallen brother, a wave of nausea sweeping over him as he saw that, impossibly, his brother was dead. But now he was amongst them and his outrage knew no bounds. With a great slashing blow of his sword he toppled Leo's killer from his saddle and without pause drove his sword down hard. A fountain of blood spurted from the dead man's throat, but he hardly noticed. A noise drummed in his ears and he looked up, toward the sound. Blinded by tears he saw, too late, that the three remaining Normans were riding hard at him, line abreast, lances couched for the kill. And in that moment he knew, as certainly as he had known anything in his life that he was going to die. And, he realised, he did not care. And with the realisation came a strange, overwhelming, elation. This then was the end. Everyone must die when their course was run; for some it was short, for others much longer. Only the manner of dying mattered. And so, he would die like a true Saxon Prince, sword in hand, fighting to the last.

"Come on you bastards!" he cried, and raised his bloodied sword shoulder high. He did not flinch as they bore down on him, nor when their lance points thudded home, hurling him downwards like a broken rag doll. His last thought before the darkness enveloped him was that Leo had always needed his firm hand to guide him. Now, in death, as in life, he would be there for him. They would journey on together…

Noon came, and went, and still the red and gold banners of Harold Godwineson continued to fly over Caldbec Hill. Exhausted Saxons, long since resigned to their fate dredged up unknown reserves of energy and willpower to stand and fight as unending waves of cavalry, hurled up the slope by William the Bastard, often in the forefront of the fight himself, were repulsed in bloody rout.

But as the hours dragged by their capacity to withstand such unremitting pressure was slowly eroded, their numbers reduced, man by man and after each cavalry charge the piles of Saxon dead grew larger. No longer was the front rank filled with housecarls for many of them lay dead, their battered and broken bodies embracing one another in the mud that held them fast. Now their places were taken by men from the fyrd, from the Sussex, Kent, or Wessex militia, or by honest peasants, come to fight for their King. One o'clock came, and then two, and still the battle raged, and the slopes of Caldbec Hill ran red with blood.

By mid afternoon Guthrum realised that his time was running out. The wound in his thigh had opened up hours ago and his leggings were soaked in blood. It was everywhere, and it continued to pump from his wound to stain the very ground on which he stood. And try as he might he could not stop it.

Just a few minutes earlier his leg had begun to feel numb and cold, and now, he realised, he had no sensation, no feeling in it at all. And it was not just his leg. His arm, his chest, his other leg had begun to feel cold, and he knew that death had him in her icy grip. Soon he would be unable to stand, and after that he would sleep forever.

But he was a warrior. All his life he had been one, had known nothing else, had wanted nothing else, save for a warrior's death. All day he had stood shoulder to shoulder with Ranulf and Cnut, proud, defiant, and the three of them had been unbreakable. The piles of Norman dead all around were testament to that. But soon, he knew, he must leave them to continue the fight without him. He did not want to go but he knew that he had no choice. And before he left them he would seek his warrior's death. He would go to join Leofwine and Gyrth, and all the others who had fallen here today. Involuntarily he gave a small sigh. It had been a good life. And it had been a memorable fight here, on this hill, and if he could have lived the memories would last a lifetime. But he would not live, for now, this hour, his time had come. He would miss Ranulf, for there was no man in the land that he admired more. But he could not stay for, like so many others, death had called for him.

As if to remind him of that his thigh pumped blood once more; thick, bright red, and he felt a wave wash over him. There was less time than he thought. He looked down the hill to where the Norman cavalry were massing for yet another assault. This time, he thought. Do it this time. His mind settled and calm he picked up his axe and waited for them to charge.

With a savage jab of his spurs Osmond de Bodes urged his sweat-covered mare up the slope of the hill. No longer grassland, the hill was now a sea of mud, slick with the blood of the dead. The mare, dapple grey, struggled to find a grip, her hooves slipping and sliding in the mud as she tried to secure a foothold on the treacherous surface. Eventually her iron-shod hooves found purchase on some firmer ground and with renewed impetus the mare plunged up the hill toward the waiting shield-wall.

Ahead of him, seemingly impervious to the slaughter, was Duke William. Three horses had already been killed under him as he led charge after charge up this cursed hill but somehow, miraculously, he had escaped unharmed, and not the slightest scratch marred his heavy features. Even so, earlier in the day rumours had spread like wildfire through the army that the Duke had been slain and the battle had almost been lost. Desperately he had ridden bare headed amongst his men, showing his face, calming the panic until the crisis was over.

Now, helmet restored and surrounded by his closest allies – Robert of Beaumont, Count Eustace, Count Guy of Poitiers, Fitz Osbern and the rest – he was urging a fresh charger forward, spearheading yet another assault on the Saxon shield-wall which somehow continued to resist them.

Osmond jabbed with his spurs again as he hastened to catch the Duke, and his mare snorted and blew with the effort as she plunged through the mud. A dying man, his leg horribly shattered, reached up imploringly for help but Osmond ignored him. He must reach the Duke, must be at his side in this next assault for all his senses were telling him that the crisis of the battle had now arrived.

All afternoon the Norman and allied cavalry had been hammering at the shield-wall and both sides were close to exhaustion. Duke William, noting the Saxon charge just before noon had adopted the tactic of deliberately feigning flight, to tempt the less disciplined of the Saxon host to break rank and pursue them down the hill, where, inevitably they were cut to pieces in his carefully laid traps. But this tactic alone had not been enough to win the day and the Saxon shield-wall, reduced in number, battered almost beyond endurance, and slowly giving ground on the flanks still held firm in the centre, still continued to defy their every attempt to break through.

Osmond dragged his sword from its scabbard as he brought his mare alongside the Duke and anxiously cast a glance across at him. He was their leader, the man that had brought them here, to this field, to this *hell*. If William faltered now they were all dead. He looked again and to his relief saw that the Duke's face betrayed no sign of fear, or exhaustion, or the weight of the awesome responsibility that he must be feeling. On the contrary all was grim determination from the set of his jaw to the fire that blazed in his eyes, locked now on some point in the Saxon ranks. And as Osmond watched he saw the Duke raise his battered shield, dig in his spurs, and prepare to do battle again.

Ahead of them the shield-wall beckoned like a great scaly serpent and Osmond felt a shiver run down his spine as he steeled himself to face its wrath. Around its foot piles of corpses, men, horses, severed limbs, littered the ground, and in the air, hanging over it all was the sweet, sickly, stench of death. He looked skywards to clear his head and gulped great mouthfuls of air into his lungs. He absently noted the sun, starting its slow downward arc to the western horizon and realised, suddenly, that time was running out. Two hours more and it would be dusk. And with it inevitable defeat.

From somewhere deep within he dredged up a final ounce of determination. Offering up a silent prayer he gritted his teeth and urged his blown mare over the last few yards to where the Saxons, spear points dulled with blood, stubbornly awaited him behind their wooden walls.

As the Norman cavalry hurled itself frantically against the shield-wall Guthrum raised his shield to deflect a lance point and summoning what little reserves of strength were left struck a fearsome blow of his own. His axe somehow found a gap in the Norman's mail shirt and, slicing through tissue and bone all but decapitated his adversary. He winced from the pain that lanced through his thigh but even as the blow was landing he finally saw the man he had been searching for, over to his right, thick in the press of men and horses.

William the Bastard, surrounded by a knot of his supporters was determinedly carving his way through the Saxon line, striking to right and left whilst all the time urging his mount ever deeper into the enemy ranks. Such was the power of his mail-clad arm that the Saxons, men from the Sussex and Kent fyrd fell like rain before his hammer blows. Here was a warrior indeed, and were they not implacable enemies Guthrum would have been proud to have fought alongside one such as he. But there was no place for such sentiments and Guthrum, through the fog of pain and loss of blood recognised that in this man, called the Bastard, lay the key to this battle.

The Saxon line could not hold much longer. Already, on the

flanks they were being pushed back under the weight of the assaults and the shield-wall, once arrow straight along the crest of the hill now resembled a crude semi-circle. Soon the King's own Standards, planted at the highest point, rear of the centre, would be under threat from those flanks, and, indeed, the King himself, for he could not leave the field of battle without handing victory to the enemy. No, once they broke through on the flanks all was lost, for there was nothing, save for a few of the King's own hearth troop to stop them striking at the King himself. Nothing at all.

He cast a glance to his left and saw Ranulf heavily engaged, desperately trying to fend off two fresh assailants eager for his death, their eyes wild as they scented a kill. Beside him Cnut, his helmet gone and blood pouring unchecked from a wicked head wound was struggling to hold yet another Norman. There could be no goodbyes. There was no time for that. Taking one last look at these men that had shared his life he hobbled away to the right, using his axe as a makeshift crutch. Immediately the pain lanced through his thigh and this time he felt it rise like a tide into his chest, a deep burning sensation that seemed to go on forever. He grimaced and, even though he did not want to he had to stop for his head was swimming.

Eventually, after what seemed an eternity the pain subsided and taking a deep breath he began to limp over to where William was continuing to carve his way into their ranks. This time, it seemed, the Normans were intent on finishing things, and judging by the numbers they were throwing into this attack they might succeed. Everywhere he looked his comrades seemed to be at bay, struggling to hold their line, the weight of numbers finally beginning to tell. But even so he knew that one blow from him would do it. One blow, well aimed, and the day could still be theirs. And then he could die. And with every painful step, with every drop of the bright red blood that seeped from his wound he clung to that thought until he saw that

William was within striking distance.

Leaning on his axe he paused to rest, to gather himself for the decisive moment. He was a dead man but he could still save his King, his friends. He looked again and saw that William was still cutting his way towards him, his sword, his whole arm, bright with Saxon blood. It was time.

Raising his axe shoulder high he pushed his way into the shield-wall until he was near the front. Impulsively he stopped and kissed the heavy blade, running a finger along the edge. When he withdrew it he saw that he had drawn blood. Still razor sharp. It would need to be. He closed his eyes for a second as he contemplated what he must do, a final moment of reflection. Soon he would be dead, gone to join his comrades, but so too would the Bastard. Judging the distance he launched himself at the unprotected flank of William's mount, his axe raised, ready to strike. Every sinew in his body screamed in protest as with almost his last breath he swung the lethal blade down, down toward the back of William's neck.

Osmond caught the movement, over to his left, from the corner of his eye. Just a blur, but it was enough. William, his attention riveted on the shield-wall had not seen it and Osmond saw all too clearly what would happen unless someone intervened. He swung his mare toward the huge Saxon and raked back his spurs, drawing blood. The mare immediately responded and as the axe blade whistled downwards the mare's flank caught the Saxon a glancing blow, turning the direction of the blade. It missed its intended target but caught the mare, slicing through tendon and muscle, bringing it to its knees in a flurry of thrashing legs. Osmond was thrown forward, over the mare's neck landing heavily, winded and dazed.

His sword gone he tried to get to his feet and realised dully that his arm was broken. He struggled to his knees, holding his arm and when he looked up he saw, too late, the same huge Saxon standing over him. His leggings were stained thick with blood and his blue eyes were vacant, as though in some faraway land. But he still held his axe, its wicked blade stained with equine blood. For a moment the Saxon swayed backwards and forwards and Osmond saw a stream of blood pump from his thigh. How he still managed to stand Osmond could only wonder. He considered lunging for him, to knock him off balance but even as the thought came to him the Saxon seemed to gather himself, his eyes focussed once more. And in them Osmond saw only sadness.

The sun's dying rays caught the heavy blade as the Saxon hefted it above his head and through the pain of his shattered arm Osmond saw with absolute clarity what he intended. Instinctively he threw up his good arm to cover his face. He had always prided himself on his courage but as the blade flashed downwards his sphincter opened and all he felt was shame…

Harold Godwineson looked all around, his keen eyes piercing the gloom beginning to settle over Caldbec Hill. To left and right the Norman cavalry were pressing in determinedly on his wings, his weakened shield-wall unable to hold their incessant attacks. Gyrth and Leofwine were dead and his housecarls, those that still stood, were all but finished. Even though his mind was dulled by the long hours of fighting he recognised one incontrovertible fact: he was losing the battle.

He removed his steel helm and wiped his sweat-stained brow with a grimy fist before pulling it on again. Over to his right the Normans were pressing again, twenty or thirty knights making a determined effort to break through. It may not be long. He had already decided that whatever happened he would stay and fight it out to the bitter end as was his right, his duty. But there were other matters to consider. His children. The Succession. If he should fall the Country must have someone to rally around, to continue the fight against the Bastard. At the moment they were safe, in London, at Westminster Palace. But if he should fall…. There may not be much time. He reached a decision. He saw Aelfgar, his constant aide during the long hours of fighting.

"Find Ranulf….. if he is alive, and bring him to me. Quickly now." Aelfgar looked at him, as though about to say something but instead simply acknowledged the command.

"Yes Sire," he said, and hurried away on exhausted legs to find Ranulf. Harold watched him go and then his attention was directed once more to his front.

The Norman archers, not seen since early in the morning were now being ushered forward to add their iron-tipped menace to that of the cavalry. As if he did not have enough to contend with. He cast an anxious glance over to his right, to where the Norman cavalry were still pressing their attack and drew *Requitur* from its scabbard. *The Sword of Kings.* He absently noted that its blade was dark with dried blood, but whose blood, and when, he could not recall. Just for a moment his mind strayed back to the day of his Coronation, to the moment he had first held *Requitur* in his hand. *The land will run with blood.* He had not been wrong. But how much blood, how much suffering, he had not foreseen. And still it was not over.

A shout from his front dragged his mind back to the present. The air hummed with noise as the Norman archers let loose their clothyard shafts, this time aiming high into the air, to let their iron tips bring them slowly down, like rain onto the heads of the Saxon housecarls. He raised his shield above his head and felt the jolt as a shaft hammered its way through the hardened linden wood. Beside him two housecarls fell to the ground, smashed down by the rain of iron, their cries drowned out by the din of the battle.

From nowhere Aelfgar appeared with Ranulf, the strain etched deeply into his lined face.

"Lord?" he said. Their eyes met and though no words were spoken each man knew the truth. The battle was lost. On the right, only yards away now the Norman cavalry were cutting their way through the resistance, bodies falling like logs as the Saxons desperate now, threw themselves before the enemy.

"My children... Godwine; the others. They must be saved..." he turned to his right, to the attack that threatened to end it all.

"Cut your way through to the north. My horse is with Edith. At the hoar apple. Take her with you. Make her go. She will protest, *but make her go*. Tell her I love her."

Behind the King Ranulf could see men running wildly for the trees, their resolve finally broken. Peasants, farmers, men from the fyrd. Not his housecarls; they would never run. Never.

"And you Lord?" he asked. For a moment Harold studied him, his blue eyes infinitely sad.

"I shall stay," he said simply. "My men need me."

The air hissed again; another flight of arrows raining down, and once more they sought cover beneath their wooden shields. Ranulf heard the scream before he saw what had happened but when he lowered his shield it was a scene he would never forget. Harold had taken an arrow in his cheek and the arrow-head, passing through the socket, had completely removed his eye. The King was down, writhing uncontrollably on the ground, his hands clutching wildly at his shattered face whilst blood poured through his fingers to stain his hands, his hauberk bright red. Instinctively Ranulf bent and grabbed him, tried to hold him whilst he bucked and writhed in his arms, all else forgotten as he tried to comfort the dying King. Harold was shouting something, but Ranulf could not make out the words. Others joined him now; Aelfgar, his young face stained with tears; Cnut his eyes wild with disbelief beneath a mask of blood. Together they cradled the King, tried to hold him as he thrashed and writhed in their arms, his agony acute, whilst around them the last of his housecarls fought to hold off the enemy.

"Hold them!"

Harold heard the words only dimly, as though through a mist. *The pain, the pain*…He wanted to massage his eye, to ease the pain, but his arm would not move. He tried to pull it clear but there was no feeling there. Someone had it held fast. A shadow crossed his vision. A cloud? Of course not, he realised, it was blood. The pain was beginning to pass, his struggles to cease. He looked up and saw them staring down at him, their faces tear stained, crestfallen. *Don't worry,* he wanted to say*, the pain is easing*, but the words would not come. He tried to reach up, to tell Ranulf, to remind him of something but again the words, the memory, were lost to him. He was suddenly seized by a thought: *Edith.* They must not let her see him like this. He would have to explain…He opened his mouth to speak but a hand touched his cheek, and he closed it again, the effort too great for him.

"*Easy Lord*," a familiar voice said. He looked up to see who was speaking but all he could see was a mist, a red mist that obscured everything. He was dimly aware that he had seen it before, but he could not remember where, or when, and perhaps it did not matter. He closed his remaining eye and it felt tacky with blood. The pain was easing now, definitely easing, but he felt tired, so very tired. He suddenly wanted to sleep but he knew that if he slept he would not wake. But he felt so tired that he knew that he must sleep, just for a few moments.…

He lay down, gentle hands cradling his head, whilst from the empty socket his blood pumped down his cheek to puddle on the ground beside him.

Ranulf knew that the King was dying. There was nothing that he or anyone could do to save a man with a wound like that. It was a miracle he still lived, if miracle was the word. He looked around anxiously. The enemy sensed victory, were closing in fast. Over to the right a dozen Norman horsemen, big men on large mounts were cutting a determined swathe through the last of the resistance on that flank, their swords rising and falling as they steadily hacked their way through. Soon, he knew, they would be upon him and that would be the end.

On the left flank also, Saxons were breaking from the line, running for the shelter of the trees, their weapons, clubs, pitchforks, discarded as they thought only to save themselves. Only his housecarls held the shield-wall intact and true to their oaths were selling their lives for their dying King.

He forced himself to look down again. Harold, his King, his friend, lay with his head resting on his lap, his greying hair matted dark purple from the blood that continued to pump from that awful wound. Ranulf saw that his own leggings were soaked in it and when he looked at his hands they too, were covered in blood. He studied the King's face, very pale beneath the red mask and saw that Harold had now closed his good eye. His breathing was shallow and laboured. It would not be long now, thank God. *Thank God.*

He looked up and his face met Cnut's. The wildness had gone from his eyes and Ranulf saw that he had taken the King's bloodied hands in his own, had them tightly clasped as though to infuse them with his strength, with his own vitality.

"Why Ranulf?" he said. "Why?" but the boy's question went unanswered for suddenly Aelfgar was on his feet and screaming for all he was worth.

"For pity's sake hold them!…Hold them!" Ranulf looked past Cnut's tear stained face to the hard pressed shield-wall and saw what he had dreaded most: half a dozen Normans had broken through and even now were heading straight for them, determinedly ignoring all else as they sought to reach the King.

Aelfgar was the first to react, and with no thought for himself flung his tired body between them and the small group of housecarls surrounding the stricken King. His sword whirled in his hand as he succeeded in bringing one mount to its knees with a slashing blow on the nose that brought both horse and rider crashing to the ground. He was about to strike again, to finish the Norman knight but before he could do so a lance point took him square in the chest, flinging him backwards in a spray of blood, ending his defiance.

But he had bought precious seconds and now four more housecarls rallied to the cry, hurrying from nowhere to place themselves between the King and the butchers that sought to finish him. One Norman was brought down, eventually, by hacking, slashing, blades, but it took three housecarls to do it, their broken bodies joining those of their comrades on the bloodstained ground as they too were hacked down, the supreme price for their blood oaths.

And still four horsemen came on: Guy of Ponthieu, Walter Giffard, Hugh of Montfort and Count Eustace of Boulogne, each with the promise of land and riches beyond imagination and the scent of blood strong in their nostrils.

A single housecarl now stood before them. He was young, and brave, but he knew that he stood no chance and so desperately cast around for help as the four horsemen bore down on him. For a moment his eyes rested on Cnut, the King's hand still clutched tightly between his own. And as Cnut returned the look a voice inside him spoke and it was as though time had stood still and he was a child again. *Remember who you are boy*. His father had said those words all those years ago when he had first learned his craft and he had never forgotten them. Never forgotten that he was of the blood - line of Canute, who was once King of England. And as the voice called to him he knew that this was the moment that he had been waiting for: the fulfilment of his destiny.

He looked at the broken body on the ground, at the ruined face, barely recognisable as that of the King. He glanced across at Ranulf. The King's blood covered him from head to foot, pumping from the awful socket that once held an eye. Ranulf hardly seemed to notice, his own face frozen into a mask, staring into the shattered face of Harold.

"Ranulf!" he said. "Ranulf! Go! I shall hold them...buy you time. Save yourself. Save the Queen....his children. Do it for me..... *do it for him!"*

Ranulf looked across, hearing the words through a fog. He had forgotten. It was the last thing, the last command, he had been given. Gently he lowered the King onto the ground and with a final glance, first at Cnut and then at the King, he left the field of slaughter.

"Remember me!" Cnut cried after him as he hurried away, his sword quickly snatched from the ground.

Cnut paused only to watch Ranulf go before he turned to confront the butchers that threatened the King. And as he locked shields with the hard pressed housecarl he knew that this was where he belonged. Here, on the field of battle, where his ancestors would watch over him and call him swiftly and assuredly into their bosom. *All my life I have lived for this.* The words came unbidden as he parried a lance thrust aimed at his heart, whilst taking a vicious sword blow on his shield. The Norman assailants were big and strong, but he did not care for he was Cnut of the blood-line of Canute and he had found his place at last. A blow to the head stunned him momentarily and he realised that the original wound had opened again. Fresh blood, warm and wet trickled down his cheek. He shook his head and as he did so he saw the young housecarl fall, hacked down by two of the knights who now turned upon him. *Four against one.* He had no chance but still he fought on. His sword was a blur in his hand as he thrust and parried the desperate blows raining down on him but it could not last. He felt a pain in his thigh, sharp, and hot, and looked down to see that a sword had cut him, but still he fought on, fighting on instinct. His sword clashed once, twice, jarring his arm to the elbow. A lance point took him in the shoulder and threw him backwards. He parried a blow to his head even as he fell, but now other blows were raining down and he could not parry them all.

Down he went under a welter of blows from sword and lance and as the ground rose up to greet him he knew he was dead. He looked to the sky and in the heavens he could see them looking, smiling down at him. They were all there, his ancestors. *So they had been watching*. And as the blows rained down he saw their hands stretch out to him, welcoming, eager for him to join them. He did not keep them waiting for long.

And as Cnut fought his last fight, Ranulf stumbled blindly through the trees, the darkness covering his retreat whilst his mind screamed in torment. The battle was lost and he had run. He had obeyed a command, but he had *run*. The cries of the dying assaulted his ears as though they were mocking him and tears blinded his eyes as he tripped and staggered ever deeper into the Andredsweald. His thoughts flooded in on him, one upon the other, as he sought somewhere to rest, to unscramble his mind, to deal with the awful events of the last hour.

Eventually, after what seemed an age he found a lichen covered log and hunkered down beneath it. It was only when he put down his sword that he saw through his tears that it was not his own but the King's sword *Requitur*. He must have picked it up by mistake. He turned the sword in his hands and saw that its blade was dulled by blood. Gently he wiped it clean with a handful of moss and as he did so his sanity slowly returned. *The Sword of Kings*. The Normans would never have it. Not while he lived. And he intended to live. To live, and to fight them with every breath in his body until they were driven from England's shores. And as he sat staring at the sword the King's final words came flooding back to him: *My children; Edith...at the hoar apple tree.* And suddenly he knew what he must do.

Retracing his steps he fought his way through the darkness to the edge of the tree line and looked for the hoar apple. He was sure it was to the right but it was so dark now he could hardly see. In the distance the cries of the dying on Caldbec Hill could still be heard ringing through the night and Ranulf knew that the sound would haunt him for years. Trying to ignore it he manoeuvred right, keeping just behind the tree line until he found the place where he thought it would be.

Cautiously he ventured out, his ears alert to the slightest sound until, finally, he recognised the twisted branches of the hoar apple. Twenty-four hours earlier the King had sat under the tree with his brothers whilst they had laid their battle plan. And now they lay dead. Slowly he made his way toward the tree expecting to see Edith at any moment. Closer and closer he circled until, at last, he could see the dying embers of a fire. But even from this distance he could see that there was no horse, no Edith, no sign of life; nothing, in fact but the twisted branches of the tree blowing in the chill autumn night and the embers of a fire lit long ago.

A hand touched his shoulder and he whirled around in panic but it was only the fingers of a branch, stripped of its leaves, catching him and holding him fast. Quickly he pulled himself free. Heart racing he plunged once more into the woods seeking cover. It was hopeless. England was doomed, her King slain, and he was lost.

To the south the cries of the dying echoed through the night, a haunting refrain that went on and on and seemed to have no end. And listening to it in his bolt-hole buried deep in the undergrowth Ranulf finally gave up. What could he do, one man against so many? The best that England could offer had been slaughtered in the space of a day, undone by the Normans' superior weaponry and armour. What hope was there? Tomorrow he would start again but tonight he would mourn for all he held dear was gone, smashed into oblivion on Caldbec Hill. Tomorrow a new age would dawn. It would belong to the Normans; to the Normans and to William the Bastard.

But Cnut's last words still troubled him, still echoed in his mind and he knew he must continue the fight. Somehow he would find a way. There was nothing he could do here, tonight. Nothing any Saxon could do, save to give his life needlessly. But there was something he could do for himself, and for another. His hand closed about *Requitur's* hilt, and taking care not to be seen he slipped away north, to find the road to London. As he did so an uneasy peace came over him, a new resolve. He subconsciously quickened his stride.

In the darkness a mile to the south the Norman army, drunk with victory, rode back and forth along Caldbec Hill celebrating wildly long into the night. Harold Godwinesons' banners were beaten down and trampled in the mud, and the wreckage of his once proud army littered the field.

And gazing down from high above, his head now anointing the point of a lance, Harold Godwineson wept tears of blood from sightless eyes, his cries silenced by the genitalia filling his mouth....

EPILOGUE

CHRISTMAS DAY

25TH DECEMBER 1066.

The sun, low in a winter sky, slanted through the stained-glass windows of Westminster Abbey throwing the brilliant colours of the glass onto the pillars and floor, and upon the sombre grey tomb of the Confessor. It also shone upon the man now seated upon the Throne of England, William the Bastard, renamed the Conqueror by his men.

In the aisles those same men, his Earls and Barons and knights stood in respectful silence whilst Archbishop Ealdred repeated the age-old questions of the Catechism and William answered as instructed. Outside, in a sullen, cowed silence the Saxon inhabitants of London stared at the ring of heavily armed soldiers stationed around the Abbey to prevent any chance of a disturbance.

It had taken William two months to butcher and waste his way towards the Capital, his mood black and grim after waiting five days at bloody Caldbec Hill for a deputation to arrive, to offer him the Crown. And when none came he determined to teach the Saxons a final lesson, a lesson they would never forget.

The remains of Harold's body, headless and disembowelled was thrown over Dover Cliffs. That done William proceeded at a leisurely pace towards London, killing, looting and burning every step of the way. Finally the Saxons had yielded, those that had not already fled north to Yorkshire or Northumbria, or into the Fens, and he had entered London unopposed to accept a Crown grudgingly offered by those still left in the City.

And now the Abbey was almost empty, save for his own men,

insignificant in the vastness of the building, witnesses to this, the second Coronation of the year. The Catechism ended and now the Archbishop prepared for the conclusion of the ceremony.

In William's left hand he placed the Orb, in his right the Sceptre. And as he picked up the Crown of England, gently removing it from its velvet cushion a great roar went up from his supporters, finding their voices at last. William knew that this was the greatest moment of his life and a smile finally crossed his granite features.

It was not to last. Outside, his soldiers, jittery and nervous, thought that a riot had started and immediately began to fire the nearby houses. Inside the abbey his Earls and Barons, fearing that they were under attack fled outside, leaving the Duke alone, deserted inside an empty Cathedral with only the Archbishop for company.

An eerie silence pervaded the vast Cathedral as the Archbishop placed the Crown of England upon William's head and William, his nerve failing him for once, shook like a leaf and wondered whether God had finally turned his back on him.

Half a mile away, across the river, in a small room at the Blue Boar tavern a young girl at the limit of her endurance gave a final, despairing push. And to her relief, in a torrent of blood and afterbirth and tears and screams her baby, expected for so long finally saw the world. The young man, looking much older than his years gently caught the child and placed it on the mothers' breast.

"A boy," he said.

The girl smiled at him, a weary, tear stained smile and then cradled her baby. He had raven hair, like her own, but his fathers' blue eyes. The baby cried, a tiny, pathetic cry from untested lungs, the first sound he had made, and the girl felt so happy she thought she would die. The man bent and kissed her gently on the cheek and then kissed his son. She saw that there were tears rolling down his

cheeks, into his beard. The man smiled and brushed the tears away.
"Hal," he said, "we should call him Hal." The girl smiled, and nodded.

"A fine name," she said. "I like that."

The man rose and came back with a cloak, which he gently placed over them both, mother and son together.

"Sleep now, my love," he said. "Sleep."

He went to the door, turning only to look once more at the miracle handed to him, to them both. The girl was almost asleep. Silently he tiptoed down the stairs and went outside. It was clear, bright, a northerly wind having scoured the air clean, but across the river thick smoke spiralled into the air and the man wondered for a moment what it signified. Whatever it was it could not harm him, not today.

He realised, for the first time what day it was. Christmas Day. He had totally forgotten. The thought stirred a memory, dulled by recent events, of the same day a year ago. The day the Confessor's message had arrived. A year. It was not possible. They had all been here then. And now they were gone: Harold and his brothers, Gyrth, and Leofwine. Even Edith Swanneshals was dead, captured at the hoar apple before he had arrived and dragged to the crest of Caldbec Hill to identify the body of her lover. Afterwards she had taken her life with poison; the runes had not been wrong.

His housecarls were all gone too, Aelfgar, Cnut, Guthrum, and so many more. *Guthrum.* How he would have loved to have seen this day. Seen the child. He missed him like a brother. Guthrum, yes, and all the others. Gone now, but never forgotten.

He wandered down to the river and watched the burning buildings, their reflections bright in the water of the Thames. Their reflection suddenly reminded him of the sun setting in a dull red glow over Caldbec Hill, and of the last desperate minutes of that terrible afternoon as dusk finally fell.

Events were clearer now, judged from the distance, from the safety of two months. How they had stood in the gathering gloom and one by one sacrificed themselves as their King lay dying, his face a ruined, bloodstained wreck, knowing that there was no chance.

Remember me, Cnut had said, his parting words before he had turned to face the butchers. He would not forget. Not whilst there was breath in his body. The Normans had cut down Cnut, cut down all of them, to a man, the last man vainly flinging himself over the body of the King, clinging to him like a limpet so that they had to hack their way through him to get to Harold. And then they had butchered the King.

Across the river the fires were beginning to spread, the crackle of burning timbers and the shouts and screams of the people masking the peal of the Abbey's bells. It could go on for months, perhaps years.

As soon as Alice and the child were strong enough he would get them out of the City and go north, or east, into the fens. They would be safe there. He would offer his services to a renegade leader and continue the fight. There would be enough of them, and one of them would surely welcome his sword arm.

He turned away from the river, from the chaos and confusion across the water and made his way back to the Inn. She would be sleeping now, Alice and her son, his son.

He climbed the stairs that led to their room, looking forward to watching them sleep whilst he kept vigil over them; a simple pleasure for the last man to bear witness to the slaughter on Caldbec Hill: the last of Harold's housecarls.

HISTORICAL NOTE

The year 1066 was a turning point in British history. Until the fateful events of that year England had always looked north, culturally, socially, and geographically. Its Kings, many of them, had come from Norway and Denmark, and a large percentage of the people, especially on the east coast, the *Danelaw,* were descendants of the Danes. After 1066, specifically after the calamitous events of the 14th October the map was turned around and England looked to the South, to Normandy, and later, to Anjou, for its Kings. Nothing would ever be the same again.

We shall never know why Harold Godwineson made the fateful journey to Normandy in 1064 that led to his captivity by Duke William and to the swearing of the infamous Oath of which so much political capital is made in the Bayeux Tapestry. Norman Chroniclers, the Bayeux Tapestry included, claim that the journey was made by Harold Godwineson at the behest of the then King of England, Edward the Confessor to confirm, in advance of his death that Duke William of Normandy would succeed him as King. And yet, if that is true, Harold is an odd choice for so important a mission.

First and foremost Edward the Confessor would have known of Harold's own ambitions in that direction and he must therefore have made a most reluctant emissary for him.

Second, of course, there is no reason at all why Harold would have agreed to take part in the enterprise for to do so would surely have jeopardised his own claim to the crown, something that given Harold's character, he is most unlikely to have done.

Third, it must be remembered that on his death-bed Edward the Confessor actually named Harold as his heir - a complete volte-face if the Norman account of events is accepted as true.

Alternative reasons, or theories, for the journey have been put forward by those sympathetic to Harold's cause, none more convincing than the simple fact that he was caught in a storm at sea, and blown off course, landing, by virtue of wind and tide on the coast of Normandy. Seagoing vessels of that age were notoriously difficult to navigate and were at the complete mercy of the winds, as is surely evidenced by the fact that in 1066 William himself, his fleet ready and itching to be off, was unable to sail because of the contrary winds which prevented him from crossing the Channel for several weeks.

Ultimately speculation is idle. The undeniable fact is that Harold was captured by William, was held as his "guest" and did swear an Oath of allegiance to him, which, whatever else it may have done, lent legitimacy to William's claim to the English Throne. Support for the claim by the Pope and by the Church of Rome was, again, vital. It is doubtful whether, without that oath and the support of the Church, Duke William could ever have succeeded.

The long-tailed star seen by Ranulf on the 24th April was in fact Halley's Comet which first appeared in the skies over England that night and shone brightly for a week. It is clearly depicted in the border of the Bayeux Tapestry and must therefore have had enormous significance for the uninformed people of the time. It had last been seen over a hundred years earlier and had heralded the commencement of the dreadful Danish invasions that had so ravaged the east coast of Britain. It was clearly regarded as an evil and unnatural omen of disaster and given what later occurred the chroniclers of the period were undoubtedly right to attach significance to its appearance.

The battle of Stamford Bridge, fought on the 25th September 1066 was, until the battle of Hastings a few weeks later, the bloodiest battle fought on British soil in over a thousand years. The fight on the bridge itself between the huge Norwegian and the Saxons who tried to force the crossing took place much as depicted in the novel. He was indeed slain by a spear in the groin, thrust upwards by an unknown Saxon who had sailed a small coracle underneath the bridge. It was a sad end for an undoubtedly brave man.

Harald Hardraada was every bit as commanding a figure as the novel depicts him. The dominant military figure of the age, Harold Godwineson must have thought Hardraada the major threat to his Throne despite the threat that he faced from across the English Channel. If only he had been blessed with hindsight. Hardraada, the "Thunderbolt of the North" could trace his bloodline back to King Canute and this gave him, by blood at least, as strong a claim to the English Throne as the other two protagonists. On hearing of his landing in the north of England Harold Godwineson must have feared for the worst – especially after the slaughter of his allies' army at Fulford Gate. It is a testament to his courage and determination that he could march his army 200 miles in five days and fight, and win, a fearful battle at the end of it.

The battle itself was again, much as depicted in the novel. The Norwegians, taken by surprise, could hardly have believed their eyes when they saw Harold Godwineson approach with his army hundreds of miles north of where they believed him to be. Without their chain-mail, left with the fleet, they were unprepared for battle and the safest course would undoubtedly have been that urged by Tostig, namely to retire to the fleet but Hardraada was not the man to do that. And so he decided to give battle, and lost – the battle and his life, killed in the thick of the action, wielding his great double handed axe when an arrow pierced his neck. What might have happened had Hardraada decided to retire, to fight on his own terms, we shall never know but it is interesting to speculate.

Tostig Godwineson was almost as bad as the novel describes him. Removed from the Earldom of Northumbria because of his brutal and corrupt rule of the people he left England in disgrace bent upon his return and upon the destruction of his brother Harold whom he regarded with loathing and jealousy. Initially he went to the Court of his brother's arch-rival, William of Normandy, seeking arms and support, and receiving little more than a few ships and men he landed at the Isle of Wight in May 1066 expecting aid and support from the people of that island. Not getting it, and acting like a badly behaved child he then embarked upon a journey of wanton destruction along the South Coast of England, ending up in Sandwich. It was only by the narrowest of margins that he escaped capture, evading Harold's pincer movement at the last moment, the sun giving away the presence of Harold's army. Eventually he threw in his lot with Harald Hardraada, only to meet his death at Stamford Bridge.

In describing Tostig's death I have strayed a little from the truth. In reality Tostig was cut down by the English not far from Hardraada's banner, "Land Waster," fighting to the end. But that would be too heroic a death for such an unpleasant character. Instead, like the bully and coward depicted in the novel, he runs from the fight, only to meet his death in any event. I apologise to the purists and to Tostig for traducing his character. I doubt that he would be grateful.

Harold's brothers, the Earls Gyrth and Leofwine did exist and though not a great deal is known of them we do know that they remained loyal to Harold from beginning to end. Gyrth tried hard to persuade Harold to remain in London, to await reinforcements, and then offered to fight the battle against William for him. Harold refused. It had become personal and it cost him his life. The Bayeaux Tapestry depicts the deaths of Gyrth and Leofwine - it mentions them by name in adjoining frames - and one can probably make the deduction that they must have died memorably, and, in all probability within close proximity of each other. The Saxons did charge down the hill much as described in the novel but there is no evidence that they were led by Leofwine or that he even took part in it. Once again, an apology is due.

The death of Harold Godwineson remains a considerable talking point even today. The "arrow in the eye" theory has, in recent years been discredited and it is easy to see why. It is known that Harold had placed his twin Standards to the rear of the shield-wall, the defensive formation that he had adopted to repel the Norman infantry and cavalry. It is also known that the Norman archers had, toward the end of the battle, begun to fire their arrows high into the air to rain down upon the men in the shield-wall. If one studies the Tapestry one can see that the man plucking the arrow from his eye (or is it his helmet?) is on the right of the shield-wall, and, possibly therefore, one of Harold's housecarls. The figure being cut down by the Norman knight is clearly behind the shield-wall and, equally obviously, is Harold himself. This figure, clearly that of Harold, once had an arrow protruding from his head or face but at some time and for some reason the arrow was removed. It no longer exists. But the tiny puncture marks made by a seamstresses needle a thousand years ago are still visible. Why was it removed? It is the abiding question for anyone interested in the ultimate fate of the last Saxon King. Are both of these figures meant to represent Harold or is only one of them he? My own view is that the figure plucking the arrow from the eye, or helmet, is one of Harold's housecarls and not Harold himself. Why depict Harold's death in two stages? Does it not make more of a dramatic statement to show Harold in one final frame, the Norman cavalry bursting through the shield-wall to cut down the King? The debate continues and the mystery of the needle marks where an arrow allegedly struck the King remains unanswered to this day, but despite my views I have remained faithful to the traditional story by having Harold first hit in the eye by an arrow and then, mortally wounded, being cut to pieces in the final act of savagery. One can only pity him.

And, indeed, Harold Godwineson still arouses sympathy even today, nearly one thousand years after his death. The treatment of the English King by the Norman victors after the battle was nothing short of barbaric. His head was roughly hacked off – it took several blows - and he was disembowelled. His penis and genitalia were removed and stuffed into his mouth and his head then paraded around the victorious army on the point of a lance. His corpse was thrown over Dover cliffs in order that he could "lie at the very frontier of the land he had tried so hard to defend." Ultimately his body was recovered by a grief-stricken mother and removed to Waltham Abbey where his remains still lie today.

Should Harold have fought the battle when he did? With hindsight, and knowing what the outcome would be there is no doubt that he would have waited. This would have allowed his tired housecarls to recover from their extraordinary efforts before giving battle again. Delay would also have allowed his allies in the north, Earls Morcar and Edwin to regroup and to march south with their forces. Delay also harmed William. With every day that passed he must have grown progressively weaker whilst, conversely, Harold grew stronger. To fight when he did was therefore a mistake and, obviously it changed the course of history.

So why did Harold fight? First, and perhaps foremost in his mind was the fact that he had just destroyed Harald Hardraada who, as stated earlier, had a fearsome reputation. Harold must have thought that if he could do it once, after a march of two hundred miles he could do it again. He was wrong. He overreached himself and was defeated.

Second, we know from the Bayeux Tapestry and from other sources that William deliberately fired the countryside south of London in an attempt to lure Harold into battle, knowing, or perhaps hoping, that Harold would not stand idly by and allow the destruction of the countryside continue. William was right.

Third, of course, it had become intensely personal between the two and William calculated, correctly, that the slightest provocation would cause Harold to give battle at the earliest opportunity to rid himself of the festering thorn in his side. One can admire William's tactics whilst at the same time understanding, and having sympathy with, the action taken by Harold. And so, on the 14th October 1066 matters came to a head at Caldbec Hill.

The battlefield still exists and is little changed from how it must have appeared all that time ago. The land in the valley has been drained, and raised about eight feet but one can still appreciate the strength of the position held by Harold. For William to succeed he had to remove Harold from the ridge which barred his path to London. And all day long he attempted to do so, battering Harold's shield-wall with archers, infantry and cavalry. The battle unfolded much as described in the novel. William had three horses killed under him in charge after charge up the hill. William did have to raise his nasal to show his face to his terrified troops who thought that he was killed. The Saxons did break ranks and charge down the hill after the retreating Normans only to be cut to pieces themselves by William's cavalry. And Harold's housecarls' did stand and die, one by one, true to their blood-oaths as the battle was slowly lost.

One can scarcely imagine the carnage, the courage it must have taken, to stand and be cut down rather than, as many of Harold's volunteers had done, run for the cover of the trees, but they did. And it is to those men, Harold's housecarls, that this novel owes its existence.

Ranulf, Guthrum, Cnut and the rest of Harold's housecarls are purely fictional characters but the lives they led, and the manner of their deaths, are as heroic as men of any age. To stand on the spot at Caldbec Hill (renamed "Senlac Hill" by the Normans and meaning, literally, "Bloody Lake") where Harold is said to have been slain amongst the wreckage of his army is a vastly moving experience and the visitor comes away with the feeling of great sadness.

Edith Swanneshals, the mother of Harold's three children actually existed and was reputed to be a great beauty. She was present at the battle and it is to her, and to Harold's injunction that she be taken to safety that Ranulf owes his life. He failed in his mission because, sadly, Edith was captured by the Normans and after the battle was required to identify the body of her lover "from marks on his body known only to her." Can any widow have ever had a sadder task to perform? Later that night she took her own life with poison.

For any student wishing to know more on the subject there are any number of excellent books presently available. And for those who want to know something of the battle that cannot be gained from books let them travel to the town of Battle in East Sussex and follow the ridge, now a metalled footpath, where Harold planted his Standards, and then head north, over the crest, to the east of Battle Abbey, to where a memorial stone and an inscription marks the place where Harold fell, and England changed forever.